For Annie, Maggie and Mairin

WITNESS

Also by Cath Staincliffe

The Kindest Thing

WITNESS

Cath Staincliffe

Constable • London

Constable & Robinson Ltd
3 The Lanchesters
162 Fulham Palace Road
London W6 9ER
www.constablerobinson.com

First published in the UK by Constable,
an imprint of Constable & Robinson Ltd, 2011

A copy of the British Library Cataloguing in
Publication data is available from the British Library

ISBN: 978-1-84901-343-7

Typeset by TW Typesetting, Plymouth, Devon

Printed and bound in the EU

1 3 5 7 9 10 8 6 4 2

Thanks to Kerrie James and Anne Gaunt from Witness Service Greater Manchester who generously shared their knowledge, experience and time with me. As ever, any errors are all my own doing.

PART ONE

Oh Danny Boy

CHAPTER ONE

Fiona

The blood didn't disturb her. Fiona was no stranger to blood: as a midwife, it came with the territory.

The boy lay on his back, one leg buckled to the side, his arms outflung. Large hands. A boy on the cusp. Like her own son. Different features, this boy was Afro-Caribbean, but the same sort of age. Even as she had these thoughts she was kneeling, assessing him; ignoring the wild beating of her heart, channelling the roar of adrenalin to fire up memory and intellect and practical responses.

Checking his airways and finding breath there, stuttering but there all the same. Warm, moist breath, the faint tang of spearmint. And his eyes on her. Brown eyes, tawny, reflecting her silhouette and the blue sky beyond her. A rim of gold edged each iris. His eyes locked on hers as she tore off her cardigan, folded it and pressed it to his chest. There were dressings in her bag, over in the house, but there was no time to fetch it. The green T-shirt he wore was now black with blood. The same blood pooled in a slick beneath his shoulders, soaking into the grass, into the hard earth among the daisies and dandelions, the clover and the plantain. His eyes fixed on hers as she murmured words of comfort and prayed for the ambulance to hurry. His gaze was a kaleidoscope of emotion: surprise, then the skitter of fear and finally the bloom of love. Bringing tears burning in her own eyes.

'It's all right, love, the ambulance is on its way, you're all right.'

His eyelids fluttered and a spasm shook his frame. She saw his eyes roll back and his mouth slacken. Felt the thready pulse at his neck race then falter and stop.

She bent over to give him mouth-to-mouth and glimpsed his young person's travel pass. His photo and name: Danny Macateer. A kick of memory. Macateer. The first twins she'd seen born by vaginal delivery. Danny and a girl, a name with similar letters: Dana? Anya? Nadia? Nadine! Must still be living in the area.

Fiona held his nose; his skin was clammy now from shock. She placed her mouth over his and breathed out, soft, steady. She had never had to do this before. Not in twenty years of midwifery. His chest moved, she allowed it to settle then breathed again. She could smell the soap on his skin, see the fine down on his cheek, the shine in his close-cut, springy, black hair.

Sitting back on her heels she felt for his breast-bone, placed the heel of her left hand on it, covered that with her right hand and laced her fingers together. The wound was somewhere on the left of his chest, close to his heart and his lung. Pumping his heart might increase the blood loss but without it there would be no chance for blood to reach his brain. She began to push, using her weight, counting the rhythm. Aware of the ground trembling, people running, approaching, a Babel of words: *shot . . . I saw the car . . . has anyone rung the ambulance . . . broad daylight.*

'Come on, Danny. Stay with me. Come on.' Fiona gave him two more breaths. Resumed pushing. The muscles in her upper arms ached with the strain, she was sweaty with exertion, her hands now smeared red, the smell of copper in her throat.

She was still trying when she heard the howl of the ambulance getting louder and louder, then abruptly ceasing. The paramedic put his hand on her shoulder, told her to move away, that they could take it from here. And she nodded, unable to speak. Placed her hand against Danny's cheek and saw his eyes unfocused, still. She bent to kiss him on the forehead. A mother's kiss.

Fiona tried to stand but her legs were numb, useless. She struggled to her feet and felt the world tilt. Dizzy. She closed her eyes.

Across the grass came a crowd, to add to the clutch of onlookers. Perhaps two dozen people, mostly black. In hats and frocks, finery and natty suits. Fiona thought of a wedding party. Then she remembered it was Sunday. Churchgoers. And in the centre of the crowd, three women. Three generations. The youngest, the boy's age. Exactly. Calling out, crying, praying aloud. Anguished. Fiona moved back, moved away and watched as the women – the mother and grandmother, the sister Nadine – fell beside him, demanding hope from the paramedics, deliverance from their God.

Fiona stood reeling under the high, blue sky, voices swooping and diving around her, while the boy was injected, defibrillated and put on oxygen. They loaded him into the ambulance.

When the police came they took her to sit in a car at the edge of the grass. She told them everything she could but the order kept getting mixed up and she left things out and had to correct herself and retell it until she had stitched together the sequence. All about doing the home visit and hearing the shot,

5

seeing through the window the boy fall, and racing out of the house. The car that almost ran her over, as she hurtled across the road, the glimpse of the driver, a white man, at the wheel. Reaching Danny.

The area had been cordoned off. They asked for her shoes. Something about forensics. Her shoes were full of blood.

She had left everything at the new mother's house when she heard the gunshot, saw Danny fall. Her medical kit, her bag. The police gave her some protective shoe covers in place of her shoes. Similar to the paper slippers patients wear for theatre. They hid the blood on her feet but were useless at protecting her soles from the gravel and glass scattered on the pavement on the walk back to the house. The police had offered to call someone, or find her a taxi home, but she needed to get her own car back, so she declined.

She knocked on the door for the second time that day. She found it hard to recall how much of the visit she'd covered: checking and weighing baby, examining the contents of its nappy and the cord. Examining mum (temp, BP, glucose in the urine) and checking how feeding was going. Leaving some time for any worries and problems to be raised. She couldn't do anything now, in the state she was in. Hygiene was one of the most important routines to establish with parents. When the new mum opened the door Fiona apologized several times.

'It's all right,' the other woman said. Her eyes kept creeping back to Fiona's uniform, to her hands, where the blood had dried like rust in the creases of her skin. Carmel shook her head. 'It's terrible. Just a kid.'

Fiona nodded fiercely. She didn't trust herself to speak. She held up her hands, looked a question, the

6

woman nodded and Fiona went through to the kitchen. She washed her hands with cold water, then handwash, until the blood had gone and they were blotchy red and white. She collected her things together and asked Carmel if she would like another midwife to call as the visit had been cut short.

'I'm fine.'

'There will be someone here tomorrow,' Fiona told her.

Fiona sat in her car. She felt immensely tired, her back ached, her stomach was hollow. She was desperately thirsty. Around the green space police tape shivered in the light breeze, glinting in the sun. The sound of her phone jolted her. She took it from her bag. Home. Owen wondering where she was. She was on a half-day, four-hour shift. Should have been back two hours ago. She couldn't face talking to him now. There were two earlier missed calls. She groaned. Go home, she told herself.

She drove carefully, the pedals biting into her feet, fearful that she would drift off and lose concentration. Everything looked so ordinary, so normal. She had an irrational desire to wind down her window and shout to people: a boy's been shot! See their faces change. Make them pause. Stupid, she muttered to herself.

She pulled into the drive and parked the car. Gathered up her bags and jacket and went in the side gate expecting the french windows would be open. The garden was empty.

Owen was in the living room, playing his games. Chisel-faced men in uniforms, men with guns, sweeping through abandoned houses. 'You could have rung,' he complained without turning round. 'I needed that money.'

Rage reared in her. Owen turned, saw her face,

took in her uniform, the blood, the overshoes. 'Oh, God.' His voice had softened.

'They shot a boy,' she began, sorrow replacing anger. Her fingers stiff, splayed bouncing on her lips. 'Your age.'

He swallowed, uncertain how to respond.

'In Hulme, on the field by the dual carriageway, near the bridge. I couldn't save him.' Tears spilt down her cheeks, blurring everything. 'Sorry.' She wiped at her eyes.

Owen was blushing, his face and his neck red. 'You could give us a hug,' she chided him. He looked at her uniform.

'It's dry,' she said.

He lumbered to his feet, came closer. She wrapped her arms around him. Still a child really, though he was taller than her now, broad like his father. She was careful not to weep all over him. They were on their own together and she always tried to remember she was the grown-up, not to expect him to meet her emotional needs. She withdrew. 'I need to shower. I didn't get any cash. It'll have to be tomorrow.'

He grunted. Went back to his game.

She undressed. Her tights were stuck to her knees with discs of blood. She peeled them off, put them in the bin. She soaped and scrubbed her hands and feet, then washed her hair in the shower. She sat down under the water, knees bent up, resting her head on them. She let the water drum upon her upper back, where her spine felt rigid, fused hard as stones. She tried to clear her mind but each time she closed her eyes, Danny swung into view: his eyes on her, that steady warmth, looking joyous almost, just before she lost him.

'I'm sorry,' she whispered over and over. Sitting there until her back was numb from the jets and the room was dense with steam.

Feeling raw and slightly giddy, Fiona sat down to eat with Owen. It was a fine June evening and they ate on the patio. The air was full of drifting seeds, woolly clumps from the stand of poplars that ran along the edge of the meadows near the river. She and her ex, Jeff, had chosen the house because of its location. They were still close to the city, fifteen minutes in the car to town outside rush hour, but had the advantages of being on the edge of the housing development with uninterrupted views across the meadows to the Mersey. A small back garden and a rather characterless semi were a small price to pay for the pleasure of being close to the open land.

Fiona doled out lasagne and handed Owen his plate, took some salad. Her son was avoiding her eyes, skulking behind his long, black fringe. Eyes studiously downcast. She felt a flare of resentment; what was he so scared of? That she might weep again or shake or show some other embarrassing emotion? Precisely that, she thought. With all the intense selfishness of a teenager, Owen hated adult displays of feeling though his own moods were mercurial and dramatic.

She cut into the pasta, scooped a small forkful up. It smelt good, her mouth watered. Then she felt a rush of nausea. She set her fork back down. 'He was one of my babies,' she told him.

Owen gawped. 'He was a teenager.'

'Now he is,' she told him. 'A twin.' She frowned, her eyes stung. Owen hastily looked away.

He cleared his throat. 'It was on the news,' he said. 'He died.'

She'd known. He'd died there, in her shadow. The sky trapped in his eyes. Everything that came after:

9

the breath she shared, the medical efforts, the oxygen and drugs, the mercy dash – irrelevant, surplus to requirements.

She felt her nose redden and the prickle of tears. Bit down hard on her inside cheek and watched as the swifts wove arcs in the sky.

Owen shovelled his food down, eating only with his fork, gulping his orange juice in between.

She cut a piece of cucumber in half. Ate that, a sliver of red onion, some lettuce. Took a sip of the Sauvignon, so cold it made her teeth ache. The meat in tomato sauce was congealing on her plate. Ask me about it, she demanded in her head. Ask me now. Just show a glimmer of interest. She wanted to talk about it, all the details, go over it. Tell him everything, not just the facts that the police wanted, but all the rest. How she felt. Ask me how I am. Ask me.

Owen pushed back his chair, the metal legs scraping, screeching on the flagstones. 'Going out,' he said.

Panic exploded in her chest. Stay, she wanted to say. Don't go. Be careful! This – the soft air, the food, home, it's a mirage. Gone in an instant. It's not safe out there.

'Back by ten,' she told him, 'school tomorrow.'

''Kay.'

She turned to watch him go: a clumsy bear of a boy. An impression strengthened by the ridiculous baggy black denims, the huge black T-shirt. At fifteen it was as if the light in him had gone out. Just a phase, everyone told her, and she hoped that was the case, and that it would not be long-lived.

She took more wine. Drank deep. Felt her edges smudge. Stayed there for a while watching the birds. Then forced herself up to go and walk Ziggy.

* * *

The dog ran ahead of her hoovering up smells, tail waving. Ziggy was a mongrel they'd rescued from the dogs' home. Owen's dog. Arranged when he was six in the wake of his dad leaving them. The dog was average, unremarkable. Tan-coloured, pointy ears and muzzle. An every-dog. The sort that could illustrate the alphabet letter D or a brand of dog food. Impossible to mistake for any pedigree breed. He was good-natured, biddable.

Owen was meant to walk him once a day, Fiona the other time. But in recent months Owen's personality transplant meant he'd given up on the walking. It ranked alongside brushing his hair and clearing up his room. Boring, beneath him.

Fiona felt a stab of guilt. Then a wash of shame. Her son was alive. She should have clung to him despite his protestations. Rejoiced. He was a lovely boy beyond the practised disenchantment, the grunts and the sneers. He was caring and honest. As a younger child he'd been avidly interested in the world and its workings, genial, prone to giggles. Easy company. He would be again, surely.

She wondered about Danny and his mother. Had they squabbled and fallen out? Was he surly and sullen at home? What had his parting words been? Something mundane: *I don't want tea.* Or edgy: *I heard you, I'll do it later!* Or poignant: *Love you, Mum.* Fiona had a sudden urge to text Owen – *Luv u.* He'd not thank her for it, would probably not even acknowledge it. His phone was always off when she tried it, or out of credit when she asked why he'd not responded to her messages. Mysterious how he still seemed able to communicate with his mates on it.

11

Ziggy waited at the bridge to see which route they were taking. Fiona signalled ahead: 'Go on Zig.' The dog waited and trotted over the bridge when Fiona reached the steps. The pub on the other bank, Jackson's Boat, once derelict, had been done up a couple of years ago and there were parties sitting at the picnic tables. The smell of fried food lingered in the air, children squealed in the playground. Back in the mists of time she and Jeff had occasionally treated themselves to Sunday lunch there, Owen in his pushchair.

The lane led through an avenue of trees, the canopies in full leaf, the track beneath still muddy in the shadiest places from last week's rains. Fiona hoped she wouldn't run into any of the regulars, the dog walkers who'd come to know each other through their animals. A rag-tag community, all shapes and sizes. She didn't want to talk to anyone. She tried to immerse herself in the natural world around her: the heady perfume of dog-roses, splashed pink among the hedgerows, the clamour of sparrows, a small tortoiseshell butterfly dancing in the nettles, the flash of orange and the blue edging far fancier than its name suggested. They crossed into the little wood by the nature reserve building and she saw a wren busy in the undergrowth and a ball of gnats in a roiling jig under the boughs of the trees. The path led on to the water park. The lake was the colour of blue-black ink, ruffled despite the still of the evening. The motorway ran at the other side, its roar ever-present. Pylons stood sentinel, their wires stretched high above the water. Bulrushes and Himalayan balsam, with its sweet, waxy scent, lined the banks. The lake was used for sailing and canoeing but the water was clear of craft now, the boats locked away in the yard on the far side near

12

the fancy motorway footbridge with its triangular frame. Now only ducks and Canada geese, gulls and a solitary heron broke the water's surface.

Ziggy ran down to the shore and barked half-heartedly at a clutch of geese. The birds ignored the dog. They were resident here all year; their marbled olive-green and white guano decorated the banks and the paths. Further along Fiona saw fishermen, hunkering down for the night, with their green tents and paraphernalia, rods already baited and propped on stays.

Fiona and Ziggy passed a man and a woman with a golden retriever. Strangers: smiles and nods exchanged. When the path left the lakeside, she took the turn up to the river. The banks had been raised for flood defences, and the broken bricks and chunks of concrete peeked through the grass here and there. A path ran along the top and another had been carved out halfway down. Fiona took the lower route, which was punctuated by heaps of debris – kindling and plastic waste – left by the storms. As they neared the bridge again, she was tiring. She stopped and stared into the river, following the ripple where some obstacle altered the current. Ziggy ran ahead then back, waited unsettled, head cocked on one side. They turned for home. The air was cooling now, the sun lost behind the tiled roofs, the swifts still in flight. She had read that they sleep in flight, roosting high above the ground, unable to fly again if they are forced to land. Ziggy waited for her at the back gate. Fiona looked up at the house. Owen was still out. She wasn't due in work till Wednesday. She must ring in the morning, tell them she hadn't finished her last visit.

She locked the gate behind them, let the dog in. She took off her trainers and cleared up the dishes even though it was Owen's job, unable to let them sit and then face another argument about it. She poured a glass of wine.

It was almost nine. She tuned the radio into the local station. Why was she doing this? Proof? Prurience? The jingle came on then the time signal. The newscaster gave her introduction, then announced the headline: *Police in Greater Manchester have launched a murder inquiry after a sixteen-year-old boy was shot and killed in the Hulme district of Manchester earlier today. The youth has not yet been named.*

'Danny,' Fiona whispered, 'Danny Macateer.' She turned the radio off and sat in silence until she heard Owen come in at quarter past ten, his footsteps thudding up the stairs, shaking the house. She stood and went up after him. Met him on the landing.

'Hey,' she kept her voice light, 'I said ten.'

He gave a sigh.

'I love you, you know,' she said quickly. 'Don't ever forget that.' He made a noise in his throat. She squeezed his shoulder. He swung past her into the bathroom, a half-smile on his lips.

She cleared up the living room, set the alarm, put Ziggy in the kitchen. Routines. Then she went to bed, promising herself that if she couldn't doze off, she'd get up and read or something. It didn't matter; she'd no work in the morning. She felt so tired, as though she'd not enough blood in her any more, insubstantial. She closed her eyes. And slept.

CHAPTER TWO

Mike

M ike's first thought was that it was a movie. Someone making a film. The guy stepping out of the Beemer, raising his arm. The retort of the weapon cutting through the traffic noise, through Joe Strummer's snarling vocals and the thrash of guitars. You saw plenty of filming in the city. Granada Studios were in town. Only a couple of miles or so from here. They used locations for *Coronation Street*, for other programmes they made. The Town Hall was popular – it doubled as the Houses of Parliament inside – all the marble pillars and stone stairways, elaborate ceilings and mullioned windows. They'd filmed across the way from Mike's one time. An episode of *Cracker*, Robbie Coltrane, the big man himself, playing the police shrink, criminal profiler they called it. Coltrane had to knock on this door and when it opened he stepped inside. All morning they'd filmed. Mike had to move his van round the corner out of the way. The little street was chocker with cables and flight cases and the crew. Must have been twenty people milling around. Coltrane did his move again, and again. Up to the door, knocking, stepping inside. Mike grew bored after a while but Vicky was fascinated. She watched from their upstairs bedroom window. Circle seats. Working out what all the crew's jobs were. Mike left for work. He had to wait for a signal from a guy in a knee-length bubble coat and headset before he could walk down the road to get his van. In case his shadow or his footsteps or something spoiled the shot.

So that was Mike's first thought: a film. But there was a sick feeling in the pit of his stomach like he knew before he'd even thought it through. No vans or cables, no UNIT signs on the lamp-posts, no clusters of make-up artists or technicians. No camera.

The lad crossing the grass, he had his back to the man with the gun. Mike wanted to call out, the word rose in his throat. NO! A warning to the lad or a plea to the shooter. The word died on his lips as the lad was jolted, spun a quarter turn then, arms flailing, fell. Lay twitching.

Mike slammed on his brakes, felt the seat belt bite his shoulder, hauled the wheel over to the left and mounted the pavement. Earning a blast on the horn from the car in his wake. He killed the engine and The Clash cut out mid-beat.

Across the far side of the recreation ground the bloke with the gun slid into the passenger seat, pulled the door to and the car set off at speed, the driver gunning the engine. The car was side on and Mike couldn't see the registration plates. Wouldn't be able to read them at this distance. There was a woman coming out of one of the houses, dressed in a blue uniform. A nurse. The car almost mowed her down, bucked and swerved past her. She was running to the boy. Mike pulled out his phone and pressed 999 as he jumped down from the van. He walked quickly, closing the distance between himself and the figures on the ground. The lad in his green top and jeans, the nurse crouched over him. Across the way, at the corner of the houses, a dog stood barking up at the roof. At something Mike couldn't see. Pigeons perhaps, or a cat.

'Ambulance,' he snapped when they asked him which service he required.

'What's your emergency?'

'There's a lad been shot on the field near Abbey Street, in Hulme. Beyond the bridge.'

'Please stay on the line.'

Mike kept walking, and the operator asked him all sorts of impossible questions about the situation and the lad's health. He tried to stay calm, to get enough breath and control the trembling in his voice as he answered her. He was close enough now to see the lake of blood, glossy in the light, and the nurse doing mouth-to-mouth. He relayed what he could see, told her what the nurse was doing. She kept him talking until the sirens materialized. He thanked her several times before sliding his phone shut. Watching the paramedics scurry from the ambulance, Mike stepped back. The lad wasn't moving. He couldn't be very old. Maybe fourteen or fifteen.

Then there was a crowd in Sunday best swarming to the field. A black woman near the front, running fast, her face a mask of fear. Mike had to look away. He tried to swallow, suddenly thirsty. He had some Coke in the van but it didn't seem right to walk away.

The black woman was on her knees by the paramedics, an older woman beside her, others around them. The woman was shouting and crying, her distress making her words unintelligible but Mike knew exactly what she meant. Any human being would: my son, my son! Mike bit his tongue, took a steadying breath.

Four squad cars arrived, and other assorted vehicles as the lad was stretchered into the ambulance. His mother, an older woman and a teenage

17

girl were directed to an unmarked car. Manchester Royal Infirmary was the nearest A&E, only a couple of streets away. They'd be there in no time, Mike thought. The police were edging people away, asking them to go to the road by the houses, to give their details.

The policeman who first spoke to him was a pudgy lad with large blue eyes. Staring eyes, like he'd had a surprise and never got over it. He took Mike's name and address, date of birth, and asked him what he was doing in the area.

Mike explained and gestured to his van.

'And can you tell me what you saw?'

'I saw the shooting,' Mike said.

The police officer glanced swiftly at him, as if to check he was serious. Then nodded and wrote something in his notebook. 'Can you come over here, sir? We'd like to take some details now.'

It was another hour and a half before they were done. There was a lot of waiting about. Mike tried ringing Vicky but there was no answer on either her mobile or the landline. Then he sat in a car with a woman who took a detailed account from him, and she seemed to deliberately take it slowly. First interrupting him and wanting him to elaborate on things, then asking him to repeat what he'd just told her. He was thirsty and asked if he could get his Coke but she wouldn't let him. She drummed up a bottle of water, warm but wet. Mike drank it all. Someone removed his shoes and returned them after taking an impression of the soles.

A lot of the questions were about the man with the gun. His height and size, which arm he raised, his stance, his clothes, his hairstyle. Mike could see the guy in his mind's eye but when she repeated her questions uncertainty corroded the picture. He was black, yes, like the boy he shot. Tall, solid build. Baggy yellow and blue clothes, like the basketball players wear. But Mike was too far away to be sure about his hair, or his features.

'Could you identify him?' she asked. It was warm in the car, even with the windows open, and tiny beads of sweat framed her forehead. Mike could smell his own sweat. Rank. He wanted to apologize for it. It couldn't be pleasant. You must get used to it, he thought, people in a state. He recalled the nurse standing up once the ambulance arrived, her hands and knees crimson and blood daubed on her uniform, a smear on one cheek. Looking dazed and lost.

'I was too far away,' he admitted.

Finally the woman told Mike he could go. They'd be in touch.

'Is there any news,' he asked 'from the hospital?'

She pulled her mouth down, took off her specs, there were deep red grooves either side of the bridge of her nose. 'They couldn't revive him,' she said.

Mike nodded once, his hands balled into fists.

He'd missed nine deliveries. He was one of the few drivers who covered Sundays – same rate, Ian never paid double time. Most of the trade was home shopping, people ordering from catalogues and, more often nowadays, online.

Ian owned the business. Mike had been a postman before that, kept it up when Kieran came along but by the time he was a year old and it was clear there was something wrong, him being so difficult to manage, Vicky begged Mike to find something with more sociable hours. Where he wasn't heading off at four in the morning leaving her to cope on her own.

19

Mike didn't mind the driving job, liked his own company, listened to music or the radio when he got bored; Radio 5 Live or Radio 4. Learnt all sorts.

With the money Vicky made from her mobile hairdressing and tax credits from the government they could just about manage. It was touch and go at times: no leeway if the washing machine packed in or the gas bill doubled. Annual holidays were beyond their means and Vicky's old banger was running on a lick and a prayer but holidays weren't really an option with Kieran anyway. Change of any sort, the slightest deviation from routine, brought out the worst of his behaviour.

Mike looked at his clipboard. Two of the parcels were 24-hour express. Timperley and over in Urmston. Opposite sides of the city. 'Sod it,' he said quietly, deciding he would make an early start tomorrow and try to clear the backlog plus whatever else was on his sheet. He looked over to the rec, the white tent which now shielded the ground where the lad had lain. 'It'll keep.'

Back home he could smell pizza. Vicky was in the garden with the kids. Megan was on the slide; she skimmed down then raced across the grass to greet him. He swung her up and she let out a peal of laughter. 'Again, Dad.'

'Later, matey, Dad's tired. Hey, Kieran.'

His son was nestled in the corner of the small area of decking, facing the walls. Mike could see the toys scattered between his legs. The bafflingly random items that Kieran formed an attachment to. A small rubber ring for a dog, a thimble, a piece of yellow felt, a plastic snake.

'Did you get the straws?' Vicky asked.

'Oh, shit.' Mike couldn't face going out again. The only way Kieran would drink was through a particular make of striped plastic straws. No others. The child would die of dehydration rather than compromise. And the only place that sold those straws was Morrison's supermarket, the nearest branch out in Reddish.

'They'll be shut, now,' Mike said.

'How could you forget!' Her eyes were blazing.

'Aren't there any left?'

They bought in bulk, a system that worked for months at a time making them complacent, not aware of dwindling supplies.

Vicky swore and stalked into the kitchen. Mike followed. 'I rang,' he said. 'You never answered.' Bit of a red herring, really, he would never have made it to the supermarket even if he had got through and Vicky had reminded him.

'Yes, well, he's hidden the phone again,' she hissed, pulling at the drawers, rifling through, just in case. Another of Kieran's obsessions: taking and hiding phones.

'And your mobile?'

'Recharging. Look!' She turned, furious, her face contorted, holding up the transparent plastic box. 'That's it!' A single straw.

Mike's mouth began to twitch, a bubble of hysteria fluttered in his chest. His diaphragm and belly convulsed. Don't say it, he thought. Don't.

'It's not funny, Mike.' She looked askance. 'It's the last straw!'

Laughter burst from him. Snatching his breath and sight and sense. And then his face was wet and his shoulders shook and he lifted his hands to his face.

'Jesus Christ,' Vicky said quietly. 'What on earth is it?'

CHAPTER THREE

Cheryl

It was hot for once and Milo was fretting after his midday nap so Cheryl texted Vinia. Asked if she'd like to hang out. Take Milo down the play park together. Vinia was cool with it. Said half an hour and pitched up in twenty which was some sort of a record. She was always late was Vinia, be late for her own funeral, that girl, Nana said. Many a time.

Nana had gone to church after giving out about how it would do the child good to visit the Lord, like she always did. How back home in Jamaica no one would dare miss church. And Cheryl nodded and shrugged and then objected that Milo had gone down and she wasn't going to wake him.

'Where did I go wrong?' Nana muttered to the mirror, adjusting the veil on her hat. 'Well?' She turned to Cheryl, one arm out, palm up, the other on her waist. Asking now for Cheryl's opinion about her outfit.

'Fine.' Cheryl nodded at the navy skirt suit. Gold buckles on the shoes, anchors on the suit buttons. Nautical Nana. 'More than fine.' Cheryl grinned.

'Splendid?' Nana demanded.

'Splendid.'

Nana clapped her hands but the gloves muffled the sound. She went to the door. 'I might go back with Rose.'

'Okay,' said Cheryl.

'There's some casserole left if you peckish.'

'Ta, Nana.'

Since then Milo had woken, grumpy at first, then refreshed, and she'd fed him a banana sandwich and some juice and changed his nappy.

He had some words now; it cracked her up to hear him. 'Woof' had been his first word and they still couldn't pass a dog, a picture of a dog, or hear a dog bark without Milo on the case.

Milo squealed when he saw Vinia and she picked him up and pretended to eat his cheeks, making him writhe and giggle.

When she put him down, Cheryl told him to get in his buggy and he toddled over to it and climbed in. Gave a little one-two kick of his legs in anticipation.

'I need some cigs,' Vinia said.

'Call at Sid's,' said Cheryl. Shorthand for Siddique's – the corner shop.

Cheryl manoeuvred the buggy out of the door and Vinia followed. Cheryl liked the heat. She'd been itching to wear her new shorts and the halter top and today was the day. Her figure was just as good as before she had Milo. Mile high legs, the agency had said, potential runway material. She'd done a few shoots, adverts, mainly print for magazines and promotions, just one for TV, but all that was impossible now, couldn't pitch up for castings with Milo under her arm.

The sun was fierce and made the colours stronger, the red of the brick walls, the green of the plants in the hanging baskets that some people had up. The sky too looked bluer, a great bowl of blue, not a cloud anywhere. Nana had a tub by the door, no garden at the front 'cos the houses opened right on to the street, and in the tub there was a rose climbing up the wall, big, creamy flowers with that smell of lemon and spice. The smell was stronger, as well.

At the corner, Vinia went into Sid's and Cheryl waited outside with Milo, watching people coming and going. Plenty of people out, making the most of the good weather. A guy walked by on the other side of the street, skinny, grimy, bare-chested and his skin milk-white, with a backpack on. A dog at his heels. Cheryl didn't know him.

'Woof!' chirruped Milo.

'Yes, woof,' Cheryl agreed.

'Woof!' Milo was alive with glee. Like he'd never seen a dog before and this was the best dog in the universe. 'Woof!' He kept it up, one dimpled finger pointing to the dog, until they disappeared round the turning. Even with the dog gone, Milo muttered 'Woof' a couple more times. Savouring the memory.

Danny Macateer came along. A good kid. He stopped to say hello to Milo.

'Why fer yer not at church?' Cheryl mimicked her nana. Danny cracked a smile. She knew he got the same from his Nana Rose, and his mum. Nana Rose and Nana had come over on the same boat, way back. Young married women moving with their husbands, answering the call for workers.

'Rehearsal,' Danny said to Cheryl.

'Safe!' She nodded with approval. 'You got any gigs?'

'Maybe Night and Day.'

Cheryl knew it, a bar on Oldham Street that showcased new talent. She'd been to a poetry slam there once.

'Way! Let us know.'

He nodded, a flush to his cheeks, still awkward with female attention. Cheryl was surprised that no one had snapped him up. A good-looker with brains

24

and an easy way to him. Staying out of trouble, so far. Killer smile. If he was a few years older . . .

'Later.' Danny put his fist to Milo's. The toddler bumped his hand against the teenager's. Tiny against the boy's paw. Cheryl tried to imagine Milo growing that big.

'Woof,' the child said.

'Later.' Danny nodded to Cheryl.

'See ya.'

He went on his way. Vinia came out of the shop, lighting a cigarette. Passed one to Cheryl. She lit up, relishing the kick in her throat, the fuzzy sensation at the back of her neck as the nicotine got to work.

They set off again, Cheryl negotiating the buggy to pass people on the narrow pavement. A couple of guys went past, eyes appraising her, one of them whistled, his mate groaned. Cheryl played dumb. Used to it.

'We're going to the park, Milo,' Cheryl said. 'To the swings.' He waved one hand.

Cheryl smiled. A lot of people would slag her off – single mum, teenage pregnancy, living on benefits – but Milo was the best thing that ever happened to her. It didn't mean she wouldn't do anything else with her life. Get back into modelling once he was in school. Cheryl did nails at home for a bit of extra cash. She had a flair for it. She could do something in that line, if the modelling didn't take off. Not just beauty though, make-up for film or TV, or music videos. See her name in the credits.

Vinia worked afternoons at H&M in the Arndale. Minimum wage but a discount on the clothes. Vinia blew most of her money on clothes there. She lived at home still. Everyone Cheryl knew was still at home. Crazy prices for flats and houses, even with

25

the recession. Cheryl didn't mind living with Nana, it helped with having Milo too, she could leave him if she had to go somewhere or she needed a break. Nana could be a bit preachy but she'd lie down and die for Cheryl.

Vinia was telling her about a jacket she had her eyes on, white denim with beading, when a car came round the corner way too fast, the engine snarling. Cheryl pulled the buggy back sharpish and leaned into the wall, away from the road. The car was a silver BMW. Cheryl knew the car, knew the two guys in it: Sam Millins and Carlton. Carlton was Vinia's stepbrother. They were both bad news. The car roared past them and took a right at Sid's.

'You heard about the Nineteen Crew?' Vinia asked her, keeping her voice low.

Cheryl shook her head.

'Fired into Sam's house last night.'

Cheryl swallowed. 'Anyone hurt?'

'Nah. They were lucky, man.' Vinia shook her head. 'But everyone's wanting payback now.'

'Wankers,' said Cheryl. Vinia cut her eyes at her, a warning. Vinia had to be careful around Carlton. He was a man with a lot of power. A dangerous man. Twenty-four years old and running the neighbourhood like some feudal prince.

Cheryl sighed. Eased the buggy back into the centre of the pavement.

'Dry clean only.' Vinia was returning to the theme of her jacket when a loud crack split the air, echoing through the sunlit streets. Vinia looked at Cheryl, Cheryl gave a slight shake of her head. This she did not want. It was never-ending. Tit for tat. Boys running wild with guns and knives.

'It came from over there.' Vinia gestured in the direction of the dual carriageway and the recreation

26

ground. She made to walk that way but Cheryl put a hand on her friend's arm.

'Wait, there might be more.'

Vinia took a drag of her cigarette and rolled her eyes at Cheryl's caution. There were no more loud noises until the same car appeared, crossing the road ahead of them. Gone round the block. It careered down the centre of the narrow road and disappeared. Cheryl could smell rubber burning and see the cloud of exhaust, hot, making the road junction ripple in the heat.

'Come on,' said Vinia.

They walked quickly to the corner then along Marsh Street to the end. Cheryl saw someone on the grass, halfway across the rec. He had a green sweatshirt on. A woman was running up to him, kneeling down. Some kids on bikes were racing to reach the scene of excitement first. Her heart thumped in her chest. 'No,' she moaned. She pulled on her cigarette, her hand trembling, took the smoke in deep.

Vinia swore under her breath.

'I'm going home.' Cheryl wheeled the buggy round.

'Don't you want to see who it is?'

'I know who it is.' Her throat hurt and she felt sick.

Vinia had her hands on her hips, glaring at her.

'It's Danny Macateer.' Cheryl's eyes burned. She threw down her cigarette.

'No!' breathed Vinia. 'How can you tell from here? We need to get a closer look.'

'I'm not taking Milo there!' Cheryl was furious. 'You think a baby should see that?' She couldn't bear the way Vinia was talking about it, the avid interest in her eyes.

'How do you know it's him?'

Cheryl didn't want to tell Vinia that she'd chatted to him. Not wanting to share the words they swapped. 'He always wears that green top. You go.' She was anxious to be free of Vinia. 'I'm going back.'

'Okay.'

Cheryl pushed the buggy as fast as she could go, biting her lips, her nose stinging, her chest aching. She burst into the house, dragging the buggy in after her. Slammed the door and sat down hard on the sofa.

Later, he'd said. *Later*. There wouldn't be any later. He'd not get to rehearse, or play the gig, or make his mum proud. It wasn't fair. The bastards had shot him down for no reason. He wasn't in with the gangs. They'd shot him. Maybe a mistake. Or just because they could. And no one could do anything to stop them.

28

CHAPTER FOUR

Zak

Z ak had spent all morning on the supermarket
car park near the precinct. He did try getting
into the precinct first, tied up Bess at the bike racks,
but the guard gave him a stone dead look and jerked
his head. 'On yer way.'

'I haven't done 'owt.' Zak protested, all injured
pride.

'And yer not going to, neither.' The guy was
chewing gum. Nicorette. Zak could smell it. Rank.
He'd got some from the GP once, on prescription,
sold it in the pub for a knock-down price.

'Yer can't do that,' Zak said. Though he knew he
could. Said it for the wind-up really. Liked the idea
of toying with the guy for a bit. Bound to be on a
short fuse, on the gum, trying to kick the smokes. ''S
a public place.'

'Wrong.' The guy gave a smug little smile. 'This is
a private development, privately owned. Anyone
may be refused entry or ejected. And I'm refusing
you.'

'Why, what's your grounds?'

'I'm not obliged to say.'

Zak snorted. Drew the roll-up out from behind his
ear and fired up.

The guy's cheek twitched, like there was a bug
under the skin. 'No smoking,' he said tightly.

Zak took a pull, released it slowly, like an old

advert, the smoke swirling up all lazy and relaxed.
'I'm not inside.'

'Within ten metres of the entrance.' The bug
jumped again.

Zak took a step back, and another drag.

The guard's jaw jerked up, his eyes darkened.

'Fair enough.' Zak raised his hand, flaunting the
ciggie. 'I get the message. You have a nice day, now.'
He gave a little bow and spun away. Walked back to
Bess. She wriggled like mad, ecstatic, as though he'd
been gone for hours. He patted her back, rubbed the
loose fur under her chin.

After that they went round the other side of the
block to the supermarket car park. He left Bess at the
far end where there was some shade.

Zak struck lucky first time: a good omen. A
youngish woman, early twenties like him, plain-
looking with a trolley full of food. He'd watched her
load her stuff into the hatchback then return the
trolley to the bays and get her pound back. He met
her halfway back to her car.

'Excuse me—' Zak was always polite – 'can you
help us out? Me mam's been taken into hospital and
I'm trying to get the bus fare to get down there and
visit. I don't like to ask . . .'

But, already embarrassed, she was fishing in her
pocket, handing him the pound coin, apologizing
that she hadn't any more change on her.

There were two advantages to working the supermarket car park as Zak saw it: first off, because you
had to use a pound for the trolley then just about
everyone had a spare quid on them and second, they
were on their way home after the big shop and
wouldn't be hanging around to see him use the same
line ten, twenty, thirty more times. Way past the point
where he'd made enough for a day-rider on the bus.

The morning went well. He'd a few who refused to acknowledge him and a smart-arse who suggested he get some money out of the hole-in-the-wall or find a job. Then smart-arse's mate joined in – offering Zak a lift, was she in Wythenshawe? Going that way. The men despised Zak, and it was mutual. Not a thought about why someone might choose to go begging if they had any other way of getting by.

He cleared £22 in an hour and a half. That'd cover food for Bess and some scran of his own: he could feel his belly growling. He'd get a tenner of weed. The price had rocketed recently. His dealer Midge had hung out for long enough but the market wasn't moving so what could you do?

There was a Pound Shop further down Princess Road, good for dog food, and a Bargain Booze next door. Café on the corner. He and Bess headed down there. He could smell the bacon half a mile away. He got a bacon, sausage and egg barm and a large cola. Ate in the café while Bess waited outside. His mouth flooded with juices at the first bite: the salt of the meat and the silk of the yolk just perfect. The woman was happy to fill Bess's dish with water. Important she got plenty to drink when it was hot. He saved a piece of sausage for her, a treat. They'd some big chocolate muffins and he got one for out. He had to eat it quick; the chocolate pieces melting in the heat.

He put the tins of dog food and the cider he bought in his backpack and went over to the park. Had a drink and a fag. He was feeling good, he told himself, everything going his way. He only had 60p credit on his phone so he texted Midge to say he'd be round later and to keep him ten quid's worth. He ought to top up his phone; he liked to keep in credit in case he got news about his mam.

31

The cider coming after the meal, took the edge off. When he was working everything was wound up tight, ready to flee or fight if need be. No knowing what might kick off. A clenched fist inside his guts. Eyes everywhere. He never let that show; it'd scare the punters off if you were all wired. Now, he could chill. The sun was fierce on his face. He slipped off his top and spread it out beneath him. Lay back on the grass. He always went freckly in the sun, burnt easily, but some sun was good for you, vitamins or something. Bess whined and wriggled closer, laid her head on his chest. He grabbed the scruff at the back of her neck. 'Good dog, atta girl.' He felt the thud of her tail twice on the ground.

A while later he decided to head off for Midge's. They cut through the estate. Some kid in a buggy took a shine to Bess, calling after her. At Marsh Street, Zak went left, saw the house at the end facing across the rec to the big road, kitchen window flung open. Singing to him. An invitation. Too good to be true? Sixth sense told him there was no one home. He went round on to Booth Street, no car outside the front. The tiny space in the back yard wouldn't fit a car, motorbike at most. Zak rang the front door bell, waited, listened. Nada.

He told Bess to sit by the gable wall. Sunday afternoon and Zak could see people crossing Marsh Street further along. He waited until no one was visible on Marsh Street itself or along the alleyway that separated the backs of this row of houses from those running parallel and tried the back gate. Wouldn't shift. He jumped up, gripping the top and hoisted himself up, trainers scrabbling for purchase. The yard was small, neat, paved with pink and white flags and a white plastic table and chairs by the back door. The wheelie bin was just below the open window. Sweet. He took a look in, listened again. Not wanting any surprises. He emptied his backpack, leaving the dog food and cider on the table.

He went in head first, lowered himself down and took his weight on the edge of the sink. Always liked gymnastics, only thing he was any good at in school. Managed to get his feet down without knocking anything off the draining board.

He swept through the downstairs first, looking for anything small and valuable. In drawers, cupboards, on the coffee table. His heart was racing, sweat sticky on the back of his neck. Found a camera, and a small bamboo box with two twenties in. He took the stairs two at a time, no telling how long they'd be out. Might just have gone for a paper, or popped round to the neighbour's.

Nothing in the bathroom. Little bedroom full of kid's stuff, bunk beds, small TV and, yes!, an Xbox 360. He disconnected it, fitted it in his bag, heavy but worth the effort. His lucky day.

In the big bedroom at the front there were a couple of necklaces and some rings, a nice little ornament, a girl and some birds, the sort people collect. Worth a few quid.

Zak glanced out of the window and saw to his left a silver BMW drive up along the top end of the rec. The car stopped suddenly and threw a load of dust up behind it. A man jumped out. A big guy with his hair cut close, a number two, and a short beard like a dark rectangle under his mouth. He was wearing a yellow vest, lots of bling and dark baggy baseball shorts, high-tops. Zak knew him: Carlton. Hard man. The car was his mate's. Carlton was holding a gun. Aiming at a lad crossing the grass, bound for the big road. The lad didn't see him.

Zak heard the crack of the shot as the kid fell.

Zak's stomach plummeted, there was a yawning inside, like a hole waiting for him. A current of fear zapping through him. There was a moment when Carlton was looking straight across to where Zak stood paralysed. Could Carlton see him? Zak was sweating more; he had that loose, sick feeling. Then Carlton ran towards the car. Zak hoofed it downstairs. He could hear Bess barking, warning him, sensing danger. There was a hessian bag hanging up in the kitchen, writing on it. Zak grabbed it and chucked it out of the window. He knew he wouldn't fit through with the backpack on, all the stuff in it, so he used an apron and rolled it into a rope, his hands shaking, fumbling. He tied one end to the pack and, standing on the sink, lowered his booty down carefully on to the wheelie bin. He let go of the apron-rope and was starting to smile when the backpack tilted sharply to the right and tumbled down on to the flags.

Zak swore, clambered up and out of the window. Slithered down on to the wheelie bin and then righted himself. He didn't stop to assess any damage but slung the dog food and cider in the shopper and then opened the bolt on the back gate to let himself out.

Bess stopped barking and wagged her tail. He headed back away from the recreation ground, into the estate. He was shaking. Got to get to Midge's, have a blow, calm down. Wishing this wasn't happening. It had all been going so well.

He heard the whoop of sirens after a while and increased his pace. By the time they got to Midge's, Zak was tight as a cat's arse, heart going like the clappers. He didn't mention the shooting, didn't want Midge to know he was there. Word would get round about it all soon enough. Zak didn't want it in his head. He just bought his stuff. Had a blunt one then and there, shared the cider.

The figurine was smashed to bits but he showed Midge the Xbox and Midge said he might be interested for his nephew. They tried it out but the bastard thing was knackered. He should have known.

That night, back in the derelict house he was dossing in, he couldn't settle. His skin humming and the ball of dread there again. Echoes bounced in his head: fists and sticks, a locked room, hot delirium. He woke in the early hours with a whimper, spitting and retching. Trying to get rid of the sensation in his mouth: the brittle, bitter flakes, the taste of salt and rubber and soil. His mouth watering and his back aching with each uncontrollable spasm. He tried to tell himself it was just a dream but he knew it was more than that.

He rolled another smoke, extra strong. Felt his skin slacken, everything melt. 'Something'll turn up,' he whispered to Bess. 'It'll be all right.'

CHAPTER FIVE

Cheryl

Vinia was back within the hour. The ambulance had taken Danny to the hospital, his mum and Nadine had gone with him. They'd turned up at the recreation ground, the whole congregation.

'Your nana's sitting with Rose. She said to tell you.'

'Why'd they do it, Vinia?'

'I don't know!' Vinia got all moody, flashing her eyes. 'And I don't want to know.'

'There's no good reason,' Cheryl said.

'It's not our business,' Vinia said flatly.

'He was just a kid.'

'Leave it.' Vinia's face was set.

'So it's all right to gossip and go over there all big eyes like some ghoul but we don't ask why?'

'Not unless you got a death wish.'

Cheryl shook her head.

'What,' Vinia demanded. 'You judging me?'

'No. But Carlton—'

'Shh!' Vinia hissed. 'Don't mess with it.'

The unfairness lodged like a weight in Cheryl's chest, like a hand tight round her throat. She knew Vinia was right. Carlton and Sam were not to be messed with. She knew nothing, had seen nothing, would say nothing. It was a senseless tragedy. Everyone would suck their teeth at it, shed tears, keep quiet.

Cheryl's phone went off. Nana.

'The boy passed.' Her voice sounded old, creaky. 'The Lord has taken him.'

'No,' Cheryl moaned.

'I'm going to stay with Rose.'

'What can I do, Nana?'

'Nothing, child.'

'Some food, the casserole?'

'You have that. The church will be bringing food for the set-up. Paulette is still at the hospital. You could get some flowers. There's money in the ginger jar.'

'Yes.'

'Sign my name as well.'

'Shall I bring them to Auntie Paulette's?'

'No. Leave them where he fell.'

'Yes.'

'God love you, child.'

Cheryl's hand shook and her eyes stung as she ended the call. She sniffed hard. Turned to Vinia. 'Danny died. I have to get flowers.'

'I'll come,' Vinia said.

Cheryl felt trapped, wanting to shake free of her. 'No need.'

'I can't go home.'

Vinia was scared, Cheryl saw, couldn't face Carlton and his boys.

'Okay.'

Cheryl bought the biggest bouquet she could with Nana's £20 note. White and red: lilies and carnations, gypsy and ferns. Milo wanted to hold them but she was worried he would try eating them or crush the delicate blooms, so she bought him a piece of red ribbon from the woman and gave him that.

She had no idea what to write on the card. Everything was either tacky or pious: *You are with*

the angels now or *At peace with the Lord.* Vinia was
no help at all: *Rest in peace* her only suggestion.
Cheryl didn't know any poems and there wasn't
much room on the card anyway.

She printed *For Danny.* She thought of his music,
his smile, the way he greeted Milo. Wrote *A bright
star.* Pictured Auntie Paulette and Uncle Stephen,
Nadine and Nana Rose without him. Added
Beloved. Signed it *Nana T., Cheryl and Milo.*

Back at the rec, Cheryl made Vinia go on ahead
and check there was nothing to upset Milo. Vinia
came back, said it was all sectioned off. A tent up,
you couldn't see anything. Loads of police around.
He lost a lot of blood, Vinia added. Cheryl didn't
want to think about that. Wished she hadn't said
that.

They didn't know what to do with the flowers.
There weren't any others. They stood for a while
until a policewoman came up. She took the flowers
from them and put them by the lamp-post on the
corner. Milo protested, held out his arms and kicked
his legs, threw his piece of ribbon down.

The policewoman came back over to them. 'We'll
be setting up a mobile incident room, here,' she said.
'If anyone has any information, anything that might
help us, in complete confidence. And there's Crimestoppers too, just ring the number. Completely
confidential as well.' She smiled. Cheryl could tell
she'd had her teeth whitened. Some patches glowing
brighter than others. 'Were you girls around earlier?'

'Nah.' Vinia shook her head. 'Just heard about it.'
Cheryl nodded in agreement.

'Did you know him?'

'Knew of him, that's all,' Vinia said. Cheryl felt
her jaw clench. Milo arched his back and yelled
again.

'And who's this?' The policewoman bent to speak to Milo.

'Better get him back,' Vinia told Cheryl, 'must be his teatime.'

'Yeah.'

The woman straightened up, gave them another smile.

Cheryl swung the buggy round and they set off. Milo's cries got more frantic as the chance of him getting the flowers receded. Fat tears streamed down his cheeks. His crying drilled into Cheryl. Boring into her bones. He was enraged and desolate. She knew exactly how he felt.

CHAPTER SIX

Fiona

F iona was dazed. The world, its minutiae, swam in and out of focus, at times hazy, then cast into sharp relief. Too harsh. Her mind was scrambled, thoughts jumbled like old sticks tangled on the river bank. On the Tuesday evening when Owen got back from school she was bewildered to find herself putting towels in the deep freeze.

She went over her memories of Danny's death, anxious that they might fade and wilt like wild-flowers brought into the house. Then she would be of no use when the police took her full statement.

She reassured her manager Shelley, who was also her close friend, that she was capable of returning to work as scheduled. Fiona couldn't bear the thought of taking sick leave, of wandering round the house like some spare part: she needed to be busy, occupied, productive.

Tuesday teatime brought fresher weather. As she walked Ziggy the first full drops of rain fell, making little craters in the dusty footpaths. The river was hungry for rain, already the level had sunk with just a few dry days. The smell of mud, brackish and chemical, was pungent in the air. They walked along the river to the east. Fiona remembered her shoes, how the police had taken them, her cardigan: she'd have to get to a shoe shop, her trainers would do for tomorrow but they were pretty tatty.

On the walk back the sky darkened, huge bruised clouds hung low overhead and the first throaty rumble of thunder sounded. Fiona increased her pace, keeping up with Ziggy: the dog hated storms.

The deluge hit before they reached home. The rain, tropical in its intensity, flattened nettles and grass, bouncing off the hard earth. It soaked through the seams in her jacket and drenched the front of her trousers, making her limbs damp and cold.

Ziggy raced ahead, waited trembling at the gate. Fiona stood a moment, turned her face up and felt the cold, fresh water drumming on her cheeks and her eyelids, sliding down her neck. Lost in the sensation.

She was all right that first day back. More or less. She accepted the words of sympathy, the shared outrage of her colleagues, with a nod and a shake of her head. *It must have been awful. That poor child. And his mother. A twin as well. Is it right you'd delivered them?* Hands on her arms, on her shoulders, a hug.

She felt a little teary but once she was back doing her visits it passed. One of her mums-to-be showed signs of pre-eclampsia and Fiona organized a hospital admission. Another had worrying levels of sugar in her urine and Fiona recommended she see her GP: it happened to some women and not others, but they needed to consider whether there was any risk of diabetes. She went about her work: changed four nappies on newborns, dressed umbilical stumps, comforted a toddler, gave an anxious mum some help getting the baby to latch on properly and removed stitches from a tear. At each house there were papers and charts to complete. She called at the

41

office at the end of the day. Shelley had checked her schedule and asked for a word.

'Do you want to swap Carmen Johnson for another second-weeker?'

Carmen Johnson was the woman whose house overlooked the recreation ground. The woman Fiona was with when she saw Danny fall. Carmen was in her second week of motherhood and now only receiving visits every other day. Soon the midwives would stop calling and the health visitor would take over.

'No, I'll be fine,' Fiona said.

'Just yell,' Shelley told her.

'I will.'

Nothing had prepared her for the impact of returning there. As she drove closer she felt her guts cramp and her palms grow hot and sticky. She admonished herself. 'It'll be fine. Don't be daft. Take it easy. It's just a place.' Fiona tried to empty her mind, let it fill with grey fuzz.

She turned off the dual carriageway alongside the rec. The tent and the police tape were gone but there was a police Portakabin at the northern side of the rectangle. And a splash of colour by a lamp-post. Flowers. She should have bought flowers! Her thoughtlessness cut at her. She parked outside Carmen Johnson's, gathered her bag and case, got out and locked the car.

She knocked on the door. Her face felt rigid, a mask. She tried to rearrange her features as the door opened. 'Hello—' The word caught in her throat, husky. She coughed.

Carmen looked perplexed, she wouldn't meet Fiona's eye. 'We're fine,' she said. She wrapped her arms around herself, rubbed at her upper arms with her hands. 'We don't need a visit.'

'It's every other day now,' Fiona explained. Not understanding. 'We'll be handing over to the health visitors soon, all's going well.'

'Look.' Carmen's eyes were everywhere, her mouth working. 'I just don't want any trouble. That's how it is.' She closed the door.

Fiona stood there, her knees weak, feeling humiliated, shamed. Her cheeks aglow, her pulse hammering. Aware at first only of the bald rejection. The door closed on her. There had been times before: women resistant to visits, not wanting interference, women with things to hide or a damaged view of professionals. But this sudden switch . . .

Then she got it. *She* was 'the trouble'. Because of what she'd seen, what she'd done. Much had already been made in the media of the community living in fear, afraid to speak out. Carmen lived here. She might have a good idea who was behind the shooting and how they ensured people's silence. Carmen was simply protecting herself and her baby.

Fiona was back in the car, still smarting, when the pain hit. A band crushing her chest, impossible to move or breathe properly. A huge weight. She could feel her lungs contracting, the terror of a vacuum developing. Like drowning. No air, no way of moving. Sweat bathed her skin, her tongue felt huge in her mouth, her mouth chalk dry. An overwhelming sense of danger, animal-keen, consumed her, urging her to flee, but she was pinned down by the pain. She was dying. Everything went dark, then red. There was a roaring in her ears and her hands and feet were nettled with pinpricks. Her knees were juddering, heels drumming in the footwell.

She gulped and found a breath, then another. The pain dimmed, her vision cleared. Trembling spread through her body. She felt sick. Her heart hurt, thudding irregularly in her chest. She couldn't possibly drive. Her eyes filled with tears.

Opening her phone was awkward but she only needed to press one button for Shelley's number.

'Please can you come and get me,' she told her when she answered. 'Get a cab.'

'What?'

'I can't drive, Shelley.' She reeled off the address.

'Why? What's happened?'

'I need to get to the hospital. I'm having a heart attack.'

The shaking wouldn't stop, and the waves of nausea. Every time she closed her eyes, with each blink, she saw a still from Sunday: Danny prone, his leg twisted at an odd angle, *blink*, the fear in his tawny eyes, *blink*, the blood in the creases of her knuckles.

When Shelley arrived she was alive with concern. 'Why on earth didn't you call an ambulance?'

'I don't know.' Because the ambulance was too much like Sunday? 'It's much better now. Perhaps it's just angina.'

Of course A&E was busy. It always was. She spoke to the triage nurse, filled in the form and took a seat in the shabby waiting area, all lumpy green gloss paint and scuffed linoleum. There were two dozen people on the chairs.

'No point in you waiting,' she told Shelley.

'I don't know.'

'I'm fine. Honestly. The pain's all gone.'

Shelley took some persuading but they both knew enough about hospitals to realize it could be a long time before Fiona was seen. 'Can you do me a favour, take my car home?'

'Of course, and let me know what they say.'

She had nothing to do. Nothing to read. She passed the time examining her fellow casualties, trying to work out what accident had befallen them. Some were easy: the schoolboy in his PE kit with a makeshift sling and the elderly woman with a grazed knee complaining to all and sundry about the kerbs. But others had hidden traumas.

The time inched by. Patients were called through to the examination bays and others took their places. They would have brought Danny here. Through the other double doors straight into the resuscitation suite. And then to the mortuary.

'Fiona Geary.'

She stood and followed the nurse to a bay. 'You'll know the drill,' the woman joked. A reference to Fiona's uniform. 'You at St Mary's?' The maternity hospital was nearby.

'Yes, on the community.' Some of the midwives worked all their shifts in the hospital. The community midwives made the home visits before and after birth, carried out home deliveries, worked with women on the domino scheme, where they only went into hospital for the actual birth. Fiona preferred work in the community. There was more freedom and greater responsibility. Less intervention. The consultants held less sway.

The nurse handed Fiona the thermometer, which she tucked under her armpit. She tested her blood pressure. Both readings were a little high. 'Any symptoms now?'

Fiona shook her head. 'Just a bit tired, a bit dizzy.'

'Any breathing trouble?'

'No.'

45

The nurse checked through her form. No history of asthma, allergies, no pre-existing medical conditions. No regular prescriptions. Any family history of heart problems? Yes, her father. Fiona felt the prick of irritation. It was already all down there in black and white, she'd filled the form in today, did they think she'd developed diabetes or epilepsy in the meantime? She knew she was being unreasonable. She double-checked the same details with her own patients. She answered all the questions as reasonably as possible. The nurse left her for a few minutes and then a doctor appeared. The doctor looked at the form and listened to her heartbeat. Then she was sent back to reception to wait.

Another half-hour passed. Fiona knew that a lot could be done with heart disease. She was a little overweight but nothing excessive. They might put her on statins to lower her cholesterol, or do a bypass. A nurse brought Fiona a form and asked her to take it to Cardiology. The hospital was a maze: annexes and prefabs had been bolted on to the old Victorian buildings, sprawling in all directions and now connected up to a spanking new extension. Complicated colour-coded signs were there for navigation.

She handed the form in to the receptionist at Cardiology and took a seat. There was a water cooler there and she was thankful to drink a cup, to clear the stale taste from her mouth.

The ECG took ten minutes. The cardio guy attached the stickers to her arms, legs and chest, and she lay down on the curtained bed while the machine took its measurements.

There was nothing wrong, no arrhythmia or palpitations, no indication of any heart trauma. No echo of myocardial infarction. The cardiologist, giving her the results, asked her to describe again the symptoms she'd had. As she did, she felt her mouth get dry and her pulse speed up, a sense of dread creeping up her spine.

'The tingling,' he asked, 'where was that?'

'My feet and my hands.'

'Any cramping in the arms?'

'No.'

He nodded, pleased with her answers. 'I think the good news is that there's no sign of a heart attack. But there is an explanation that accounts for all the symptoms you describe, and that's a panic attack.'

Fiona stared at him.

'Have you been under any particular stress recently?'

'Yes,' she whispered. Felt her tongue stick to the roof of her mouth.

Another nod. 'Your GP will be able to help,' he carried on, 'discuss the treatment, ways of managing it. It may be a one-off. Some people have an attack once and that's it.'

But the rest? She was appalled. It could happen again.

She went to the walk-in clinic at her GP's practice the following morning. Dr Melling wasn't her regular doctor but she couldn't wait for an appointment, she had to see someone straight away. When Fiona tried to explain what had happened, starting with Sunday, the words clotted in her mouth and she was alarmed by tears in her eyes.

'Take your time,' the GP said.

'The boy that was shot on Sunday,' Fiona said.

Sympathy rippled across the doctor's face. It made Fiona feel worse. She gave the gist of the story. 'Then

47

when I went back I had this, erm, this panic attack.' She felt small and frail as she spoke. 'The doctor at the hospital said sometimes it just happens once. But it was so awful . . .'

'Have you heard from Victim Support?'

Fiona nodded, a letter had come yesterday.

'They can help. Or we have a counsellor here, if you'd like someone to talk to. Just let me . . .' She turned and hit some keys on her computer. Read up a bit. 'Cognitive behaviour therapy can be very useful, that's what Hazel's trained in, good success rate reported. The other usual treatment is anti-depressants. Some patients find a dual approach most useful.'

Fiona listened to her talk about side effects and the need for gradual withdrawal. 'It may be that you'd prefer to wait and see if there is any recurrence.'

'No,' Fiona said quickly. The prospect of that terror clawing through her again, the flailing fear, the feeling that she was dying, was untenable. She asked for a prescription and said she would like to try the CBT. Dr Melling said there might be a wait but Fiona would get a letter as soon as an appointment was available.

Fiona filled the prescription at the pharmacy next door to the surgery. *To be taken with food*, it read on the label. She wasn't hungry but she wanted the medicine so managed a couple of oatcakes and cheese.

She prayed the drugs would work quickly to protect her from the panic returning. She also hoped they would stop the pictures that were lodged in her skull. The relentless carousel of images shuttering on and on. *Blink*, Danny's palm on the grass. *Blink*, his eyes rolling back in his skull. *Blink*, his mother on her knees, her face torn wide with grief.

CHAPTER SEVEN

Mike

I an was ready to sack Mike. He'd had customers on his back: several express deliveries not received, the firm's golden guarantee rendered worthless.

Mike explained the situation and Ian had nowhere to go with it. Took a while for his body to catch up with his brain: face still grimacing, shoulders flexing as he processed the fact that witnessing a murder probably did count as a rock-solid excuse. Mike promised to stay late, clear his backlog, half-hoping Ian would give him a break, put some of his sheet on to one of the other couriers, but Ian just nodded and clapped him on the back. Trying for matey. Failing.

Word spread fast and a couple of the lads caught up with Mike in the loading bay. Mike was holding court describing the scene, telling it like a story, when Ian came out of the office, hitching his pants up. Already had the gut of a man ten years older.

'Best get on.' Mike broke up the little gathering before Ian could. 'Shocking, no two ways about it. I tell you.' He headed for his van.

'Never seen a dead body,' one of the younger men said.

Mike just caught the backchat as he clambered into his cab. 'Hang around here any longer and we'll all see one.' The gale of laughter.

Mike felt a quickening in the pit of his guts. The shadow of the time before. The other boy who'd died, his father running into the street with his son in his arms. Mike pushed the shadow away, shaken, and stabbed at the button on the radio. Retuned to XFM, local rock station, Elbow singing 'The Seldom Seen Kid', plaintive riffs and Mancunian lyrics.

Vicky had been great. They'd fed the kids, got them to bed early. Mike had surreptitiously washed Kieran's straw, turned it the other way up so the boy wouldn't find the faint indentations his teeth had already made. Later Mike had snipped half a centimetre off the end so it'd look fresh enough to do for breakfast in the morning.

With the kids out of the way, she'd sent him for a shower. 'You don't half reek, Mike.' And when he came back she gave him a cold lager, sat him down, wanted to know everything. When he got ahead of himself, she interrupted, pulled him back to the right point.

'It's bloody awful,' she said when he'd done. She held his gaze. 'You okay?'

He tipped his head.

'Do you want to get off down the pub for a bit?' He met up with the lads a couple of times a week.

'Nah.' He nodded at the fridge. 'I'll have another can. Maybe an early night.'

'Oh, yeah.' She walked to the fridge, got the beer, turned and faced him. Grinned, one tooth snagging on her bottom lip. 'What sort of early night?'

'Bring that over here and I'll show you.' He felt the heat of anticipation in his groin.

Vicky giggled, popped the ring pull and took a swig. Walked over to him, nice and slow, her hips swaying, the fine, straight blonde hair swinging in time.

She sat astride his legs, took another swig and handed him his drink. Her eyes were dancing. She smiled and reached for the buttons on his jeans.

50

* * *

Thursday the police wanted to see him. The murder had been all over the papers. A boy gunned down on his way to a band rehearsal. A lad who had a bright future by all accounts. Well liked in school, never in trouble. Planned to do a course in sound production and dreamed of being a successful musician. Mike had never done much at school. Just the thought of the place brought back memories he'd rather not have, set the swirl of unease moving inside him like dirty water, dampened his day.

They couldn't tell him how long he'd be there. And the answer didn't change when he explained things were a bit tricky work-wise. He agreed to go in for one o'clock, hoping an hour would cover it and he could call it lunch.

It was like he'd never spoken to the officer in the police car, the woman. He had to start from scratch. Sat in a meeting room with a copper who was a few years older than Mike. Grey hair but well turned out – suit and white shirt. He slipped the jacket off once they were settled. Joe Kitson, a detective inspector. 'Call me Joe,' he told Mike. Mike appreciated the informality. Understood it too. People would open up to you more if you were on first-name terms.

Joe asked Mike to talk him through what happened. Then he wrote down what Mike had told him. Checking sentence by sentence. He wrote on a laptop, fast, read back each complete paragraph and made sure he'd got it right. Joe didn't talk much but he had an easy way to him, a good listener, not only for the statement but for the other stuff Mike mentioned: the situation at work, the shock he'd felt when he realized he was seeing it for real.

Then Joe printed it all out on a special form and asked Mike to read it, and sign and date it at the bottom. He'd give evidence if the case came to court, Joe said, Mike understood that?

'Yes, of course,' Mike said

Joe explained what would happen next. The police would be gathering as much evidence as possible to try and bring charges against the culprits. It would probably be a matter of months rather than weeks before they knew whether they had enough to mount a prosecution.

Joe told him that they intended to keep the witnesses' identity secret to minimize any chances of coercion. He asked Mike not to advertise the fact he was giving a statement and might be called as a witness. Joe gave him his card, told him to get in touch if he had any questions, any concerns.

'What do you reckon the chances are?' Mike asked as Joe walked him out. 'Reckon you'll find out who did it?'

'Oh, we've a pretty shrewd idea of who's behind it,' said Joe. 'What we have to do now is see if we can prove it.'

'Did you trace the car? You'd think a Beemer like that'd be a doddle to find.'

Joe smiled, shook his head. 'Sorry, I'm not allowed to discuss the investigation with you.'

Mike nodded. 'Need to know basis,' he said. Some line off the telly. He felt a prat as soon as he said it.

'That's right,' Joe agreed. They shook hands at the front desk. 'Thanks for coming in, and I hope we'll be in touch later in the year.'

Mike had lost an hour and three-quarters and missed two calls from Ian. He rang his boss.

'Where the bloody hell are you?' Ian barked. 'I've had Sandringham Way mithering about a new laptop for the past hour, stayed off work to take delivery.'

'Almost there,' Mike lied, 'five minutes.'

'Keep your bloody phone on!' Ian ended the call.

Mike sighed, slid a CD into the player. Jumped to Track 4, prepared to sing along with Jagger: 'Hey You Get Off My Cloud'.

CHAPTER EIGHT

Zak

Topping up his phone had used up what was left from the supermarket money. And he only made a tenner on the stuff from the house. Everyone had a camera these days and the people in the pub slagged off the one he was flogging: no video and only two megapixels, they'd better on their phones. The jewellery brought a bit more.

He bought half an ounce of Golden Virginia and some Rizlas, a bottle of Lambrini. In the shop they were talking about the murder. Zak didn't want to hear it. Made him remember the way Carlton had looked at him, trapped in the window. And if Carlton knew Zak had seen him shoot, what then? He'd be coming after Zak before too long – to shut him up.

He was living in an old house near Plattfields Park. Not on the council estate but the other side of Wilmslow Road. The place was scheduled for demolition, chain link fencing and warning signs. Zak wasn't much of a reader but he could tell what the red and white sign with the picture of an Alsatian meant. And he knew it was just for show. Any hint of a real guard dog and Bess would have let on.

There was a gap below the fencing at one side where a part of the low garden wall had collapsed. He only needed to shove some bricks aside to wriggle under and Bess had followed.

The house was full of damp and the garden thick with saplings and brambles. Now they were in leaf and hid most of the building. It looked blind: sheets of chipboard nailed over the windows and doors. When he first found it, he could see they'd been there a good while. Broken guttering poured rainwater on to the sheet over the side door and the wood had gone black and green with mould, the bottom swelling with rot.

It hadn't taken Zak much effort to work one edge loose, lumps of wood crumbling off like Weetabix and woodlice scurrying away. A couple of kicks had got him through the brittle door behind.

Now, when he came and went, he could swing the chipboard out a couple of feet and push it back in place. From any distance the property still looked secure.

No electrics so it was pitch dark day and night, and full of creepy crawlies, but it was safer than the streets.

Zak had nicked some candles from the health food shop. Big, fat yellow ones that burned for hours. The driest room was at the back. The old dining room. He'd got his sleeping bag in there and there was a massive fireplace where he could burn stuff. The smoke came back in the room but it was worth it to see the flames dancing and feel the glow of heat. The place was stone cold even now in summer and come winter he thought it'd be unbearable. Unless he got hold of some sort of arctic clothing, bearskin or summat, like explorers use. He'd have to move on. Maybe find out if his mam was sorted out now and move back there.

Zak had never been upstairs. Part of the staircase had come down and there was no easy way up. The floors were probably all rotten up there. The first night he'd heard noises upstairs. Come awake so sudden, Bess had growled, picking up on his fear. He'd listened awhile. Scratching sounds. He didn't think it was rats or he'd see them downstairs too and Bess would have been after them. Maybe squirrels? Or pigeons in the roof.

Even with its gloom and damp he liked the vibe of the house. He liked to imagine it full of people. A family and all their mates. Bess by the fire or under the table when they sat down to eat. Plates piled high. And a swing in the garden and a Christmas tree, a real one in the corner.

He'd shifted Christmas trees last winter. A mate of Midge's had a batch going for a song. Midge did him a sign on cardboard and the mate dropped them off at dawn, on the corner where a lot of commuters would be driving past into work in town. Norway Spruce, they were. £25 for five foot. Undercut all the other outlets. They were bound up tight, easy to slide on to a roof rack or in a car.

'Just don't let 'em open them,' Midge's mate warned him.

'Why's that?'

He tapped his nose. 'And any you don't shift, just leave 'em. No returns.'

Zak had sold nineteen by eleven thirty. Made a shedload of dosh. He left the last one for himself. Levelled it on his shoulder and walked back to the place he was staying. A little terrace in Fallowfield. The small bedroom at the back. No room for a tree there, and all the other rooms full of blokes over from Bulgaria, sharing three or four to a room, but he could stick it in the yard. He left it while he went to Aldi, got some decorations and a fairy, some stuff like Bailey's seeing as it was that time of year.

He'd taken the tree out and cut off the netting and stood it up. Stared at it and heard the laughter from the kitchen doorway behind him, two of the lads. One of them slapping his knees and wheezing. Zak stared at it. Branches at the top lush and green and a skirt the same round the bottom. In between a naked trunk. A great gap where the middle should be like something had eaten the best bit.

He carried on. Put the baubles on top and bottom, left the tinsel hanging down to fill the hole. All the while the men almost hysterical behind him. Better than nothing. They shared a toast with him once he'd set the fairy on top.

Now he lit a candle, fed Bess and rolled a joint. Drank some of the Lambrini. Grew sleepy. He slid into his sleeping bag and Bess padded over to join him. She circled a couple of times then plumped down, stretched out by his side. Head on her paws. Zak always left the candle going, to take the sting out of the darkness. Not enough to see much by but he wanted the light to stop the dreams. That and the booze. It didn't always work. It could happen any time, a beast with a gaping, black mouth, swallowing him down, where it was suffocating and cold and no one could hear him crying.

His bones ached, an icy, needling pain too deep to reach. Scars from the crash. He didn't like to think about that. It didn't do any good thinking about that. When they lifted him out and he was yelping with the pain. The look in their eyes: he knew it was bad, he must be very bad. And one of the men turned away, Zak saw his nose redden and his mouth tremble and saw the man was crying. Then Zak had wanted to cry too but his tears didn't work any more.

He closed his eyes and imagined the house on a summer's day, a barbecue in the garden. Zak flipping burgers and Bess waiting for any crumbs. His mam at the table with all the others, catching his eye and smiling at him.

Zak drifted off to sleep. Met his dreams. Found himself running, darting, dodging. The mud sucking him under. Stones thudding into him. Twitching and jerking as he slept. His restless movements echoed by the dog at his side.

CHAPTER NINE

Fiona

Fiona was rarely ill and Owen didn't know how to react. She'd taken sick leave and explained everything to Shelley, who stressed that she was to have as long as she needed and not try and rush back to work.

Over tea that same day she told Owen. 'So, I'm going to be at home and I've got some tablets from the doctor. I'll be seeing a therapist as well.'

His face, what she could see of it, froze. His eyes met hers. Dismay. A slight curl to his lip.

'Lots of people do,' she said amused, 'you don't have to be bonkers. Have you any plans for the weekend?' She changed the conversation, letting him off the hook.

'Maybe Central.' The indoor skate park in town. Skateboarding was the only active thing Owen showed any interest in, and because it got him up and away from his video games she supported him to the hilt. That meant shelling out for all the gear as well as the boards and fittings. The bulky shoes with their lurid patterns (Etnies, Vans, DCs), the fluorescent belts and garish socks, the particular brands of hooded jackets.

And of course the hair, straight and dark. Owen's natural colour was mid-brown but now he dyed it black with Fiona's assistance. She helped him apply it, wiped the splodges from his neck and ears, reminded him when twenty-five minutes was up. How much longer would he let her help? 'Have you got homework?' she asked him.

Owen shrugged.

'Well, you don't go anywhere until you've checked and you've done it.'

Owen kept eating.

'Did you hear me?' She was irritated at how he ignored her.

'I'm not deaf,' Owen retorted and got to his feet, scraping the chair across the wood flooring.

'Well, don't act like you are then,' she said sharply.

Owen glared at her, his face reddening.

Fiona couldn't bear it. She raised a hand, fingers spread, trying to be reasonable. 'Maybe it's about time I trusted you to do your homework,' she said, 'without any nagging from me. Okay? So it's up to you from now on.'

He waited, shoulders slumped, head on one side, mouth open, a study in tedium, to see if she had finished. Then he walked away. Her eyes prickled, she sniffed hard. It won't always be like this, she reminded herself. It will change.

After tea she read the local evening paper. All week she had been devouring coverage about the murder. Each time she found an item her heart would swell and her throat tighten. Often she would weep, the tears always so close to the surface. She read and reread, hoping to find something there, some meaning, some understanding. She drank in the details about the boy and his family: his parents Paulette and Stephen, Danny's twin sister Nadine, also a hard-working student who wanted to make films, the grandmother Rose. Fiona pored over the pictures, the school photographs, the family occasions.

Tonight the article carried a photograph of the family in mourning. Dark clothes and harrowed expressions outside their church. Preparations were under way for the funeral. Momentarily Fiona considered going. But the germ of the idea was crushed by the weight of fear. It might prompt another attack. The GP had told her that it could be a couple of weeks before the medication started working and she should avoid stressful situations. It felt craven, cowardly, but she could not risk it. Both for her own sake but also because she knew it would be unforgivable if she went and the worst happened and she distracted attention from what really mattered. The burial of a child.

She didn't like to throw the papers in the bin, it seemed irreverent. Instead she cut out the articles about Danny first and put them in a large envelope. She left it in the dining room, with her work files. She did it secretively, waiting until she was alone, though she wasn't sure why. Perhaps it seemed ghoulish.

Fiona no longer trusted herself to drive. The car brought associations of both the murder and the crippling panic. So when the police wanted her to go in and make a statement she asked if it would be possible to do it at her house. She might have been able to work out a bus route or hire a cab but if going over the incident made her ill with anxiety she wanted to be under her own roof. The man she spoke to, DI Kitson, agreed and turned up promptly on the Tuesday afternoon.

Joe was a nice man, softly spoken. She'd expected someone with more bluster or drive, someone sharper round the edges. He put her at her ease and set up his laptop to take notes. She liked the way he listened to her, really listened, instead of simply waiting for her to stop talking so he could start, which is how many of her male colleagues in senior positions behaved. And he thought carefully when she asked him questions rather than jumping straight in with a response.

He had a sketch of the area – the main road and the recreation ground. The houses and their back yards all marked off exactly like the diagrams on house deeds. He took it a stage at a time, asking her to show him where she was when she left the house, after she crossed the road, when she reached Danny – and what else she saw, who else she remembered each time. She was back there, *blink*, the sun hot on the nape of her neck and her hands on Danny's chest, *blink*, his blood still warm on his T-shirt. She felt sick, felt her gullet spasm and her ears buzz. She made a noise and he saw. He knew.

'Breathe out,' he said, 'slowly. Good, that's good. Wait, shallow now.' It was ironic – exactly the sort of coaching she would use with one of her mums in labour.

He repeated the words until she'd calmed. 'I'm sorry,' he said, 'something like this, it's a terrible thing.'

'I have a son,' she said. A sudden urge to confide. Wiping at her face with her fingers.

He nodded. He knew of course, that was one of her background details.

Joe explained there were two areas he wanted to focus on more closely, to see if she could add anything further: one was the car that had almost run her over and the other was the man behind the wheel. She'd already described a silver BMW. He asked if she could recall any details.

'I didn't see the number plate.'

'What about the windscreen, the tax disc?'

She shook her head. 'It was so fast.'

'Any decals, decorations, anything dangling from the rear-view mirror?'

It was a blank. All she could see was the sheen of the glass and the glimpse of the man.

'What did he look like?'

'He was white, a slim face, a wide mouth.' She had practised this, gone over it again and again in her mind's eye, determined not to let the snapshot fade. 'Very short hair, pretty really, like a male model. Good cheekbones. I'm sorry.' She laughed at herself and Joe gave an easy grin. 'A bit like Johnny Depp,' she added. 'That sounds so stupid. But that's who he reminded me of.'

'That's very good. Anything else? Clothes, hands?'

'I only saw his face. He braked, I jumped back, there was this moment—' her voice shook and her mouth felt dry – 'we were just staring at each other, both shocked.' She recalled the way he glared at her. 'And then he drove on.'

'And the other man?'

'I barely registered him. I could tell there were two people in the car but I only saw the driver.'

Joe shifted in his seat. Typed a bit more into his laptop. Then he explained that he'd like her to try and identify the man she saw but she would have to do that at the police station. It was important to make sure it was done above board, the right checks and balances. 'Someone else has to do it, I'm not allowed.' He smiled. 'Make sure I don't tip you the wink.'

Fiona felt uneasy. 'I don't know.'

'We could pop along now,' he said quietly. 'No fuss, no complicated arrangements. Be back within the hour.' His eyes were greeny grey, the colour of shale, of bay leaf.

Later she thought he had planned it like that, making it easier to do because she wouldn't be anticipating it, wouldn't have a chance to get cold feet.

Still she hesitated. 'But if I . . .'

He read her mind. 'You find it's too much, I'll bring you straight home.'

She agreed. Wanting to be brave, wanting to impress him. Pathetic, she told herself.

The drive took only ten minutes and when they got to the police station it was all set up. Joe left her with a jovial, whiskery man and a younger woman. There was a monitor for her to watch and a camera would record Fiona's reactions for evidence.

'What we have are eight video IDs,' the man said. 'I'd like you to watch them, all of them, and only at the end tell me if the man you saw driving the BMW is among them and which number he is. You can look again at any of the images and we can freeze them for you too, if you ask. You can't ask me any questions and please take your time. Is that all right?'

It was and the woman set the camera going.

They were like moving mug-shots, Fiona thought to herself, the men looking straight ahead then turning this way and that for the profiles. The men were all white with short hair. She saw him, number four, with a lurch of recognition. Then did as instructed and watched the rest. None of the others came close. 'Number four.' Her voice sounded dusty. 'That was him.' The man put number four back on the screen. He had large, dark eyes. A sensuous mouth, the sculpted face. Dress him in ringlets and kohl, pantaloons and a frilly shirt, and he could be Captain Jack in *Pirates of the Caribbean*.

'You're sure?'

'Completely.'

'Thank you.'

The woman stopped filming. Then Fiona had to answer several questions and her answers were recorded on forms: when and where she had seen the man, how close she had been, whether her view had been obstructed and so on.

Joe met her afterwards. He had already spoken to the man conducting the identification.

'How did I do?' Fiona asked.

'Very well,' Joe smiled. 'You identified Sam Millins. He's known to us already and his name is high on the list for this inquiry.'

She soaked up his air of satisfaction. She wanted to please him. 'Were there other witnesses?' she asked.

Joe nodded. 'One, so far. We hope there will be others.'

'In the paper, they talk about people being afraid to talk to the police.'

He sighed. 'That's our biggest problem.'

She told him about Carmen Johnson: how the new mum turned Fiona away, unwilling to be associated with her.

After Joe had dropped her home, Fiona found herself wondering about him: whether he was married and had children, what he did outside work. And whether she would see him again.

CHAPTER TEN

Cheryl

The tradition was to celebrate the one who had passed for nine nights. No one seemed to know why it was that number, not even Nana who usually couldn't shut up about the old country customs back in Jamaica.

The Macateer house was full of people. Some had come up from London and Bristol and Birmingham, branches of the family Cheryl didn't even know. It wasn't just for family either, everyone in the community turned up. No invitation needed. Some nights it was hard to figure out how they would all fit in: it wasn't a big house. But they did and the food and the drinks kept coming. Plates of fried chicken and fish, curry and patties, rice and peas, loaves of white bread and big, fat sponge cakes.

The place was noisy with chatter and laughter, got raucous as the evenings deepened and more rum and Red Stripe was consumed. People sang old tunes, hymns, gospel, some nights they'd put music on and dance. Cheryl wondered how Auntie Paulette and Nadine and the others could stand it. Didn't they want to grieve in peace?

'That come later,' said Nana, 'after the funeral. All the time in the world they have then.' She was up most nights, sitting beside her friend Rose, slipping to the kitchen to clear up paper plates or wash glasses. With so many there of Nana's own age

Cheryl saw her in a different light. She was the most outspoken, prickly even. She'd say a thing and then there'd be a pause and someone would cut their eyes at her but Nana would stand her ground. Little things or big, it didn't seem to matter. She was loudest of all talking about what had happened to Danny and how shameful it was that people were running scared, keeping quiet. 'Like a new set of chains, slaves to fear,' she pronounced one night, just as Cheryl was preparing to head back home to put Milo to bed. Late already and Milo grizzling in her arms. Rose nodded at Nana's words but other people murmured, disliking the sentiment. There were people in the room linked to Carlton, though neither he nor Vinia had been down. Auntie Paulette kept saying she didn't want anyone at the funeral that was part of the gangs but the gangs weren't a fixed thing. Not like joining the gym or enrolling at college. No membership cards or contracts. Some people were there for life, or death, calling the shots and making the money, but the younger kids might run an errand now and then, hide a gun or deliver a package. Might do a favour for a friend or a cousin and never a thing more. Others would start their own operation, something small that wouldn't disrespect the main players. Most of the people in the room had a notion who'd killed Danny Macateer. And Cheryl knew for sure. Even though she hadn't seen them fire the gun. It sat inside her like something rotten, a clump of dirt making her sick.

The day of the funeral was dull but dry, the sky a grey, wool blanket trapping the air which smelt of steel. Outside the church a crowd of reporters with cameras filmed everyone arriving. They kept a distance, behind the railings across the road, and they were quiet, though there was the click and flash and ding and sizzle as they took their pictures. The church was full, people standing at the back, and folding chairs brought out to create extra rows behind the pews. As people arrived there were greetings, men shaking hands and hugging each other, acquaintances waving, people who hadn't met at the nine nights smiling in surprise and recognition. Cheryl's heart kicked when she saw Vinia and her mother: had Carlton come? Of course not, he'd be a fool to do that for all his front.

Cheryl, Nana and Milo were three rows back, behind the immediate family who would follow the coffin into church. Above the altar hung a huge banner, a picture of Danny. It wasn't a formal one, not a school photo or a pose from a family wedding, but something more relaxed. As if someone had just caught the moment: Danny, his head tilted a little, his eyes alive with merriment, his smile wide and open. The life in him! *Danny Martin Macateer*, read the words beneath in black edged with gold, *1993–2009*. It brought a lump to Cheryl's throat, it hurt to swallow.

'Who took the picture?' she asked Nana, who'd been party to many of the arrangements.

'Nadine.'

Cheryl wondered what it was like to lose a twin. Had they shared that special bond you read about? When Danny was shot, had Nadine felt it? Or sensed something really bad was going down? She'd been in church at the time, had she turned dizzy or felt a spike of pain pierce her heart?

Music started up, some piano sounding sweet and low, and the procession came down the central aisle. Reverend James and then Danny's coffin, a huge bouquet on top, yellow roses, white lilies, green ferns and golden dahlias. The family followed and slid into their places. Cheryl could see Nadine's back, the arch of her neck, the shape of her head, so like her brother's.

There were prayers from the Reverend and readings from the Bible then testimonials. People queued up to speak about the boy, to make jokes, and share memories, read poems and quotes. Mr Gaunt, Danny's music teacher, spoke and Mr Throstle the school head whose voice wavered towards the end of his praises. Danny's uncle and his cousin took a turn, then another cousin. Danny's band played a song he'd written, the little guy on the drums, his eyes red from weeping. Bobby Carr, the community leader, spoke about the peril that stalked the streets and the need for hope and vision, the need to take the guns from the hands of the boys who were lost and brutalized and deadly and give them work, hope, life. He promised Danny Macateer should not die in vain. Cheryl clamped her teeth tight together and felt the acid rise behind her breastbone, the sweat prickle around the edge of her hair.

Finally Nadine walked to the front. She looked a thousand years old, her eyes bottomless. She raised her face to speak then faltered, shook her head and covered her mouth. Murmurs of support echoed from the congregation. She tried again, her voice just audible. 'This is how I remember Danny, my brother. His spirit is with me still. He will always be with me.'

A large screen to the left of the altar lit up and a cascade of images and music unfolded, fragments from Danny's YouTube pieces, home movies, band practice. Danny fooling around, showing off, Danny concentrating, one arm rubbing the back of his neck, Danny singing, his eyes closed, mouth close to the mic, Danny trying to moonwalk, Danny with a wig on performing a speech from his drama course, opening a Christmas present. Laughing, head flung back, arms wide. The life shining from him. The picture froze and Reverend James thanked them all and invited them to the burial at Southern Cemetery.

Finally, as the procession followed the coffin out of the church, faces blurred with grief, 'Abraham, Martin, John' soared, filling the space, Marvin Gaye's song about how the good die young. Cheryl sobbed and clung to her nana and Milo crawled between them pulling at their sleeves, disturbed by all these tears.

At the cemetery, a couple of miles south of the church, Milo was restless and Cheryl let him wander about while they lowered the coffin into the grave and Reverend James spoke again. The mourners sang at the graveside – one of the cousins had printed off hymn sheets. The day was still, muffled, but the voices sounded raw and broken. Cheryl couldn't sing. Her chest felt too tight.

They waited until the grave was filled. Cheryl knew there were old stories from the islands of the dead trying to walk again, or of robbers taking the body, and people were still superstitious even in a different country and modern times.

Back at the church hall, Milo staggered about between legs, under the buffet tables, fractious and full of temper. Cheryl took him out and pushed him in his stroller round the car park until he fell asleep. After that, for the next two hours, even the sound of the band playing didn't wake him.

The day wound on, the lights came on in the hall, half the guests were outside smoking. Cheryl had lost count of the people she'd spoken to, the cigarettes she'd had. Vinia had been cosying up to one of the boys from Birmingham, even though she knew he was due to be a daddy with another girl.

When they finally left, Vinia walked back with them. A starless sky. The streets looked tired in the sodium light, jaundiced. Cheryl wanted Vinia gone but Nana asked her if she'd like to stay and she said yes, double quick.

Milo never stirred when Cheryl put him in his cot. He'd got his second wind late afternoon and been on the go ever since, playing hide and seek and tig with the other kids. Cheryl looked at him lying there, his cheek sticky with sugar from some cake, his knees grubby, the curls at the nape of his neck tangled. He was perfect. Beautiful. Every time she saw him afresh she felt the glow in her heart, the big, hot, rush of love for him.

Nana was sitting in her chair, eyes closed, head resting back while Vinia made some tea. Nana looked old, the skin slack on her jaw, draped loose on her neck. Her brow and the sides of her mouth, deep furrows. When she opened her eyes to take the mug from Vinia, Cheryl saw that the whites of her eyes were yellow.

'It's a terrible thing.' Nana blew on her tea.

Cheryl and Vinia murmured in agreement. Though Cheryl felt like strangling her if she said it again.

'And no one speaks up. Someone knows.'

'It's not easy, Nana,' Cheryl said.

'I ain't saying it's easy but it is right. There is right and there is wrong.'

'It was a lovely service.' Vinia tried to head Nana off but she wasn't for turning.

'It wasn't easy for Dr Martin Luther King but he speak out,' she began the litany. 'It wasn't easy for

Nelson Mandela but he never give in. Never.' The skin on her face wobbled as she shook her head for emphasis. 'Years in prison.' She was on a roll now, jabbing her finger at them, her frown deeper, voice husky like she was wearing it out. 'It wasn't easy for Rosa Parks but she stood up.'

'No, Nana, she sat down.' Cheryl quipped. She'd been reared on the stories of these heroes, Rosa Parks refusing to go to the back of the bus, parking herself on one of the 'white' seats, a civil rights pioneer. Vinia laughed.

Nana snorted her displeasure, her eyes grew hard. 'There's talk your stepbrother might know something,' she challenged Vinia.

Cheryl tensed, pressing her toes into the floor. Was that why Nana had asked her friend if she wanted to stay? To try and shame her into saying something?

'That's crazy,' said Vinia. 'Stupid talk.'

'No way!' Cheryl backed Vinia up.

Nana sipped her tea. 'Sad day,' she said and struggled to her feet. Cheryl didn't know if she meant the day was sad because of the funeral, or because people were afraid to speak about the murder. 'Goodnight and God bless,' she told them.

'G'night,' Cheryl said, hands cupping her own drink, the heat hurting her fingers, studying the tremor on the surface of the tea, unable to meet Nana's eyes.

CHAPTER ELEVEN

Mike

Mike woke suddenly at five. Bolt upright in bed, slippery with sweat. He grabbed a breath, listened, wondering whether Megan had cried out, though she usually came into their room if she'd had a bad dream and wriggled between them. No one got much sleep after that, her elbows and knees sharp as tacks. Plus she snored. A four-year-old! Mike asked Vicky once if they should get her checked out. Vicky rolled her eyes and told him to forget it: they'd enough on their plates seeing doctors for Kieran, Megan was just fine.

The house was quiet. Vicky, beside him, turned over and pulled at the duvet. Mike lay back down and closed his eyes. Had he been dreaming? He didn't usually remember his dreams. Now he sensed an aftertaste, like a blurred reflection of something wrong, something shameful. The old sour feeling from way back, times he didn't want to think about. He wiped it away, steam on a mirror, and tried to sleep; if he got back off sharpish he'd have another two hours.

Their routine proper began at seven. Kids up and dressed. Breakfast, packed lunches. At twenty past eight Vicky did the school run. Kieran was at Brook School, a place catering for children with Autistic Spectrum Disorder. There'd never been any sugges-tion of him going into mainstream schools, his needs too varied, too complex. Stick him in the local primary and he'd have sat in the corner for six hours, unreachable.

The staff at Brook were fantastic. Kieran had his own programme, a combination of one-to-one and group sessions to assist with his physical, mental and social skills. He'd come on in leaps and bounds, now able to greet people he'd not met before and sometimes answer simple questions. They all knew there were limits to what Kieran would achieve. He'd never live independently. Probably never take a bus ride unaccompanied. That frightened Mike more than anything. That when he and Vicky went, not to be maudlin or owt, Kieran would be in the care of the state. You couldn't put that on to Megan, she'd have her own life to lead, maybe her own family. Might live abroad or anything.

Vicky had been home with Megan for three months after she was born but they couldn't manage without Vicky's income. She'd asked her mum to have Megan while she visited her customers but her mum's health wasn't great so it was a relief when they got a place at the childminder's and were able to claim the fees back. Now Megan was at the nursery attached to the primary school and thriving on it. Vicky worked school hours and some evenings when Mike could sort the kids.

Mike let his thoughts drift. Wondered if a holiday might possibly be an option this year. Some last-minute bargain break. It would mean organizing respite care for Kieran. They'd only done that once before and they weren't sure whether the pain was worth the gain. The stress of worrying how Kieran was, the guilt of being off on the beach, at the café or in the pool without him. Vicky had missed him, grown tearful by the end of the stay, homesick for

74

the lad. Mike too, though not so bad. 'It's been good for Megan,' he told Vicky, 'look at her.' She was laughing and splashing in the toddler pool.

'She's happy anywhere,' Vicky said.

The alarm woke Mike just as he slipped away. He came swimming to consciousness: his mouth dry, his head aching. He wondered if he was coming down with a cold. Too bad. They didn't do illness. Couldn't afford to.

At the loading bay, Mike checked off his delivery sheet and packed the van so he'd got the parcels in the right sequence Most of it was short-run stuff, within ten miles of the depot. But he'd one delivery out into Cheshire, beyond Bollington. That'd make a change. The winding lanes instead of city bottle-necks. A bit of scenery. He'd aim for that in the middle of the day, have his butties in a lay-by somewhere. It was shaping up to be fine: a few clouds but no rain forecast.

Ian was prowling around looking for an argument so Mike got his stuff packed and didn't hang about.

It took him forever to make his first two drops. Extensions to the tram network meant diversions and road closures, forcing the heavy traffic into a smaller number of routes. He made a stop in Ancoats where the process of converting crumbling warehouses from the rag trade into luxury gaffs for professionals continued even in the teeth of the recession. Then he crossed town to Salford Quays, where the BBC's Media City was nearing completion.

Coming back into Manchester took him along Princess Road and past the recreation ground. There was a mobile cop shop there now and placards on

the lamp-posts: *Witness Appeal, Serious Incident.*
That's when he saw the car.

Up ahead of him, taking a right, a silver BMW
X5. He felt his guts clench and a jolt travel the length
of his forearms. He checked his mirrors, indicated
and nipped out. If he could just get the number plate.
There were two other cars between him and his
quarry, waiting for the lights to change.

He could get a picture. He rooted for his phone
and pulled it out, switched the camera on. The traffic
lights went red-and-amber then green. The Beemer
moved at speed into the side road. One guy inside,
but the angle of the sunlight cast reflections on the
driver's window and Mike couldn't make the man
out.

Halfway down the side street one of the other cars
slowed to park. No indicator. Mike swore at him and
swung out to overtake, his pulse jumping, just in
time to register the Beemer perform a U-turn.
Heading back towards him. Mike jammed on his
brakes and grabbed the phone. Suddenly he was
slammed forward, his head glancing off the windscreen, the seat belt biting into his shoulder, head
snapping back and a burning at his wrists. He heard
the sound of metal and glass and the whoomp of the
impact, as the car behind him rear-ended his van.
Then the whoop of an alarm, fast and urgent,
howling in his ears, matching his heartbeat.

CHAPTER TWELVE

Zak

He'd watched the taller girl get some money from a hole-in-the-wall and reckoned it was worth a shot.

'D'you wanna buy a dog?'

'Why, what's wrong with it?' The smaller one had mean eyes, little slits all suspicion. He had 'em pegged as sisters.

'Nothing. But I can't look after her any more. Just been chucked out my flat, I haven't got anywhere to stay. I hate to let her go.' He shuffled, stuck his hands in his pockets, swung his head to the side and down.

The taller one was stooping down, patting Bess on the head. 'What's her name?'

'Bess. She's a lovely nature. Lab cross.' He'd no idea what with but she was big and golden. 'She's had all her jabs,' he added. 'She was my dad's then he died and I took her.'

'Aw.' The taller one straightened up, her eyes soft, 'I want her to go to a good home.'

'How much?' demanded the little one. Then she cast an eye at her sister. 'Mum'd die.'

'She'd come round,' the taller one said, smitten.

'She's a good guard dog,' Zak put in. 'She'll bark if you want her to. Better than an alarm.'

'She's lovely, Shiv.' She grinned at her little sister. 'What's she eat?'

'She's not fussy but lamb's her favourite, any brand.'

'How much?' repeated Shiv.

'Twenty-five.' It was nothing. You'd pay ten for a rabbit in the pet shops. Zak hoped he'd get twenty.

'How old is she?' Shiv asked.

'Nearly five.'

'What's that in dog years?' The tall one was petting Bess again.

'Thirty-five,' said Zak. 'You times it by seven. Labradors, they live to fourteen or fifteen so she's only a young one.' Zak was aware of a pair of CSOs strolling up the precinct in their high vis jackets and dark caps. He wanted to make the sale before they got too close. 'She's well trained, tell her to stay and she won't budge. Sit there all night, she would.'

'What do you think, Shiv?' Her voice was bubbly with excitement, a smile flickered round her lips.

'Mum'd kill us.'

'Go over there,' Zak suggested to the tall one, 'then call her.' The CSOs had stopped, were talking to one of the African lads flogging brollies.

The girl walked over to the shop doorway. Bent down. 'Come on, Bess.' Bess ran over and stood at her feet. The girl clapped her hands. She walked back, Bess at her heels.

'Twenty,' Shiv said to Zak.

Zak made out he was torn for a moment. Looked at Bess then back to the girl. Nodded. The taller one burst out laughing. She took a fresh note out of her purse and Zak thanked her. He knelt down, hugged Bess, ruffled her head.

'You'll want her lead.' He pulled the coil of rope from his pocket. 'She's fine without but some places you have to put them on the lead. You're meant to round the shops.' He hooked the lead into the ring on Bess's collar.

'When's her birthday?' Shiv asked.

'Next week, August 10th. She'll be five then.'

'She's a Leo,' the tall girl said. 'Sociable, out-going.'

'Sounds right,' Zak smiled. The CSOs were on the move again. 'Look after her, won't you?'

'We will,' chorused the sisters.

Zak left them and walked up the tram platform. In the reflection of the glass he saw them set off towards Boots. Shiv went in the shop, the other girl waited outside with Bess.

A few minutes later, Shiv came out and they linked arms and walked further along. Then they went into the market. Zak slipped down from the tram stop and ran along the road to the alley that led into the middle of the market. He stopped at the bottom of the alley. The stalls were close together and the aisles between them narrow. He couldn't see the girls. Had no idea where they were but that was okay. Better in fact.

He whistled once, three shrill notes, and within seconds Bess was hurtling into the alley, no lead attached to her collar, not any more. Zak always made sure to fix the lead on with a soft, thin wire ring, little more than fuse wire that would open with the slightest tug, let alone the frantic yank when Bess heard him whistle for her.

He and the dog walked smartly up the alley and then down the steps to the canal. Out of sight, together again, and twenty quid richer.

Zak wondered if they'd put out a reward for information about the murder. If it was big enough, really really big, then it might be worth him coming forward but he'd want guarantees as well. Carlton saw him, he was sure of that, would know him by

Bess down there barking when it all kicked off if nothing else. Zak tried to steer clear of Carlton and his like but they made a point of knowing who was doing what on their turf. Zak was small-time, no threat to them. But if the cops did offer a reward, like they did when no one snitched, then he'd need a new identity, a place to live, somewhere for his mam and Bess. If the reward money was a lot, and it'd have to be a lot to break the silence, then maybe they'd go abroad, somewhere nice like Ibiza. Party all the time. Have a place by the beach and a pool. He could be a DJ, just for the fun, wouldn't need to work if the reward was big enough. He was imagining this when he saw the lads. Four of them on bikes, hoods up, circling round the end of the street like hyenas waiting for carrion. There was no way he was going past them, even with the dog at his side.

He spun on his heels and began to retrace his steps but one of them noticed him. He heard a yell, a ripple of sounds, the threat in the air like electricity, pricking his skin and pressing inside his skull.

He picked up speed but heard the air move behind him, the whirr of wheels, the clatter of gears.

'Oy, dosser.'

'Eh, tramp.'

Then the thud of something on his back. The rattle of a can hitting the road. A gale of laughter.

He turned now, pulling Bess in front of him, his hand in her collar.

'You got a light?' The lad had a shaved head, skin the colour of porridge, his neck was a mix of fuzzy tattoos and angry pimples. Zak stared. Stupid question, he knew it wasn't a light they wanted.

'Yeah.'

Zak pulled out his lighter, tossed it to the guy who caught it, dropped it, drove his heel down on to it and mashed it into the ground. 'Whoops!' He grinned. There were brown lines on his teeth. 'What else you got?'

'Nothing.'

'Empty your pockets.' A ginger lad, freckly. They'd no fear of Bess, barely cast her a glance. How could they tell she was soft? If he had a pit bull would they have left him alone?

Zak brought out his tobacco in one hand, a twist of draw, all he had left, in the other.

'Wacky backy,' the Asian guy said. He let his bike drop, stepped up to Zak. He had a scar by his eye, the line paler, puckered. He took the tobacco and the draw. 'And the rest,' he said.

'That's it.' Zak could smell the guy's aftershave, the sweat beneath it.

'Phone,' the first guy commanded.

'I need my phone.' Zak tried to keep calm, like it was a fact not an argument. 'My mam, she needs it to keep in touch with me.'

'His mam,' jeered the Asian lad.

'Mummy's boy, is he,' the ginger lad said. Then spat on the floor.

'She's in hospital. A big operation.'

'Give it here.' The Asian lad moved closer. Zak pulled his phone out. That raised a laugh. Old and scratched, chunky too, the sort you couldn't give away.

The Asian lad threw it to Ginger who rode off down the road with it before coming back and chucking it to the one with the tattoos. He peered at it, pressed some buttons. 'Let's have a chat to Mummy, then.'

Zak felt his bowels loosen with fear and a sullen rage burn his gullet. 'She's on the ward,' he said. 'Her phone'll be off. Give it here.'

'No can do,' the guy said. Then he lost interest. Dropped the phone and positioned the front wheel of his bike on top of it, then lifted and slammed the bike down. The phone skittered off across the tarmac. One of the others, the one who hadn't done much, put his bike down and got the phone. Dropped it down the drain. 'You should upgrade.'

They howled with laughter. Before they stopped, the Asian guy had punched Zak hard and he was falling backwards. Bess was barking. The others moved in. The next blow caught his ear. He rolled away, curling as small as he could, his arms trying to protect his head. A kick to his kidneys, one to his arse, pain rippling, throbbing. Black and red in his head.

Memories: metal on stone, the smell of his own dirt. His mouth was full of the bits again; chewy wisps of thread and the rigid shavings of rubber. The flavour of soil and sweat and elastic bands. Sometimes the tang of blood. Some of his teeth had gone. His gums were sore. In the daytime a band of light spangled golden around the door. If he wriggled and stretched out his leg, a line of it would fall across his foot. A beam of warmth. But at night it was dark as soot.

Then the lads were gone. He heard them pedal away, jeers fading. He lay there, the grit stinging his cheek, trembling and nauseous. They could have killed him, another few kicks in the right place. He could be lying dead. Like Danny Macateer. Never see Bess again, never see his mam. A ruptured gut or a knife in the throat or a bullet in the back.

Slowly he got to his knees, nothing broken, though his ribs hurt when he took a breath and his wrist was killing. Bess licked his face. He should train her to fight, he thought, train her to rip their throats out, take their faces off. Maybe he should muzzle her, make her look vicious. Whip the muzzle off next time he was threatened. Get a gun. Something to scare the shit out of them.

When he was fully upright, his head spun and he was sick, a thin stream of bile, bitter as anything. His eyes stung, he rubbed them hard. He'd have to get a new phone.

He still had the twenty in his shoe. That was summat. He'd drop in on Midge, get a little something, a drink too. Long as Midge didn't go on about the murder. He got his supply of drugs from Carlton, he'd be listening to all the gossip like the rest. Zak's ear felt hot and wet; it was bleeding. He'd try the corner shop, they didn't bother with a dress code. Serve anyone.

Could have been worse, he told himself. All the same he'd steer clear of this part of town for a while. No sense in asking for trouble. Wankers.

PART TWO

I Heard it Through the Grapevine

CHAPTER THIRTEEN

Fiona

I t was the middle of autumn before Fiona saw the cognitive behaviour therapist. In the intervening weeks she experienced two full-blown panic attacks. The first was in the post office of all places.

She had assumed the sickening terror was linked to Danny's death, the area it happened and by extension the car where the fear had first consumed her. So walking to the post office to pay her car tax hadn't worried her in the slightest.

The post office wasn't even noisy. But it was crowded and hot and cramped. A line of people snaked zigzag style in the cordoned-off aisles. There were two counters working but one clerk seemed to be stuck weighing a mountain of small packets for a customer. No one spoke and the air was tight with impatience. Fiona tried not to breathe in the stale smell coming off the elderly man in front of her. She could see the grime on the collar of his coat and the flakes of dandruff dotted through his hair. The woman behind her wore industrial-strength perfume which was even worse than the musty man smell.

Fiona felt herself gag. She cleared her throat then felt the ground tilt away, thick sweat broke along her hairline, on her scalp, under her arms. The fear came rolling like a wave, unstoppable, all-powerful, climbing her torso, robbing her of breath, of sense. She thought she would wet herself.

She turned abruptly, pushing past the queue, fighting her way to the door. Outside, she doubled over, her heart thundering in her ears, her mouth gummy.

'You all right, love?' A white-haired woman with a shopping trolley put her hand on Fiona's arm. Fiona couldn't reply, her throat was locked, her chest exploding. She knew there was something she should do, something to remember, but her mind was tangled.

Suddenly her stomach heaved and she vomited on to the pavement. The woman took a step back. 'You'd better go home.'

Fiona gulped, nodded, her mouth sour, her nose and throat stinging from the acid.

'Can you manage?'

Fiona coughed. Her breath came fast, rapid. Stars bursting in her eyes, then she remembered: *breathe slowly*. Joe's words, the policeman. Fiona tried to master her breath. Took a sip, shuddered, took another tiny sip. Little bird breaths.

The woman frowned.

'I'll be all right, thanks,' Fiona managed. The woman wasn't convinced but she gave a quick nod and set off with her trolley. Fiona sipped again. Waited until she felt able to move. Then walked home, her legs unsteady, her breath rank.

You might never have another, the cardiologist had said. Liar, thought Fiona, and now what?

Almost as great as the fear of a repeat attack was the dread of becoming housebound. She could live without town and shopping (there was the internet for that) and even without work, which had surprised her as she'd always loved her job, but not being able to walk the fields and the woods, or set out along by the river: to lose that would be intolerable. So the afternoon of the post office meltdown, even though she still felt sick and scalded, she forced herself to go out with Ziggy.

Apprehension wormed about in her stomach and her back was stiff, her thoughts edgy, as she set out. She watched Ziggy trot from scent to scent and they made their way to the nature reserve. There were blackberries, fat and shiny, alongside the path and she had a spare plastic bag in her pocket. She tasted one, the flavour deep and fruity, a perfect mix of sweet and tart. She picked lots, savouring the occasional bite of a thorn from the brambles, her fingers turning purple, gritty with specks leftover from the flowers. She attained a sort of equilibrium. When the bag was half full, she stopped. The juice drying on her hands was sticky.

Sticky like blood. A stab of horror. She flashed back to that day, the shower, peeling the tights from her knees. His eyes, the boy's eyes. She slewed her mind away, catalogued what she could see, determined to root herself in the here and now. The horse-chestnut cases still green and heavy in the tree; the sycamore leaves dying at the edges, splashed with sooty fungus, tar spot, there every year, though it never harmed the trees; the hen blackbird, dusty brown, seeking food in the mulch beneath the hedge; the whine of a wasp, drunk on rotten fruit. The gradual dying of the year. But this would all renew, return. This was her church. She fought for control and clung to her harvest. With some apples she could make a pie, or a crumble. She wiped her fingers on a tissue, texted Owen, asked him to get some Bramleys and some cream; there was a small supermarket on his way home.

Walking back, Fiona ran into the old American couple with their terriers. She smiled and nodded, her teeth clenched as they nattered about the weather and the deterioration in the quality of the kennels they used. By the time they moved on, her jaw ached with the effort. But she had coped.

Owen arrived back without any apples or cream.

'Oh, brilliant!' She rounded on him. 'I texted you.'

He stared at her, affronted. 'I didn't get any text.'

'How come?' she demanded. 'How come you never get my texts? Or do you just ignore them?' Her voice rising. 'I can't make apple and blackberry pie with no bloody apples.'

'Big deal.' He slung his bag down, kicked off his shoes.

'Pick them up,' she yelled. 'Put them away.' She heard the shrill of her tone, hated it.

Owen flushed, glared at her from under his fringe.

She put a hand out, grabbing the post at the bottom of the stairs. 'Look, I'm sorry. It happened again,' she said quietly. 'In the post office, another panic attack.'

'Not my fault,' he muttered and went upstairs, leaving his bag and shoes where he'd dropped them.

Three weeks after the post office and she was feeling much better. The medication seemed to be doing its work. She had some minor side effects, nausea and a dry mouth, but overall she felt calmer and safer. She was doing her best to keep a structure to her day. In the morning she did chores, the ongoing housework, then all the things there had never been enough time to do. She was clearing the spare room, sorting through old sports equipment and extra duvets, games and toys that Owen had outgrown, spare shoes. She found a set of watercolours and dabbled at them but her efforts only irritated her. The daubs on the page bore no resemblance to the pictures in her head. They'd been a present for Owen but he'd never shown any interest. If Owen had an artistic bone in his body it was a small and well-hidden one.

The idea of learning a craft, finding a hobby, appealed to her. Something for the afternoons, and those evenings when she wasn't interested in what was on television. At school she'd loved pottery, the heft of stone cold clay in her hands, the giddy spinning wheel, the magic of the kiln. They'd made coil pots and ornaments, hedgehogs and little dishes shaped like leaves. Pedestrian. But she'd used clay for her O level art project. Made a large vase, the green slip glaze on it luminous, as vibrant as she could get it. Her parents had displayed it on their sideboard but she'd no idea what had happened to it. After they'd both died, when she'd cleared out her mother's retirement flat, there'd been hardly anything left.

Pottery was impossible on her own at home. No wheel or kiln. The only place would be a night class and that meant going out, meeting people. That frightened her. She completed jigsaws and worked in the tiny back garden. She tried sudoku and cross-words but the afternoons began to yawn and her walks with Ziggy grew longer.

Since the post office she practised walking to the local shops and back every other day. Her own form of behavioural therapy. At first just there and back. Then going into one place and buying something. Then a couple of places. She managed fine. Taking things gradually and helped by the medication, she grew more confident.

Shelley had been more than happy to come round and visit. But she thought Fiona might try going out with her now. A meal maybe? Fiona liked the idea. She was lonely and the thought of Shelley's anecdotes from work, gossip about the other staff, her smiles, a restaurant meal, would be a welcome change. Would Shelley come to Chorlton, so Fiona could walk there? Could they meet early before it got too busy? Sure. Shelley agreed to all her conditions.

Fiona never even made it to the restaurant. And what made it most devastating, once she'd weathered that black, bleak, overwhelming anxiety and the indignity of cracking up in public, was the fact that there was nothing, not one, single, identifiable element that she could seize on to explain why the attack had come on in that place, a quiet junction of two suburban side streets, or at that time. If there was no particular trigger that set her off then she could be rendered disabled and petrified, suffocating and gripped by dread, anywhere, any time. Nowhere was safe.

CHAPTER FOURTEEN

Mike

With the neck brace on and a sling to support his dislocated left shoulder, Mike wouldn't be up for driving for several weeks. Ian told him he'd have to let him go. Lay-offs were on the cards anyway and it wouldn't be fair to the other lads to keep Mike's place open when he couldn't pull a fair day's graft. Mike could hear the relish in Ian's voice, bubbling under the surface of the words. Ian ran on spite: Mike knew his boss had never forgiven him for the missed deliveries on the day of the murder. And now Ian had his revenge.

'I'll try the post,' Mike told Vicky. 'See if anything's coming up for when I'm fit.' But they were letting people go, too. Combining rounds so posties had longer routes, longer hours, heavier mailbags. Some desk-jockey spouted how a walking pace of four miles an hour should be standard in the postal service, it would improve efficiency and keep the staff fit.

Mike tried the other contacts he had but it was the same story everywhere: short rations, hard times.

He went down the Jobcentre and found out what he could claim and when. He and Vicky spent a whole weekend filling in the forms. Pages and pages. They had to let the tax credit know their circumstances had changed. They applied for free school meals for the kids and got them. Mike had balked at that when Vicky first raised it.

'School dinners?' He looked at her.

'Why the face?'

'They'll get picked on,' he said. 'The kids on school dinners, they were always the losers.'

'That's daft,' Vicky countered.

'Cheap pies and soggy mash,' he tried, knowing that was a lost argument.

'Not now. Decent meals. And they'd only need a snack at teatime. Every penny counts. We might get free uniforms as well.'

Mike ran a hand over his face and sighed, stared at the fridge behind her, the garish magnets and the kids' paintings.

'You'd rather they went hungry?' She was riled, her eyes sparking a warning.

'No,' he protested.

'Well then?'

'Just do it!' He flung a hand at the school meals form, pushed away from the table and walked to the fridge.

'Bit early, isn't it?' Her voice tight as he opened the door.

Swearing, Mike slammed it shut, the fridge rocking, bottles and jars inside clanking.

That he should come to this. A man unable to feed and clothe his children. After years of solid hard work, careful budgeting. Years of being prudent and reliable, responsible and honest – and for what? Now he couldn't even provide for his family.

The dole officer had the decency to be honest with Mike about the prospects. Over fifty people chasing every vacancy, more if it was above minimum wage.

'Anything you can do to improve your profile would help.'

He gave Mike leaflets and offered him a special assessment interview. The lad was friendly, polite and sympathetic but they both knew he was on a hiding to nothing with Mike.

Mike's dad had been on the dole for a couple of years back in the eighties. He'd become depressed and irritable, carping at Mike's mum about the meals she scraped together, bossing Mike about more than usual. He was in danger of turning into his father. An appalling thought.

Danny Macateer's murder was on *Crimewatch*. They showed a re-enactment, and some of what Mike had told Joe Kitson was repeated.

'I told them that—' he turned to Vicky – 'about the car, the colour of the guy's clothes.' He'd a sense of delight, a glow of excitement, daft but there all the same.

Vicky looked like he'd slapped her.

'What?'

Kirsty Young on the telly was talking about how someone must know something, asking them to pick up the phone.

'The reason no one's come forward is because it's a gang thing,' Vicky said.

'The lad wasn't in a gang, they said that all along,' Mike told her.

'But those that did it are, and no one will dare say anything. If they do they'll be punished.'

'It's not right.' He shook his head, not seeing where she was going with it.

'What if they come after you?'

'Me? Don't be thick!'

'Listen.' Her face was white, naked. 'That's what they do. They have ways of finding out who's a witness and then they get to them.'

'What ways?' He couldn't believe this.

She closed her eyes tightly, her fists balls of fury. 'It doesn't matter what ways, they just do.'

'Suddenly you're an expert on gang crime?'

'Everyone knows!' Her voice grating. 'They'll threaten you, make you stop.'

'No,' he argued, putting his hand on her knee trying to calm her. She shoved it away.

'They could.' She was taut, ready to snap.

'Vicky.' He caught her hand, held it between his own. 'They've not even charged anyone yet. They're still appealing for help. It means they haven't got enough to pick the bloke up, not enough evidence. People like us don't get targeted; he won't know us from Adam.' He spoke faster as she tried to interrupt, emphasizing his words, as if the right stresses could force her to change her mind. 'But until there's a trial there's no risk at all. The only reason they'd put the frighteners on someone would be to stop them testifying, and then it'd only be those people they knew. Others in the neighbourhood, families and that. And there is no trial.' He bent his head, forcing eye contact, her hand warm in his. 'There probably never will be. Okay?'

She gave a half nod, nothing wholehearted but enough to make him relieved. On the television, the team had moved on to an armed robbery.

'I can put another channel on.' He held up the remote.

'I'm not bothered, now,' Vicky said.

Mike applied for every job going. He used the advice he got from the lad at the Jobcentre and drew up a CV. He worked out a batch of answers to use for the various questions like: *What do you think you could contribute to our company? What are your strongest*

96

qualities? and *Tell us about your hobbies and pas-times.* Why some manager in a call centre had the faintest interest in Mike's hobbies was beyond him but he played the game. He didn't get any interviews.

Some mornings he went to the local library, read the newspapers. Every two weeks he had to go in and sign on and have a jobsearch review: give evidence of three steps he had taken each week to prove he was actively seeking work. It was better than in his dad's time when they queued like cattle at the dole office every week and were viewed with suspicion and condescension by the staff. Mike had gone with his dad once. The place had been full of people whose lives were fragmenting or already in chaos. The air was sour with the reek of poverty, unwashed bodies and clothes, cigarettes and alcohol. The kids there were wild with boredom, their antics prompting the parents to lash out with angry slaps. The men were crazed with frustration, some of them tanked up already. A fight had kicked off and the clerks had sealed themselves in the back and the security guards turfed everyone out until things were sorted again. They filed back in, queued again and finally got seen by some pinch-faced woman whose attitude sugges-ted she tarred them all with the same brush. The feckless, the undeserving poor.

Where Mike signed on now was a purpose-built facility with brightly upholstered chairs, wooden coffee tables, counter staff trained to smile. The culture had shifted even if some of the clients looked like those Mike remembered: the long-term unem-ployed, the very poor, the ill-equipped. The rest were a hotch-potch: men and women like Mike slung out of work after half a lifetime never missing a day, professional types with their shiny shoes and crisp shirts, or students highly qualified and hungry for a job. But even with the carpeted floors and the computer terminals and the fancy logos Mike felt the desperation among the people forced between its doors. He hated the place and how it made him feel.

A month after the *Crimewatch* appeal, and Vicky had taken on more clients. Mike now walked Megan to school and picked her up, while Vicky drove Kieran in. She'd got extra work from two residential care homes for the elderly. The Perms, she called them. They all wanted the same hair. 'Will we be the same?' she asked Mike one Saturday teatime as she got back. 'Well, you'll be bald, but will I suddenly want to look like my grandma?'

'Bald?'

'Thinning on top, now.' She nodded at his head. 'Ten years be nothing left.'

'You going off me?'

'Never.'

'Prove it,' he said.

'Now? The kids are in the garden.'

'A quickie?'

She rolled her eyes but the smile breaking on her face gave him his answer.

It was on the local news, after the national headlines. A reward had been offered for information leading to the arrest and conviction of Danny Macateer's killers. Vicky turned to watch on her way out of the room with the dustpan and brush. Mike saw the tension grip her shoulders, saw her lift her chin. But she said nothing. He thought of the shooter, the man he'd seen raising the gun. Was he watching this? Did it make him feel big? Was he sure he could keep

98

people quiet, confident no one would dare speak out and he'd get away with it, or was there that little bit of him waiting for a knock on his door?

He didn't deserve to get away with it. Scum like that. Whatever Vicky thought, if the police caught him then Mike would be there like a shot. Swearing on the Bible, saying his piece. Doing all he could to help put the guy inside for life.

CHAPTER FIFTEEN

Cheryl

Nana hadn't been feeling too good. She took herself off to the doctor's and when she came back she told Cheryl that they were sending her for tests.

Cheryl felt something twist inside her. 'What kind of tests?'

'I don't know, I ain't no doctor. They just want to check all is as it should be. I's not getting any younger.' Nana was folding and unfolding a tea-towel. Cheryl wanted to grab her hands, stop her.

'I could come with you,' Cheryl offered, feeling clumsy, not sure how to be.

Nana sucked her teeth and told her she could manage just fine, fine and dandy. 'Could be weeks, they said, for the appointment.'

Milo fell over, stumbled backwards and bumped his head on the corner of the couch. All cushioned there – so he was fussing more than hurt. Cheryl scooped him up, kissed his cheeks. 'Hi, Nana, say hi!' she coached him, swinging him towards Nana.

Nana clapped her hands. 'Here's Milo.' She stroked the child's face. 'It's still dry,' she said to Cheryl. 'You taking him out?'

'Storytime at the library then maybe the park.'

'Good. Get some bread on the way back.'

'And milk?'

'Yes.' Nana went to her bag.

'I've got some,' Cheryl said. 'My benefit's in.'

Nana nodded, took a coin from her bag anyway, gave it to her. 'Get him an ice-cream or something.'

Cheryl sat with Milo and half a dozen other mums and toddlers on the carpet in the children's section. The librarian, Maeve, made the story come alive, even for the littlest ones who were more inclined to crawl away or try to eat the books. She pointed out the details in the big picture book, repeated the simple sentences and encouraged any and all contributions from the children. Each week she finished with some action rhymes which the mothers could repeat at home: 'Pat-a-Cake', 'Incy Wincy Spider', 'Five Little Speckled Frogs' and 'The Wheels on the Bus'.

Milo crooned along, shouting loudly the words at the end of each line.

When the session was over, Cheryl hung around until the rest had gone then asked Maeve if she could book on to one of the computers. Maeve scanned her card, put her on terminal two and told her to yell if she needed any help. Cheryl picked out a couple of board books for Milo, nothing he could rip up, and settled him at her feet.

She launched the browser then glanced about: someone else on a computer further along, a couple of people scanning the fiction section and three students working at the tables. No one near enough to see.

Cheryl typed in the search bar and hit enter. She felt the skin on her arms tighten and her stomach shrink as the results appeared. Sitting up straighter she clicked the link to the Greater Manchester Police website. Danny's name was there on the right under *Featured Appeals*.

Weeks had turned into months and Cheryl had waited for things to change. For the raw, tarnished feeling she had, like she'd done something awful, to evaporate but it remained. It took the shine off everything. It made her throat ache, like she wanted to cry and couldn't. It had taken her long enough to accept it was because of Danny, because she had no guts, no honour, she was just like everyone else, weak and useless. There were times she hated Nana for her certainty and her principles and her preaching. Knowing she couldn't match up, came nowhere close.

Cheryl swallowed, she pressed her knees together and followed the link. There was Danny's picture, the same one that had hung over his coffin at the memorial service. Cheryl read the text.

Sixteen-year-old Danny Macateer should have been starting his A-level studies this September but on Sunday 20 June Danny was shot once in the chest as he crossed the recreation ground by Booth Street in Hulme. He was taken to hospital where he was pronounced dead on arrival.

Detectives have renewed their call for people to come forward with information about Danny's murder. They are keen to speak to two men witnessed at the scene in a silver BMW. To date neither the car nor the gun used in the shooting have been recovered.

The promising music student was on his way to a band rehearsal when he was gunned down. His twin sister has spoken of the terrible gap that has been left in her life and that of Danny's family. At an emotional memorial service, teachers, friends and relatives queued up to pay tribute to the boy who had so much to look forward to.

Detective Inspector Joe Kitson, who is leading this investigation, said: 'We know that there were several people out that Sunday afternoon who may well have seen the car, or the men who carried out this devastating attack. If you were in the area please tell us what you saw, even if it seems insignificant, as it could be crucial for our inquiry.

'We need your help to find Danny's killers and bring his family some justice. If you are afraid to come forward for any reason I would like to reassure you that we have protective measures in place so no one ever needs to know who you are.'

A £20,000 reward is available for anyone who provides information leading to the conviction of Danny's killers.

Twenty thousand. More than Cheryl would ever see in a year but not enough for someone to move away, buy a house, start a new life. Blood money.

'Okay?' The voice made her jump; she hit the mouse, closed the browser and swivelled to see Maeve, whose arms were full of books.

'Fine,' Cheryl replied, her heart bucketing in her chest, a feeling like bubbles popping in her veins.

'Good.' Maeve smiled, moved away.

Cheryl took a moment, waiting for her heart to slow, then went back to the site. There were two numbers at the bottom of the appeal, one for the police and the other for Crimestoppers. She could tip them off, just give them Carlton and Sam's names, no more than that but it might be enough for the police, enough to stop Cheryl feeling so shabby. She got out her phone, checked she wasn't being observed and then stored the first number in her contacts list. Her fingers felt thick, uncoordinated, and she kept making mistakes.

'Woof.' Milo had found a picture of a dog.

'Yes, woof.' Cheryl nodded at him.

She opened the Safety menu on the browser and deleted her browsing history. Logged off.

Outside there was a strong wind and the clouds above, big dimpled shapes, were moving fast. It looked like it would stay dry. Cheryl persuaded Milo into his buggy and buckled him up.

A shadow fell over her from behind. 'All right, Cheryl?'

Carlton! She rose, losing her balance. He shot out an arm, catching her elbow. 'Easy now.' He smiled, a quick easy glint of white teeth, one gold cap. Carlton was a big man, pumped up from time spent at the gym and the regular use of steroids, according to Vinia. He wore a plain white tee and a thin leather and linen jacket, double-breasted, elaborate, expensive. His trainers were gold Pumas, like the ones Usain Bolt, the fastest runner in the world, won the Olympics in.

He let go of her elbow. 'Where ya bin hiding?'

Cheryl laughed. 'No place.' What if he took her phone? Found the number? 'Just taking Milo to Storytime.'

'Ya don't come round no more.'

When she did use to call on Vinia he'd leched her with his eyes, passed ripe comments, smacking his lips. It made her squirm. She'd always made sure to stick close to Vinia, not be caught alone with him.

Cheryl felt the hairs on her arms rise. She knew she must be very careful, and sly and sweet. 'Responsibilities now. No partying no more.'

'That right?' He locked his eyes on hers. His were

104

bright, glassy, a seed of anger sharpening them. She forced a glow into her own, giggled, girlish.

'Milo, he keeps me busy.' She edged aside a little so Carlton could see her son.

Carlton hunkered down, his great hand outstretched, cupped, rested like a cap on Milo's curls. 'Hey, lickle man.'

Cheryl's throat closed. She wanted to slap him away. He waggled the child's head a little.

'Yah!' Milo made some sort of greeting.

Carlton laughed, a guffaw that crackled in the air, sudden and loud. 'Yah! I hear you, man. Fine soldier you make someday. Yes!'

Over my dead body, vowed Cheryl. She felt bile in her throat. Recalled Danny, his fist bumping Milo's. She stretched her face to frame a smile for Carlton.

'What's Mama say?' He turned from Milo to her, beamed up at her, his eyes fierce, dangerous.

Cheryl laughed as though the thought of Milo being one of his foot soldiers was the funniest thing on the planet. Laughed way too long, high and brittle, but dared not stop.

Carlton stood, nodded to her. 'Don't be a stranger, you hear me?'

She nodded. Was still nodding and grinning like some ventriloquist's dummy as he strode away, his bulk rolling from hip to hip, his head swaying on his neck.

Cheryl imagined Milo grown, a gun under his bed, his arms engorged with muscles like Carlton's. Milo shot up and bleeding. Herself, like Paulette, burying her boy.

In a corner of the park, while Milo clambered on and off the little play-boat structure, Cheryl punched in the number for the police. She listened to it ring once, then twice, then a voice came on the line.

Cheryl didn't speak, she listened to the voice, all the reassurances it gave, listened to the silence, watched Milo steer the captain's wheel. Her jaw was rigid, her belly ached, her knees trembled, she was so frightened. Then she ended the call. Deleted the number, feeling shaky and sick, and her eyes hot with angry tears.

CHAPTER SIXTEEN

Zak

H e'd done something to his wrist, well – not him
but the lads who'd given him a kicking had.
And it still wasn't right. He'd waited a few weeks but
if he tried to lift anything it gave way. The pain made
it harder to sleep at night. There was a drop-in clinic
near the precinct so he left Bess at the house one
morning and went there. Early October and drizzle
like fog that caught in his throat. Made his cough
worse.

The nurse asked him to move it this way and that,
pressed it and pinched it, told him he needed an
X-ray, he should go to A&E. Zak said he would but
could she strap it up for now or give him something
for the pain? She put on an elasticated bandage and
told him to try paracetamol – no more than eight in
twenty-four hours. She said again he really needed
an X-ray. It could be broken.

He didn't bother with A&E, decided it could wait
a while longer, might sort itself out. He wore the
bandage though, he thought it might help when he
was trying to raise some cash, make people more
sympathetic. Didn't work out like that: for all those
that felt sorry for him there were another crowd who
thought he'd been fighting. Like homeless and drunk
and violent were all the same thing.

He did end up in A&E. Collapsed on Corporation Street with pneumonia and pleurisy. He was

coughing and fighting for breath, his chest sucking, a stabbing pain behind his shoulder blade and his skin on fire, but he wouldn't go in the ambulance without Bess.

They argued the toss with him, one of the paramedics going on about hygiene and risks and procedures. The other persuaded Zak to let him call a friend (Midge) who could take Bess to the PDSA, explain the situation. Zak didn't like it but it was the best offer he was gonna get. They left Bess with a CSO who'd wait for Midge, and had the PDSA address.

It was all a bit hazy at the hospital, he kept nodding off like he was stoned but he hadn't taken anything. He had one of those blue blankets with holes in, he liked the feel of that, and the way they were all treated the same, all the patients. Might have been bankers or beggars, it didn't make no odds. They were all in pain, all needed help.

They took his blood and gave him loads of X-rays and told him he'd be in overnight at least and a doctor would see him in the morning. They rigged him up to an oxygen cylinder with a little gadget to put in his nose and started him on tablets.

There were three others in his ward room, two old fellas who slept a lot and a young bloke who only appeared for meals and at bedtime, pushing a drip. One of the nursing assistants told Zak the man had a thing going with a woman he'd met on admission. Kept nipping off to see her.

The doctor didn't get to him till the next after-noon. She closed the curtains round his bed, giving them some privacy. 'We're treating the pneumonia and pleurisy with antibiotics and it's likely to take a couple more days before your symptoms improve. You've also a fractured wrist which appears to have gone untreated.'

Zak shrugged. 'Can you fix it?'

'I think so. A plaster cast should sort you out – there doesn't appear to be any infection there. You're lucky. How did you break it?'

'Slipped up.' Zak thought of the beating he'd had. That cold, sick feeling.

'You've not been treated here before so we don't have access to your medical records but these older injuries . . .'

'Car crash,' Zak explained, his good fingers working, hard to keep still.

She waited a moment, he could see she had her doubts, but in the end she went along with it. 'Nasty.'

'Yeah.'

'You're homeless at present?'

'Yeah.'

'I can refer you to Manchester Housing, or one of the other agencies for help and advice.'

Zak dismissed the idea. 'You're all right.'

'Sleeping rough isn't going to do anything for your health.'

Zak squirmed. Waited for the lecture on smoking. Instead she asked if he was a drug user.

'Nah.'

She didn't believe him, went on, 'Because there's a very good rehab scheme we have links with.'

'I'm fine.'

'Smoking cessation?' She was almost smiling.

Zak laughed and it set him off coughing, the blade turning in his back.

She had one more try, 'You're twenty-two. Another ten years and it'll all be that much harder. There is help available.'

'Yeah,' he said, meaning no.

She sighed and got up, tilted her head.

'I'll tell 'em you tried,' he said, 'on the customer satisfaction survey. Got my vote.'

Apart from fretting about Bess, Zak had a rare old time. A decent bed, hot food. He still sweated all night and the pain in his chest was worse, he was coughing up stuff the colour of rust, but even so. He didn't mind the broken sleep, it was better than the dreams. One time Carlton had the gun, he was pointing it at Zak. And Zak was talking fast, babbling that Carlton had got the wrong person. Pleading with him. Sometimes it was a gun and sometimes it was a big knife going right through him. Then another time he was locked in the dark, struggling to get up, he couldn't move, not his legs or his hand, nothing. He was buried. The dark was soil clogging his mouth, his nose and his lungs.

On the third night, Zak finished his tea – chicken casserole, potato croquettes and broccoli, lime jelly and sponge fingers with grapes – and went out for a smoke. He was off the oxygen. It took over ten minutes to walk through the maze to the smokers' corner. Midge had sent him the PDSA number. After he'd lit up, he rang 'em again. Bess was fine. He thanked the woman and apologized for bothering her, promised to let her know soon as. Could be the day after tomorrow.

Turning to go in, Zak felt a glow, warm inside. Peculiar. In bed that night, while one of the old fellas snored and the other muttered at him to put a sock in it, Zak figured out what the feeling meant. Safe. In here, turning in for the night, waking up in the morning, there was no fear. Except for the dreams. He was safe.

CHAPTER SEVENTEEN

Fiona

The therapy wasn't quite what she'd expected. No digging into her childhood or searching questions about her relationships or how she expressed her emotions. Instead Hazel Fuller began by taking an account of the circumstances surrounding her first panic attack.

As soon as Fiona began to speak, her mind flying back to that hot summer day, the boy on the ground, she found herself growing tense, her muscles retracting, her breath out of synch, words tangling.

'I'm sorry,' she said, 'it's still so—' She stopped, wrestling tears. 'I'm frightened it's starting again.' She was stupid, a child in the dark. How had she grown so weak?

'A natural fear,' Hazel reassured her. 'Relax your hands.'

Fiona looked down at her fists, clenched, the knuckles white. Consciously she opened them, palms up.

'And your feet.'

Fiona laughed, spread her toes, turned her ankles.

'Breathe out.'

Fiona obeyed.

'Wait,' Hazel cautioned. 'Drop your shoulders.' She nodded. 'Now, a steady breath in and draw it down into your diaphragm. And hold, and release.'

Once the breathing had calmed Fiona, Hazel

explained that all their sessions would be looking at practical techniques that Fiona could use.

'What do you know about CBT?' Hazel asked.

'I've read a bit online,' Fiona told her.

'Then you've probably seen that there are two elements to CBT – changing how you think and changing how you behave. We enable you to accept that however unpleasant the symptoms are they will pass, that you will not die or have a heart attack, that nothing is physically wrong. And we look at the physiology of what is happening – understanding that helps put it in perspective. As far as behaviour goes, we examine patterns that aren't helping your condition and teach you ways of controlling your anxiety and rehearsing responses to hopefully minimize the number of attacks.'

Fiona nodded. Grateful.

'You're on antidepressants?'

'Yes.'

'Those combined with CBT offer the greatest chance of improvement according to the latest studies.'

'Good.'

'You're a midwife,' Hazel observed.

'Yes.'

'Think about your work, times when something unpredictable happens, when the mother or baby is at risk and you need to act quickly. Can you give me an example?'

'A C-section, emergency Caesarean.'

'Go on.'

'If we see signs that the baby is in distress, or we lose the heartbeat, then we have to get the mother into theatre as soon as possible.'

'A lot of adrenalin?'

'God, yes.'

'What's that like for you?' She seemed genuinely interested.

'A bit hairy at times but it's important to reassure the mum, not to frighten her.'

'And while you're doing this what's happening to you, physiologically?'

Fiona thought. 'Pulse speeds up, heart too, my mind seems sharper. I think I read somewhere the adrenalin helps you remember things, concentrate better. A survival mechanism?'

Hazel nodded. 'Now think of something else. Think of losing your temper. Big time.'

Fiona thought of shouting at Owen about the apples and cream.

'What's the physiology there?' Hazel asked.

'Hot. Sweating, my head buzzing, pulse quicker, everything brighter. It's the same,' she concluded.

'The same response,' Hazel acknowledged. 'Fight, flight and fornication.'

Fiona laughed. 'I knew this – my training.'

'Of course. But it's hard to hold on to when you're so anxious. A panic attack is a flood of adrenalin; it brings all the same changes as you'd find if you were having a blazing row with someone. Or a passionate encounter.'

Chance'd be a fine thing, Fiona thought.

'The lack of context makes the panic attack both disabling and traumatic but fundamentally there is nothing happening in your body, in your muscles and your central nervous system, that doesn't happen at other times in response to particular situations – like the emergency Caesarean.'

'But it feels so different.'

'Exactly. And our goal over the next few weeks will be to repattern your thoughts about it and re-educate you.'

Fiona left with a set of daily exercises to do. She felt buoyed up by the session, especially at Hazel's optimistic view of the likely outcome of the therapy.

That afternoon Fiona bought a home hair-colour kit from the chemist's. She really needed a haircut as well. She was blessed with straight hair but as it had grown longer she'd taken to snagging it back in an elastic band. Until she felt ready to make an appointment at least she could banish the grey hairs salted through it.

She was waiting for the colour to take when Owen got in.

'Can you do mine?' he asked her.

'Have you got a kit?'

He groaned. 'Didn't you get one?'

'No. It doesn't seem five minutes since last time.'

'The brown's showing.'

'Well, go and buy a kit and I'll help you. They'll still be open.'

He didn't reply but slumped noisily into the kitchen while she went upstairs to rinse the mixture off. She left it down and let it dry naturally while she started tea. Owen loved curry so she'd bought some lamb at the butcher's and a huge bunch of fresh coriander from the Asian grocer's. She sealed the lamb and fried the onions and spices, added to-matoes and lemon juice and put the dish in the oven to cook slowly. It was dark by six when she drew the curtains and set the table.

Owen appreciated the meal, cleared his plate of seconds, grunted his thanks and left.

'Dishwasher,' she reminded him on his way out of the room.

'I know!' he shot back at her.

*   *   *

After walking the dog, she watched a film. She woke feeling disoriented, befuddled. It was eleven thirty, the house was quiet. Owen must be in bed. He never came in to kiss her goodnight any more. She missed that, the physical connection, however brief. She knew he had to grow up, grow apart from her, but hadn't anticipated how much it would hurt. She was lonely. Lonely for love and physical affection. Aware of the sentiment of self-pity she scolded herself – she'd so much to be thankful for: a healthy son, good friends, the house. The money she'd inherited from her parents together with a contribution from Jeff, by way of payment towards Owen's upkeep, meant she'd paid off the mortgage years ago. Since then they had managed on her modest income.

Fiona wondered if she should push Owen to get in touch with Jeff again. Maybe reviving his relationship with his dad would help him in the messy business of growing up. Contact between father and son had dwindled over time. Jeff had a second family now, much younger, and lived in Jersey. Jeff was punctilious about birthday and Christmas presents. He and Owen had exchanged emails regularly at first but that had trailed off. By the time he was twelve Owen was refusing invitations to spend the holidays with Jeff. But it would be so much easier, she thought, to be sharing all this, the animosity and teenage tantrums, with another parent.

In the bathroom there were dark splashes on the sink and the clothes basket and the floor by the toilet. Fiona reeled, grabbed the sink and felt the blood pound in her neck. Owen was hurt, blood everywhere, what had he done?! Cut himself, slit his wrists?! *Blink*, his blood on her hands, *blink*, his eyes

115

rolling back, *blink*, the spasm that shook him. No! She remembered Hazel. Took a slow breath, took it deep. Stared at the black stains and smears and realized it was hair dye not blood. He must have done it himself while she was watching TV. She shuddered with relief. She rubbed the blot from the sink but the marks on the basket and the floor were permanent. Still shaken, but hugely relieved she hadn't had a full-blown attack, she didn't trust herself to tackle her son about it yet. Tomorrow would be better.

She showered quickly, towelled herself dry, brushed her teeth. Her hair was shiny, the shade a rich brown. Like chestnuts. If she bought some to roast would Owen eat them? Probably not, with adolescence had come the same finicky appetite as toddlerhood. Junk food and sugary snacks were high on the list of favourites.

She lay in the dark but sleep wouldn't come, her nerves alive and singing, muscles clenched, her mind darting here and there. She pulled on some clothes and went downstairs. The house was cooler already, made her shiver. She practised her CBT exercises then tried to read. At four in the morning, swaddled in blankets, she took out the folder, Danny's folder, with all the clippings she had kept. There had been nothing in the papers for weeks now. Four months on and no one had been arrested. She traced a finger round the boy's photograph, gazed at his smile, at the expression in his eyes. Waiting for dawn.

CHAPTER EIGHTEEN

Mike

They had a break-in. Opportunistic. Mike had left the lounge window open. He'd simply not noticed. Set off to pick Megan up from school, rain pissing down and the sky dark as slate. It had rained all day, all week. Patches of water standing on the bit of lawn in their back yard. Their coats steaming on the radiators every night. They only put the heating on for a couple of hours, trying to make savings. Later they sat watching telly with their warmest clothes on, sharing a fleece throw for a blanket.

Mike had done a load of washing that day and had put the heating on early to dry it. The window was open to get rid of some of the moisture in the air, though given the outside was like a hundred degrees humidity anyway who knows if it helped. They'd already spots of black mould in the corners of the kitchen.

The burglars had been in and out in the half-hour Mike had been gone. He didn't notice at first, came in with Megan, her chattering still, unbuttoned her coat, then his own. Took her through to make her some toast and on his way saw the gap where the telly had been, the aerial cable dangling, DVD player gone, DVDs scattered on the carpet.

Mike swore.

'Where's the telly?' said Megan.

'It's gone.' Mike's brain was already adding it all up, looking across the open plan room to the windows.

'Where's it gone?'

'Don't know.' Mike walked over; saw the drops of water, streaks of mud on the window sill, and marks on the carpet.

'Why?' she asked.

'Because.' His head was too busy to be dealing with her an' all. 'Look, just give us a minute, Megan.'

Megan sighed and moved to her toy box.

Mike checked the kitchen. They'd left the micro-wave and there was nothing else worth taking. Upstairs looked untouched. No insurance though. They'd let that lapse when it came due for renewal.

How would they manage without a telly? It kept the kids quiet, even Kieran could be soothed by putting on a familiar DVD. Mike and Vicky too, barely any social life but a bit of something on the box or a decent movie was one of their few pleasures.

He made Megan's toast, gave her some juice and rang his brother Martin. Martin made a living on eBay, pretty much, that and car-boots. He always knew where you could pick up a bargain. Mike explained his predicament.

'Aw, mate!' Martin commiserated. 'How'd they get in?'

'Lounge window. Never thought. Only gone twenty minutes.'

'Leave it with us, see what I can do.'

Martin rang back within the hour. He could get them a digital set but it wouldn't be flat screen, DVD player too. Might have a couple of pixels out but the lot for £95. Cheap as chips. But Mike had nothing. No contingency, no rainy day fund. He imagined saying no, turning down the chance, and then the weeks to come with the four of them out of sorts and climbing the walls.

Mike took a breath. 'I haven't got the readies at the moment.'

'No problem.' Martin was quick to step in. 'I'll sort it. Pay us back when you can.'

Which could be never, thought Mike, the prospect bitter in his mouth. 'Appreciate it,' Mike told his brother.

'Probably be tomorrow,' Martin added.

'That's great. Thanks, mate.'

Mike had expected Vicky to go ballistic when she heard. He even thought about lying to her, for like a nanosecond. Knew he couldn't get away with it. But instead of blaming him, letting some steam off and giving him a good bollocking for being so thick, she went white. Locked on to the thieves.

'While you were getting Megan?' she said quietly. 'So they must have been watching the place.'

'What?'

'Waiting for you to go out. Knowing your routine.' A big frown on her face. Her lips bloodless. 'Watching us, then coming in here and taking the only things we've got that are worth anything.'

'Vicky, I'm sorry.'

She wasn't interested in him, in apologies. 'They targeted us, Mike, don't you see?'

'They were probably just passing,' he said. 'An open window, it's asking for it. It's down to me, I'm sorry.'

'Just passing!' The incredulity laid on heavy. 'Why would anyone be just passing here, in the pouring rain? It's a cul-de-sac.'

'There's the alley, they could have been cutting through.'

She stopped, her face alert, like she'd just heard

something. 'They must have had a car. That telly's too big to carry.'

'Not impossible.'

'And the DVD player.'

'There might have been two of them.' As soon as he said it Mike knew she'd turn that round to support her theory. 'Look,' he hurried on, changing tack, 'they didn't take anything else. No mess, nothing broken. Martin will sort us out.'

'You don't care.' Her face was flushed now.

'What?'

'Strangers, some low-lifes who've been watching the place, have been in here, touching our stuff, watching us, waiting for you to leave.' She'd never been the hysterical type and this sudden melodrama made Mike feel peculiar.

'They haven't even been upstairs,' he said.

'What if this is about the murder?'

'What?' He shook his head.

'About getting at us, getting at you.'

'Vicky they nicked the TV, what are you on about?'

She stared at him, her mouth twisted with distaste, derision.

'Look.' He stepped closer to her, put out a hand, touched her shoulder. 'I know it's a bit of a shock but let's keep it real. Some scallies took the telly. End of.'

'No, it isn't,' said Vicky, 'not by a long chalk.'

And she wasn't wrong.

The other side of Christmas, not that there'd been much festivity in their house but they'd done their best to make it a happy time for the kids. Megan was young enough to be pleased with simple things, cheap toys off the market, the idea of it all. Kieran liked the music. Favourite Christmas songs on his old CD player. Mike and Vicky had debated whether to get him a new one but decided not. The lad loved his old one and they'd learnt the hard way not to force change on him. Getting him into new clothes as he grew bigger was challenge enough. They bought him a second-hand mobile handset in the forlorn hope that it would stop him hiding theirs. And there was one thing that would guarantee his pleasure. An addition to his collection of miniature steam trains. The engines were his passion.

The Museum of Science and Industry in town was a godsend. Full of working engines in tram sheds and railway memorabilia, it was one of the few manageable destinations for family outings. And it was free.

They'd gone there again after Christmas. Kieran's face went still with appreciation as they stood in the great engine hall or went outside to watch the Planet locomotive chug its way past. His attention was fixed as though he was breathing in essence of steam train.

The families had bought presents for the kids, too, of course and they'd had a big get-together at Vicky's mum's. Mike was glad when it was all over and they were back to routine. He hoped he'd get a break in the New Year; find a job, anything for now.

Then, a Wednesday in January, close to teatime, Vicky rang him. Her voice shaking. 'Mike, we've been in an accident.' Her and Kieran. She'd collected the boy after work, was coming home.

Mike went cold right through. 'Are you okay? And Kieran? Are you hurt? What happened?'

'We're okay,' she said. 'They drove right into us, Mike, on Chester Road. They just drove right into us.' Mike's throat went dry. He could hear Kieran in the background. The repetitive noise he made when he was upset. Like a moan, half a word. A chant.

'Who did?' She didn't answer. He thought they'd lost the connection. 'Vicky? What about the other car? Have you called the police?'

'They didn't stop.'

'Have you called the police?'

'No. They just kept going, Mike.'

'We still need to report it. We can claim, even if they didn't stop. That car's your livelihood.'

'I don't want to report it.' Her voice was edgy. She carried on speaking, her voice lower. 'It was a warning, Mike. Another warning.'

'What?'

'From the gangs. Because of you.'

Mike felt like his head was going to explode. 'Oh, for Christ's sake.' He couldn't think where to go with this and he hated the stream of fear in her voice. 'Look, will it start?'

'I don't know.'

'Where's the damage?'

'The back, the driver's side.'

'Try it. If it won't start I'll come and get you in a cab.'

He heard her breathing, then the sound of the engine turning over.

'Have you got lights?'

'Yeah.'

'Check the brakes.'

'Fine.' Her voice trembled.

'You feel all right to drive?'

'Yes.'

'Okay. Any problems ring me back. Come home and we'll talk.'

* * *

122

It wasn't so much a talk, more of a rant. And Vicky didn't even wait until the kids were out of earshot like she usually did. Laying into him about the risk he'd taken.

'Vicky, wait.' He held up a hand to stop the barrage of words. 'It was an accident, that's all. A road accident. Some prat too young to be behind the wheel, or off his head.'

'It was a silver car,' she said.

Mike wanted to laugh. 'There are thousands of silver cars.'

She stared at him. Her lip trembling.

'A BMW?' he demanded.

She hesitated then said yes. He thought she was lying.

Megan was calling. 'Mummy, Mummy.' Wanting help getting her toy cooker out. The noise was a little drill in his head. Vicky was ignoring her. Kieran sat in the corner, zoned out.

He softened his voice. 'You're shaken up.'

'Don't try that,' she snarled.

'What?'

'I know what happened, you weren't there. First they break in and rob us, now they follow me.'

A dart of dread pricked in his belly. 'They were following you!' He couldn't help the ridicule in his tone, didn't know how else to deal with this fantasy.

'They must have been.'

'No.' He shook his head.

'They're dangerous, Mike. They want to stop you. They drove us off the road.'

'Mummeee!' Megan began to scream.

Vicky's face was all screwed up, her eyes shining, the glint of tears. 'Next time they could kill us.'

'Vicky.' He couldn't reason with her. Maybe when she calmed down. He turned away, went to pick up

Megan, who was bawling now and kicking at the plastic cooker. 'Here.' He hoisted her up on to the crook of his arm, her face all wet and snotty. He got a tissue, wiped her face, turned her for a cuddle.

'You've got to pull out,' Vicky said. 'For the kids. For me.'

Mike's throat ached. He patted Megan on the back. She laid her head on his shoulder, the sobs had stopped.

'The lad died, Vicky. I saw it. I told the police. That's all there is to it.'

'And you want us to be next?' Spit landed on her chin.

'Don't be daft.'

'That's what'll happen. Walk away.'

'You're upset.'

'Stop telling me I'm upset. Course I'm bloody upset. Some gangster just piled into the car. The car with your wife and your son inside.'

'It's nothing to do with the gangs,' Mike shouted and Megan started in his arms and began to grizzle again. 'How would they know anything about me? My name, where I live, who you are? That's confidential. Only the police know that. They haven't even charged anyone yet. There may never be a trial.'

'Someone could have seen you. When you were there, that day. Seen you giving your statement.' Her breath was coming in little bursts, the words broken up. 'Please, Mike!'

He couldn't pull out. This meant so much. This was his chance to make things right. Payback. Like an exorcism, cancel out the time before. The time he'd said nothing, done nothing. Played it safe. He couldn't change what had happened, but this time he'd been given the opportunity to stand up, to do the right thing.

124

'They don't know me,' he insisted. 'And if I did pull out how would they even know? What do you want me to do, string a bloody sheet up outside, Mike Sallis is a coward, Mike Sallis won't be giving evidence?' She had no answer to that. 'This is all in your imagination, Vicky.'

'What, I imagined getting rammed by a car, did I? I imagined swerving and nearly crashing?'

Megan wriggled in his arms, her cries getting louder. 'Vicky, let's talk later. It's just coincidence. Bad luck.'

'Why are you being like this?' She spat the words at him.

He felt bile rise. Set Megan down, ignoring her howl of protest. He moved towards Vicky, his skin hot, his arms shaking. 'I'm doing the right thing,' he said tightly. 'If one of our kids was hurt . . .'

Vicky flinched.

'. . . I'd want people to come forward. Any decent man—'

'Don't talk to me about decent. What's decent is protecting your own family, being a proper father and husband. There will be other witnesses. Let them do it.'

Mike shook his head. The thought of pulling out made him weak with shame. Like a dog sidling away, wriggling its back end, craven. He'd lived with that feeling all these years. Now another boy had died and he could pay penance. 'You have to let me do this,' he told her.

Her face hardened.

'We can ask for protection, if that'll make you feel safer. I can ring them now.'

She shook her head. Wiped her hand roughly at her face. 'Your choice, Mike. If you carry on, you do it without us.'

CHAPTER NINETEEN

Cheryl

Cheryl had made £30 doing nails that week. Not all profit if you counted the cost of the acrylics and the varnishes and everything. But still a welcome contribution to the household. The television licence had to be paid and even though Nana had been buying stamps at the post office towards the gas and electric, the bill was much bigger than last winter.

Milo got ill in the New Year; his temp high and him sleeping so much, Cheryl got really worried. She called the health visitor and asked her what to do. Flu and winter vomiting sickness were both in the news. The health visitor asked her a couple of questions about rashes and his neck (to rule out meningitis, she said) then told her to use Calpol and plenty of fluids and not to take him out. Nana saw how scared Cheryl was and told her Milo was a fine strong boy. She reminded Cheryl of how sick she had been when she caught glandular fever at the end of primary school. And how the only thing that would cheer her up was lying on the sofa watching the *Rug Rats* cartoon on telly.

After four days Milo started eating again, but he still had a rattling cough. Nana caught the cough. It kept her inside too. She said the cold wind set it off. She didn't even get to church. She sent Cheryl to the health food shop to buy black molasses and liquorice roots. She boiled up some mess that looked like dirty car oil and stank the house out. A tonic.

Nana Rose, Danny's grandma, came round to visit. She'd gone so thin since the murder and her back was bent as though it was too heavy to bear. Nana scolded Rose for venturing out and risking catching the flu but Nana Rose hushed her. The two of them sat side by side on the sofa, holding hands, watching *Doctors* and turning over for *Sixty Minute Makeover*. Cheryl tried to imagine herself and Vinia growing old like that. Couldn't see it. Nana Rose would go back before it got dark at four o'clock.

'Back home,' Nana said, 'it hardly change, sunset near to six every night.'

'Warm all year,' Nana Rose added.

'You had hurricanes though,' Cheryl said.

'Oh, yes,' Nana said. 'Tearing the roofs off and everything blown every way.'

'Were you scared?' Cheryl knew the answers but knew too that Nana and Rose grew happy and mellow remembering home. Cheryl had asked Nana if she'd like to go back for a visit but Nana said it was all changed now. Cheryl thought she'd like to go, take Milo when he was bigger, see where they came from.

'Yes, we would go in the root cellar of the farm next door and when the wind was shrieking the boys would say it was Satan flying in the wind.'

'Poppa Joe's car!' Nana Rose giggled.

'Ay! Poppa Joe's car went up in the tree. So high. And the land there was too swampy for them to put any machines on to reach for it.'

'And when you came here it was cold?'

'Like the North Pole! Ice and snow and frost on the windows – on the inside.'

Cheryl made them a cup of tea and Nana Rose told them that the school was building a music centre in Danny's memory. It was to have spaces for rehearsals and a recording studio and would be open to all of the community not just the school students.

Cheryl left Milo with Nana while she went to the supermarket. In the taxi back the guy was going on about another shooting. Somewhere on the Range. He meant Whalley Range. 'The Range' made it sound like a Western, thought Cheryl. Clint Eastwood and Brad Pitt with stetsons. Men of honour cleaning up town. When really the Range was mostly just a poor neighbourhood and the gunfights as pointless and sordid as Carlton shooting Danny. Stupid and deadly.

She didn't mention the rumour to Nana but watched the local TV news later. Another lad, nineteen this time, shot leaving a bakery. Cheryl didn't recognize the name or the photo. The report ended with a reminder that police were still investigating the murder of Danny Macateer, seven months earlier.

Cheryl felt ashamed again. The Macateers had to live knowing who was behind Danny's death but helpless to do anything about it. Everyone just went about their business, all of them in on the dirty little secret. And Carlton and Sam Millins carried on cocky as ever. Big men, hard men, safe behind the wall of silence. Cheryl didn't like to think about it all, doing an ostrich act like everyone else, but the guilt stuck with her, she just couldn't shake it off. And there was anger too, useless anger, that it had to be this way.

That Saturday, she and Vinia had a proper night out. Some Breezers at home first, while she did Vinia's nails and Vinia helped her choose which dress, with which belt and which shoes. Nana sucked her teeth at Vinia's low-cut top and said she'd catch her death of cold.

'Not if I find me a nice big man to keep me warm,' Vinia joked.

'Be careful,' Nana told Cheryl.

'Promise,' she answered.

They got the bus in, standing room only, everyone piling into town. The club was in The Printworks, three floors, three different sound systems. They knew Tony on the door from school. Not a big guy, fine-featured, soft-spoken, looked more like a dancer than a bouncer. They had a quick catch-up then he sent them in. They headed for the middle floor. Dubstep. The heavy bass pulsed through Cheryl; she felt it vibrate in her belly and her throat. She and Vinia found some friends and joined up. Drinks were pricey but they bought orange, topped it up with vodka from the bottle in Vinia's bag.

The place was filling up, the music so loud that it was impossible to hear anything. Lip reading and sign language the only way to communicate. Vital conversations had to take place in the corridor or the loos.

In a break between dances, breathless, her heart thudding, Cheryl went out to have a smoke. She passed him on the stairs. He was coming up them, two at a time. Dark golden skin, short brown dreads, almond eyes set off with rectangular glasses, bright blue frames. He wore a simple white short-sleeved shirt, black denims, baseball boots. Flashed her a smile.

Outside she wondered about him: if he was available, if he might be interested, if he was meeting someone.

She stood with Tony and smoked and listened to the racket from inside the club. It had begun to rain, a fine drizzle that settled on her bare arms and shone like glitter. Her hair must look the same.

Back inside she saw him on the stage, on the decks. 'Who's he?' she mouthed to Vinia, pointing at the guy. Vinia shrugged. The girl beside her pulled out a flyer and pointed to a name on the line-up: Jeri-KO.

Cheryl moved closer to the stage, raising her arms above her head as the music gained momentum. Waiting for him to see her, watching for any obvious girlfriend.

Jeri-KO raised his hands, the lights flared white behind him, drenching the audience, casting him in silhouette. He pivoted on the spot. His profile was all smooth planes. The music thundered under Cheryl's feet, Jeri-KO was dancing now, a voice sample streamed in above the rhythm 'We know what we want,' boomed a deep West Indian voice, 'we want to run free, we want to fly high, we want to get lost in the beat.' Drums crashed in and the crowd roared. Cheryl threw back her head and swung her hips to the rhythm. A strobe began casting them all as automatons, jerky stop-motion images. Cheryl closed her eyes and danced, the percussion like waves and the melody soaring over the bass.

When Cheryl opened her eyes and joined the rest of the club in applauding his set, his eyes found hers. She sketched a nod, a smile wide on her face. He blew her a kiss.

In the loos Vinia was having none of it.

'He blew me a kiss.'

'He can't see a thing in the crowd, girl, mistake you for his long-time girlfriend.'

'You're jealous,' Cheryl smirked.

'Nothing to be jealous of.'

Cheryl stretched her mouth in the mirror, touched

up her lipstick. She stepped back, swivelled side on and stood tall. She looked fine. Vain maybe but hell – got it, flaunt it. 'You wait and see,' she told Vinia.

But when Cheryl went back in he was nowhere to be seen. She felt her anticipation drain away. A little romance would have been nice. She was so lonely sometimes, sure there was Milo and Nana and Vinia but that wasn't the same.

Now she felt tired and thirsty. She wove her way through the dancers to the bar, waited to be served and asked for a glass of tap water.

Turning back, she caught her heel on something and stumbled forward, losing hold of the glass. It was only plastic so it didn't shatter but the water splashed all over the back of a woman in hot-pants.

The woman swung round and glared, shouting at Cheryl who backed away saying sorry, her eyes pricking.

Cheryl found Vinia and told her she wanted to go but Vinia wasn't ready. She dragged Cheryl into the corridor. 'It's only just getting going. Stay.'

Cheryl sighed. 'I'll get a cab,' she said.

She stood with Tony. The taxis were slow. 'Be about twenty minutes for a private cab,' Tony told her. Cheryl was debating whether to walk along and join the queue at the rank for a black cab, wondering whether that would be any quicker, when he came down the hill at a bit of a run. Slowing, his face opening with a smile as he saw her.

'You're not going, are you?' he asked. She couldn't place his accent.

'Thinking of it.'

His tongue was caught between his teeth. White teeth. He laughed.

'I thought you'd gone,' she said, knowing this was risky, showing too keen an interest.

'Took some of my gear back to the hotel.'

'You don't live in Manchester?'

'Bristol.' He looked about, sniffed. 'We could get something to eat?'

'Cool,' she said, 'yeah.' She turned to Tony. 'Where's open now?'

He made some suggestions. Cheryl nodded, barely taking them in.

'Thanks, mate,' Jeri-KO said. Then to her, 'Sushi sounds good. Okay by you?'

Cheryl knew what sushi was, raw fish, Japanese food. Never had it. 'Good, yeah.' She turned to Tony. 'See you.'

He winked at her. 'Take care.'

Cheryl felt the fizz of excitement inside, the dizzy sensation like she'd faint or fall or float off.

'Is Jeri-KO your real name?'

'Jeremy – I prefer Jeri. And you're Cheryl.'

She stopped, surprised. 'How do you know?'

'I asked around.'

She smiled. And he took her hand.

CHAPTER TWENTY

Zak

The house was gone. Zak stood there for a minute blinking as if his eyesight had just packed in and would start up again any second and hey presto, there'd be the view as it should be, the house and the trees and everything. Not so.

There was a pile of bricks in the centre of the plot and wooden joists and bits of window frames stacked to the side. All the brambles and the saplings had been stripped away and the bigger trees by the perimeter fence had been pruned. There was a big brazier too, blackened, and Zak caught the whiff of burning wood still in the air.

Zak shivered. The weather was bitter, his wrist ached with the cold, a gnawing pain and he wanted to rub it warm but it was still clad in the plaster cast.

He looked again at the house and shook his head. His sleeping bag had been in there, the spare clothes he had. He knew it would have been freezing in the winter but he could have burned stuff, made like an Indian in a tepee. Now he'd nowhere.

He walked to the PDSA, stopped a couple of passers-by with the mam in hospital story and got £1.50.

Bess was mental when she saw him. Wriggling and licking his face. He knew they didn't have set charges, 'cos it was for poor people who couldn't pay for a proper vet, but they liked you to make a contribution. He gave the woman his £1.50, said sorry it wasn't more.

It was growing dark already as they left. Zak weighed up his options: a shop doorway or Midge's. He rang Midge. 'Just a night,' he asked. 'I'll find somewhere tomorrow.'

Midge hesitated. Zak waited, hoping.

'Can't be any longer,' Midge said.

'Course not. Thanks, mate.'

There was a girl living with Midge now, Stacey, and she didn't take to Zak, wrinkled her nose and went off to the bedroom when he got there. Midge raised his eyebrows and said she was a mardy cow but not to take any notice.

Later Stacey went out, trimmed up like a Christmas tree, all shiny and gaudy. Midge gave Zak a fiver and he went for chips and jumbo sausages and curry sauce (no sauce for Bess).

Midge had to stay in; he'd business to do. People calling round to score.

Zak and Midge had a blow after the chips. Started Zak's cough off but he liked the blurry feeling that followed, made him dopey and giggly.

One of Midge's customers brought a couple of big bottles of cider with him and they shared them and watched *Top Gear* and a *Bear Grylls* rerun, surviving in the jungle. Zak got the giggles, then the munchies, but Midge said they had to leave some stuff for Stacey.

Zak slept on the sofa, Bess alongside him on the floor nearby. Midge had turned the lights off but the curtains were sheer and the street light, a fierce blue-white, filled the room with a glow.

In the early hours he heard Stacey come back and clatter around. He smelt toast and bacon and his stomach growled. Bess twitched, raised her head and looked at him. He put his hand on her head for a bit. Then she relaxed again, settled back with a sigh.

Zak had a dream he was with Bear Grylls in the jungle. Bear was picking grubs off the floor and eating them. Zak felt sick and Bear was yelling at him, 'Eat it or starve, see if I care!' Then Bear was hitting him, hitting his head and making him feel even more sick. Zak woke up and he was glad he was in Manchester, on Midge's couch, even if he was dead cold.

In the morning he didn't see Stacey but Midge made him a fried egg buttie and a coffee. Zak took his pills. Midge asked him what they were but told him there wasn't much of a call for them. Midge dealt in temazepam and co-codamol as well as weed and E's. Zak thought he'd keep them anyway, try and sort his chest out for good.

'Where you gonna go?' Midge asked him.

Zak shrugged. He hated the hostels and they wouldn't let him in with Bess, anyway.

'Maybe another old wreck.'

Midge narrowed his eyes. 'They've boarded up the Narrow Boat,' he said. Zak imagined the pub, dark, smelling of old fags and beer. Better than nothing.

'Need somewhere I can get into without too much bother.'

Midge waggled his head. 'They've put grills up.'

They were watching *Jeremy Kyle*, the people screaming at each other, some lard-arse whinging about his girl's spending habits, and there was a knock at the door. Midge let the lad in and took delivery of an M&S carrier. Paid him. When the boy had gone, Midge told Zak he was one of Carlton's runners. 'You know they put a reward out for Danny Macateer?'

Zak felt a shimmer of unease. Did Midge know something? Had Zak let something slip last night? He'd been pretty wrecked – he hadn't said anything, had he? Something slithered inside him, a worm in his belly.

'Twenty grand,' Midge said.

'You'd have to be mad,' Zak said. 'Even if you did know something.'

Midge agreed. 'Never live to spend the dosh.'

Twenty grand. Zak's head swum with pictures. A little flat and him and Bess with all their own stuff. Fridge full of food, the heating on, a power shower. Two bedrooms, one for his mam. He thought of Carlton raising the gun, the lad spinning and falling. Bess barking. Imagined himself turning down a road one day, brought up short, two lads with guns in their hands. Zak putting his own hands up as if palms could stop bullets. The jolts as one then another punched through him. A waterfall of fear and pain and Bess barking, barking as his sight went.

Zak shivered. 'Suicide,' he agreed. No one would ever give up Carlton, no matter how high the reward.

That afternoon he set out, went by the Narrow Boat but the grills were heavy duty, a professional job. You'd need power tools to break in there. He walked all round for hours but didn't see any likely spots. He sat with Bess in the launderette to warm up a bit. The smell was good in there, clean and soapy. He was starving by teatime. He did an hour on the supermarket car park and made a few bob. Bought a double cheeseburger and shared it with Bess. He thought about trying town. They were still building stuff round the canals but the trouble was the security in the new places was really tight. Dogs and nightwatchmen and cameras. A condemned building would be better.

He got the bus over to Longsight, got off on Dickie Road by the street market and walked along Stockport Road to Levenshulme. One or two places did seem derelict but when you looked closer you'd see movement inside, or steamed-up windows, and know better.

Zak's feet were hurting. He'd got a blister on his little toe. It grew dark and began to rain, soft and fine like a net. He bought some Lambrini and tobacco and Mars bars and food for Bess. Then he found a cardboard box left out for the recycling. Off a new dishwasher. Still pretty dry. He took that and went up to Levenshulme train station. Once the platform was empty, he clambered down on to the tracks and underneath the platform where he could rig up a hidey hole. The cardboard flattened out was their bed. He'd have to get a sleeping bag sorted in the morning.

He slept fitfully. After eleven nothing stopped at the station but the trains ran all night; the vibration singing in his bones before he could even hear the engines, then the rattle and crash and roar and the dust as they came racing through. Freight trains. He couldn't tell what they were carrying, some had old-fashioned trucks but others were long lines of containers, some with signs he thought might be Chinese.

He'd have to find a place to stay. He'd never make it sleeping rough. The knife in his chest was twisting again and he couldn't stop shivering, his skin was greasy from the trains, he felt like he'd got diesel in his lungs. He cuddled up to Bess, desperate to get warm. She whined and licked his face. Good dog. He closed his eyes and felt the tickle of her fur on his cheek, breathed in her doggy smell and listened to a police siren whooping through the night.

CHAPTER TWENTY-ONE

Cheryl

Vinia told Cheryl that she'd heard Carlton and his boys talking about the latest shooting and the chat coming round to Danny. Carlton bragging how that had sent a message plain and clear to the rival gangs.

'What message?' Cheryl asked. 'That they're stone killers and they don't care who they hit?'

Vinia cut her eyes at her, pulled her hand away. Cheryl had manicured Vinia's nails, was now doing the base layer. 'You want me to tell you or you just gonna keep interrupting all the time?' Vinia snapped.

'Don't have a fit,' Cheryl said.

Vinia huffed.

'Just tell me.'

'He said Danny wasn't a player but he was a blood relation to some of the Nineteen Crew. Taking him out would show them this was war. No rules all's fair.'

Cheryl looked at Vinia. 'By that reckoning, makes you fair game an' all. Relation of Carlton.'

'I ain't agreeing with it,' Vinia protested, 'just saying, that's all.'

Cheryl hated Carlton for what he'd done, probably hated him more because they were all so weak and helpless around him, no one to raise a voice. Except Nana and even she wouldn't be so stupid as to do it in the man's hearing. How come Nana was so brave? Had she been born brave or did she get braver as she grew older?

'You seeing Jeri soon?' Vinia held her other hand out. Cheryl checked the nails were dry and began applying the next coat. Vinia wanted sunsets on each nail: *real bright, you hear me.*

'He wants me to go down to Bristol next weekend.'

'You go, girl.'

Cheryl hummed. 'I'd have to leave Milo, two nights. Nana'd be wiped out. One's enough.'

'She can nap in the day,' Vinia pointed out. 'You not interested,' she joked, 'move over and make room, honey. I'll get me some.'

Cheryl was unsure, uneasy about going. Not just on Nana's account neither. She liked Jeri, she liked him so much, but sometimes she wondered why he bothered with her. She'd gone over to Liverpool one time, when he was working, spent the night in a smart hotel and he'd come to Manchester again, a rare Saturday night off when he'd met Milo and Nana.

Nana had gone into holy-roller mode, quizzing Jeri about his folks and his church and all. He was polite with her but didn't pretend to be religious and Nana made it clear that he was a great disappointment in that regard. She seemed to think his work as a DJ was akin to some loser on a boom box in a shebeen, even when Cheryl explained that Jeri was playing in proper clubs and on the radio and not some illegal drinking den. 'Got bookings all over, Nana, Ibiza, Japan even. He pays tax. It's a really good job.'

When Jeri came to Manchester they stayed at the Hilton on Deansgate. Cheryl knew Jeri wanted to impress her and he did. It was expensive, even for

139

someone like him who was used to hotels. She loved it. The bed big as a boat, the yards of carpeting, the thick white bath towels. They ate in the restaurant there that evening, views looking right out over the city. She felt ignorant and clumsy at first, seeing the formal tableware, the bright expression of their waiter in his fancy apron. But Jeri put her at ease, had the same easy friendly manner with everyone, not stuck up. He told her he'd once been a waiter, knew what it was like to get snobby customers, the sort that liked to make you feel small, like they were better than you. She imagined Carlton there in the restaurant, how it would all be about face and impression, scoring points. Every interaction a power play.

When Jeri talked about his music, his face came alive, bright with excitement. 'Still can't believe how lucky I am,' he said. 'Started out at school, playing on borrowed decks, got to do a couple of music festivals, promoter caught me, liked what he saw and next thing he's got me a spot in Monte Carlo. Kid off a shit estate up there spinning tunes and they're all going for it – fat cats and the yachting brigade – chanting my name!'

'Yachting?' Cheryl laughed. 'But you still live in Bristol?'

'Love it. Moved house though – like a shot. You come down; I'll give you the tour.'

She smiled. 'Rags to riches.'

'Summat like that,' he grinned back at her.

They'd gone back to their room and got to know each other real well in that wide bed. Jeri laughed when he came, Cheryl cried when she did. And that was just fine.

She was falling for him deep and that was scary, she didn't see how it could work, him jetting here and there, a big name on the dance scene, and her stuck in Hulme on benefits with Nana and Milo.

Bristol was a step too far too soon. Going there would show she was committed and surely it wouldn't be long after that, knowing he had won her, that Jeri would cool and turn, moving on to the next girl who caught his eye.

Cheryl finished painting Vinia's sunsets and made a cup of tea. The milk had run out so she left Vinia blowing at her nails and went along to Sid's for some.

It was a foggy night; she could smell yeast on the air from the lager plant up on Princess Road. The fog hung in shreds round the street lights and distorted and muffled the sounds: traffic from the main road, footsteps and the cough of a car engine that wouldn't start.

Cheryl bought cigs and some Murray Mints for Nana. She was 2p short but Sid let her off.

'I'll bring it next time,' she promised. She knew he sent money home to Pakistan.

'Don't be daft,' he told her, 'it's only pennies.'

Sid was there from seven thirty in the morning till eleven at night, seven days a week. Cheryl wondered how he stood it – the boredom – even with his telly tuned to some Urdu station.

Cheryl had just left the shop, opening the packet to have a smoke on the way home, when the shot rang out. Jesus! Deafening. A boom that she felt through the soles of her feet, in her teeth. She ducked, instinctively, and ran back into the shop. 'Oh, God! Oh, no!' Her heart thundering in her chest, her muscles spasming with fear.

'Hey!' Sid was all concern.

'They're shooting!' she shouted. Dread burning in her blood: guns blazing, someone getting killed.

141

'No – listen.'

She did, heard a cracking sound, then a droning whistle.

'Fireworks,' he said. 'The big one was a mortar.'

She felt like weeping.

'It's against the law to sell them at this time of year,' Sid said.

'It's against the law to shoot people too,' she snapped, cross suddenly, fed up with it. 'That doesn't stop 'em.'

Sid laughed and Cheryl started too, wiping her face and sniffing, still trembling.

'Are you okay?' he asked her.

'Yeah.' Just scared. Always scared. This was how it would be, she thought, on forever. Like Sid in his shop, day after day, year in year out. Suffocating. Waiting for the next time, the next crack of gunfire, the next death, and the one after that. A whole life holding her breath.

While Milo listened to *Each Peach Pear Plum* at Storytime, Cheryl looked up the number on the library computer again. Nana was at the hospital seeing one of the doctors there. She didn't want an audience, thank you very much.

Home again, Cheryl rang the number, her head buzzy and a knot in her belly. When she spoke her voice sounded weird, like it didn't belong to her. 'I know who shot Danny Macateer,' she said, 'but if they find out I've told anyone they'll kill me.'

She was standing in the front room, at the window, gazing through the net curtains. Nana had the winter ones up, thick, lace effect, a flower design. Cheryl watched a woman walk past carrying shopping, looking worn out.

The man, his name was Joe, told her they would protect her identity.

'I can't move away,' she said, 'I've got family.'

'That's fine,' he said. 'No one in the area will ever know that you helped us. You will be an anonymous witness; no one will know who you are.' He thanked her for coming forward, said he understood how difficult that must have been. But how important it was. 'We will need you to come in and make a full statement,' he said. He told her where the police station was and said she could choose a time to suit her.

'This afternoon,' Cheryl said. She'd go crazy if she had to wait overnight. She had someone coming for nails at one. 'About three. I've got a little boy; I'll have to bring him with me.'

'No problem,' said Joe. 'Take my mobile number. It's always on, you can get me wherever I am.' He read it out. Then, 'Can I take your name?'

Cheryl felt a chill inside, a giddy feeling, like she might fall over. 'Do you have to?' Couldn't she be anonymous to him, too?

'I will need it for your evidence but it won't be shared with anyone else. I guarantee that.'

He waited.

Cheryl looked back into the room: at the mantelpiece with Nana's fancy gold-coloured clock, her own school photos on the wall, the embroidered mats on the back of the sofa that Milo always pulled off. Within her the fear that if she told him her name there would be no going back. That the room and everything else in her life might be lost.

She pressed her lips tight together, heard her breath shudder. Then the sound of the man's breath at the other end of the line. She thought of Danny singing his song and the way her legs had weakened

143

when she heard the firework. She thought of Milo. Imagined him not coming home one night. Imagined him growing up without the gangs at his heels. 'Cheryl,' she said. 'Cheryl Williamson.'

Cheryl didn't know which bus would take her to the police station, or if they even ran on time. So she decided to walk. She guessed it would take about half an hour. She fed Milo early and changed his nappy, got his bag sorted and some juice to take. He had his nap while she did a French manicure and pedicure for a friend of Vinia's. The girl paid Cheryl and gave her a couple of quid tip, which was cool.

Cheryl was just going to get Milo up when there was a knock at the door. She thought perhaps Vinia's friend had forgotten something. A man and a woman stood there. In suits. Her first thought was Jehovah's Witnesses but they weren't smiling so they couldn't have been selling anything.

The woman stared at her. 'Cheryl Williamson?'

They knew her name! Cheryl felt her stomach drop. Were they from the police? Had Joe sent them? Was it a trap?

'We're from the Department for Work and Pensions. Can we come in a moment?' The woman wore dark lipstick, purple, too severe for her face. The man was young and fat with baby blue eyes; he carried a file.

'I'm just going out,' Cheryl said.

'That'll have to wait,' the woman told her.

Cheryl let them in; she didn't know what else to do. Perhaps if they were quick she'd still make her appointment. 'What's it all about?' Cheryl tried to keep the apprehension from her voice. Maybe it would be some scheme they wanted her to go on,

144

access into work or something. But who'd look after Milo? And she'd miss him; he was only a baby really.

'You claim Income Support,' the woman said, 'we have copies of your files here. Your benefit is means tested and you have a duty to report any change in circumstances, including any additional income.'

The man patted the file with one dimpled hand. Cheryl felt her face grow warm.

'You declare that you have no income from employment but that isn't true, is it, Miss Williamson? You are running a business from home.'

Running a business! Cheryl nearly laughed but knew that would be a stupid thing to do. 'No, I'm not,' she said. 'What business?'

'You're denying it?' The woman motioned to the man and he opened the file and passed her a piece of paper. She had a fancy pen and wrote something down. 'A nail salon,' she said with an edge and made a point of looking over at the trolley in the corner where Cheryl's polishes and creams, glue and false nails and tools were all kept in plastic containers. See-through containers. 'Benefit fraud is an extremely serious offence.'

Fraud! How did they know? Had someone shopped her? She felt grubby; they thought she was a scrounger, milking the system, making a mint. It had never been like that, she just tried to help out a bit so they could cover the bills, get things fixed when they broke. Twenty quid here and there. She kept looking down. 'I'm going to be really late,' she said. 'Can I do this tomorrow?'

'Other work to do?' the woman said smartly.

'No, erm, hospital.' Cheryl felt sick. 'I'll have to ring them. Explain.'

'Hospital?' The woman frowned. 'An appointment?'

145

Cheryl didn't want her checking up. She stalled for a moment: 'Just antenatal group. But I'd better let them know.' The woman couldn't check whether she was pregnant, could she?

The woman nodded. 'We could be some time.'

Cheryl rang the number Joe had given her, and he answered quickly. 'Hi, it's Cheryl Williamson,' she said. 'I was coming in for three but I can't come now.'

'Can you tell me why?' He sounded alert, secretive.

'They, erm, the benefits people are here.'

'Cheryl, where are you?'

Didn't he believe her?

'I'm at home.'

'I don't have your address.'

She hesitated, gave it. The woman was watching her. Had she twigged it wasn't the hospital? 'Thanks,' Cheryl said. 'I'll try and make it next time.'

It can't have been more than five minutes and he arrived. He wasn't like she'd imagined, he sounded younger on the phone but he was quite old with grey hair and a lot of wrinkles round his eyes. Laugh lines. Cheryl wondered what he had to laugh about, doing a job like that.

The door had woken Milo. Joe introduced himself to her visitors, then suggested Cheryl see to the baby and leave Joe to have a word.

She left the living-room door open a bit and as soon as Milo stopped crying, Cheryl sat on the stairs with him.

The benefits woman was spitting mad. 'You can't just tell us to back off,' she was complaining. 'Have you any idea what benefit fraud costs the nation every year?'

Joe said something back, too quiet for Cheryl to catch the beginning but she heard the rest. 'And if

146

you insist on interfering with a witness, I can have you both arrested.'

'You can't do that!' Purple lips was outraged.

'Oh, yes I can. Though I'd rather not. It does seem rather extreme.'

Cheryl couldn't resist, she walked downstairs and back into the room with Milo. The couple from the benefits were on their feet, she had circles on her face like she'd been slapped and the big guy was putting the file back together. Neither of them spoke as they crossed to the door. Joe gave Cheryl a little nod.

The woman turned back and spoke to Cheryl. 'This hasn't gone away,' she said. 'I'll continue to monitor your case and if you carry on working illegally while claiming benefits we will know about it. You will eventually be prosecuted. I can assure you of that.' Then she opened the door and they left.

Joe gave a big sigh. 'If we only put as much effort into making the rich pay tax . . .' He shook his head. 'How are you doing?'

'Okay,' said Cheryl.

'And who's this?'

'Milo,' she answered. Milo played shy, burrowing into Cheryl's shoulder.

'I can give you a lift down to the station,' Joe said.

Cheryl's belly cramped at the thought of anyone seeing them. She hesitated. He must have seen she was worried because he went on, 'Plainclothes car, round the corner. And now I have a cover story. Anyone asks, I'm a benefits fraud investigator.'

Cheryl smiled.

Cheryl had to tell him everything. How she knew Danny, and Carlton and Sam Millins. Where she'd been when she spoke to Danny, what they said.

Exactly what she saw as Carlton drove his car towards the rec. Where Vinia was, who else was around.

'If you tell them where I was, they'll figure out it's me,' she said alarmed.

'Anything in your statement that could be used to identify you will be excluded. So, we might say you were near the shop but not that you were with your friend, or that you had a baby with you.'

A couple of times, when Cheryl thought about what she was doing, what might happen, she nearly lost it. She'd get up and walk about; like she'd explode if she didn't move. Joe calmed her down. Kept telling her all they could do, would do. She wouldn't even go in the witness box, just give her evidence on video. Carlton and Millins would never see her. Even her voice would be changed.

'Make me sound like a man?' She'd seen stuff like that on television, people in silhouette with growly voices.

'Maybe.'

He said she'd be able to leave Milo at the crèche at the Town Hall while she gave her evidence. No one would ever know she had done it. He also told her that she was very brave – courageous, he said. And that it took a special sort of person to stand up for justice. Cheryl shushed him, feeling embarrassed, a lump in her throat.

Vinia rang her that evening. 'Where were you?'

Cheryl froze. 'What?'

'I came round, you weren't in. Your mobile was off.'

'Hospital,' Cheryl said. 'Nana had tests.'

'Nana was back,' said Vinia, suspicious.

'Yeah, I just missed her. Got lost, you know, now they've got the new bit open, it's massive, I was wandering round all over.'

Vinia grunted. 'You fancy coming out? There's a twenty-first party on.'

'Nah,' Cheryl said. 'Milo's teething again.'

'Man!' Vinia complained. 'More teeth! You sure that boy is a child and not some sorta crocodile?'

Cheryl giggled.

'Later, girl.'

'Later.'

But it was early the next day, very early for Vinia, who never dragged herself out of bed before noon. 'Cheryl . . .' She sounded weird.

Cheryl realized Vinia was crying. 'What is it?'

'It's Carlton. They've arrested him, the police.'

'What for?'

'What do you think! Sam too. They were both here. They came first thing, it was still dark. My mum's going mental.'

Cheryl's pulse rocketed, she felt her heart play catch up. 'Do you want to come round?' Say no, Cheryl prayed.

'Maybe in a bit. I'd better stay here for now. Somebody must have shopped them, that's what the others are saying.'

Cheryl's tongue was thick in her mouth. 'No one'd dare.'

'There is a reward,' Vinia pointed out, sounding sharp again, more like the old Vinia.

'Maybe they found the gun or something,' Cheryl said.

'Nah,' said Vinia, 'someone's looking after it; word is they still got it.'

Suddenly Vinia seemed to know a lot of stuff. Cheryl imagined it; the rest of Carlton's crew flocking to regroup, swapping theories, backing each other up, all paranoid about who grassed them up. Vinia telling them how it went down, the early morning raid. Them trusting her, Carlton's sister.

'Must be hard for your mum,' Cheryl said. Thinking at the same time that surely Vinia had some relief that Carlton was now locked up. That the man and the trouble he brought might be taken out of her life.

'Thing is,' Vinia sniffed, 'me and Sam, we been hanging out. Get him on his own, he's all right.'

'Since when?' Cheryl couldn't believe it. She didn't want it to be true. 'You never said.'

'Just recent.'

'How come you didn't tell me?'

'I was going to tell you last night but you wouldn't come out.'

'Oh, Vinia.' Cheryl felt sad. And freaked out – Vinia and Sam Millins together.

'Lousy timing, huh? A couple of times together and now what – prison visits?'

'You're not gonna stay with him?' This felt bad, very bad.

'I ditch him now, I think his friends are going to have something to say.'

'That's crazy!'

Vinia didn't answer. Cheryl heard her gulp. 'Oh, Vinia, oh, man, I'm so sorry.'

'Me an' all, girl. Double that.'

CHAPTER TWENTY-TWO

Fiona

J oe Kitson rang on Valentine's Day. 'You'll be getting a letter but I wanted to let you know in person,' the detective said. 'We've charged two men with Danny Macateer's murder.'

Fiona's stomach flipped. 'Oh, God! But that's great – that you've got them.' She had continued to follow the news reports on the inquiry but there had barely been anything in the local papers recently.

'It is,' he answered. 'They were key suspects from the start, Derek Carlton and Sam Millins, gang leaders, but we had a bit of a breakthrough and the Crown Prosecution Service is keen to go ahead. There'll be a trial at the Crown Court here in Manchester – the men will plead not guilty. You'll be called as a witness.'

Fiona felt dizzy but she had known this might happen all along.

'We need to check your availability,' Joe said. 'We're looking at September.'

'September!' Six months away.

'Couldn't be any sooner. Have you any holiday plans, family weddings and so on?'

Fiona saw her year stretch ahead – a blank calendar, Owen's school terms the only route markers. It was as though their social life had withered and died without her on the ball to arrange things. Not even a holiday planned though Owen needed some respite from school or the computer screen. 'I've nothing planned,' she told him, 'but I'll be back at work by then.'

Fiona had been in to talk to Human Resources about a phased return. The CBT and the medication had helped. She'd not had an attack since the New Year. And she'd come round to the view that she no longer wanted to put her life on hold indefinitely, just in case she might have another attack. She told them she'd like to start off on the hospital rota. A choice she never thought she'd make: giving up her patch and the autonomy of being out in the community. Back inside the hospital maternity care was still skewed in favour of intervention and medicalization; the doctors and consultants dominated the culture, the approach.

'That's good. NHS?' Joe checked.

'Yes.'

'They'll usually pay your wages while you're appearing as a witness but if not you can claim.'

'What happens now?' she asked. Suddenly edgy, the court case looming like a threat.

'I'll get back to you when the dates are agreed and you'll be invited for a pre-trial visit. It's certainly worth doing, gives you a chance to see the court and ask questions about the process. There will also be a needs assessment – someone from the Witness Care Unit will be in touch to see if you need transport or childcare and to arrange special measures.'

'What?'

'Arrangements we make for vulnerable and intimidated witnesses.'

Fiona was stung, thinking for a stupid moment that he was remarking on her character.

But he went on, 'In a case like this where there's gang involvement, witnesses are regarded as vulnerable and intimidated. So we take special measures to protect them from intimidation and to make sure they can give evidence safely.'

All the talk of safety made her nervous: she felt an unwelcome tingling in her wrists, her nerves pricking and a pressure building in her skull. Fiona thought of the young mother who had refused her entry in the wake of the murder. *I just don't want any trouble. That's how it is.*

'What sort of measures?' Her voice shook. She imagined herself and Owen in some shabby safe house, guards with dogs at the gate, bored minders playing cards.

'You'll give your evidence from behind screens so although the judge and jury will be able to see you, the defendants and their supporters won't. You will be anonymous: Miss A or whatever.'

Fiona saw Danny's face again, the line of his jaw, those golden eyes, felt the slick warmth of his blood on her hands. Her pulse kicked. She wrenched herself away, concentrated on stretching her neck, relaxing her feet, her diaphragm.

'Fiona?'

'Still here.'

'I want to thank you,' he said. The sincerity, the kindness in his tone brought sudden tears. Daft. 'Without you we'd never have got this far. And with your help we'll put these guys away for a long time. Is there anything else you want to ask me now?'

She sniffed, cleared her throat. 'No, that's all fine.'

'Well, any time. You have my number. And thank you again.'

A hard frost still lingered at the water park. Iced puddles were cracked into milky patterns, and the mud on the rutted paths was rimed white. Ziggy barked for the ball and his breath rose like little swags of mist. An easterly wind poked freezing fingers into the slightest gaps in Fiona's clothes: at her wrist when she raised her arm to throw Ziggy's ball and at her throat where her coat wasn't snug enough. She should have worn her scarf. The sky was pearly white, stippled grey here and there, the cloud cover so dense that she could not gauge the wind in it.

Bullfinches and great tits flitted among the bare branches in the copse, robins combed the ground. No sign of spring here yet. In the larger trees the bowl-like birds' nests and the larger squirrel's dray were visible. Close to the open water of the lake she found the wind too ferocious, stinging her eyes and making her nose numb. She called Ziggy to head inland to more sheltered paths.

Perhaps they should book a holiday, Fiona thought. She'd made desultory conversation about the idea at Christmas but Owen didn't seem interested in anything she suggested. Perhaps if he brought a friend, she thought now. Just a week. Even that would be costly, the boys would pay full fare if they flew anywhere. Or somewhere at home – an English seaside break: rain and steamy cafés. The smell of vinegar and candy floss. Owen and friend could go off exploring on their own. And what would she do? The thought of being trapped in a B&B or a holiday cottage with two bored teenagers for seven days in a row made her heart sink. America then? She had cousins in Maine; Owen could hang out with their kids. The travel would cost more but they wouldn't have to pay accommodation. They would perhaps need to dip into Owen's university fund to pay for it.

Fiona stopped and watched a kestrel hovering overhead. The bird hung, a black silhouette against the bright sky. Then plummeted. Rose with something in its talons. A mouse or shrew.

'You get any Valentines?' she joked with Owen at teatime.

He didn't answer, just the usual drop-dead glower.

'If we had a summer holiday,' Fiona said, 'maybe you could bring a friend along.'

Owen gave her a sidelong glance, frowning.

'Just something to think about,' she said.

'Where?' Owen asked.

'Don't know,' Fiona rushed on. 'The seaside or up to Scotland. Or Maine, to Auntie Melanie's.'

'America?' A whiff of interest.

'Nothing's decided. Just be nice to have something to look forward to. But if we did go to America we couldn't really afford for you to bring a friend, not unless they could pay the fare.'

Owen nodded. He went back to his shepherd's pie, scooping it up on his fork, his knife untouched. Why did she bother ever setting him a knife, he never used one.

'The police rang me today.' Fiona realized she wanted to tell him before he left the table. 'They've charged someone with Danny Macateer's murder. There'll be a trial.'

'You'll be a witness?' Owen spoke with his mouth full.

'Yes.'

'Who did it?'

'They're called Derek Carlton and Sam Millins; they're part of the gangs. The police had a pretty clear idea of who was behind it all along but they've only now got enough evidence to charge them.'

'How come?'

Fiona shrugged. 'He said a breakthrough.'

'Maybe they found the gun,' said Owen. 'Or DNA.' Fiona relished his contributions, these rare and fleeting times when he reverted to human form and was sociable and articulate.

'Maybe,' she smiled.

Owen was out that evening, he'd gone to a competition at the skate park. Fiona was reading but her concentration was all over the place. Joe Kitson's phone call was repeating in her head. All the talk of special measures and protection. She thought of the man she'd identified, the driver of the car, Sam Millins. He had driven the car to the recreation ground and waited at the wheel while the other man shot Danny. They were dangerous people. So dangerous that she had to be hidden from view when she gave her evidence.

A noise from the back of the house jolted through her and she sprang to her feet, gasping in fright. What was it? Was there someone outside? She crept over to the french windows and looked out. Nothing to see in the dark, just the glitter of frost over everything and the bare black arms of the magnolia tree raised to the sky.

CHAPTER TWENTY-THREE

Zak

Zak and Bess were sleeping in an underground car park, below a block of flats, been there almost two months. Zak had gone in there one night, after Christmas, walking in through the automatic gates after a car, figuring that the worst that could happen is the driver chucks him out.

He found a store cupboard down there, tucked away in a corner. Full of cleaning materials and things. He thought he'd struck lucky, it wasn't locked. He moved some stuff about a bit to make space to lie down. He just fitted if he curled his legs up. Then the door opened and there was a guy in brown overalls and a Hitler tache looking at him. The caretaker, a can of woodstain in his hand.

Zak scrambled to his feet. 'Soz, mate, just looking for somewhere to kip.' Bess got up, wagged her tail.

'How d'you get in the gate?' the bloke asked.

'Followed a car in.'

The bloke shook his head. 'Thick as planks, half of 'em. And then they wonder why they get robbed.'

'I'm not on the rob,' Zak protested.

'I could turn a blind eye,' the bloke said. 'Few nights, you make it worth it.'

Zak knew he meant for money. He only had about £4 in change. He dug in his pocket, held it out.

'No notes?' the bloke complained.

Zak shook his head.

'That'll do you for tonight but I'll be wanting more.'

Zak nodded. 'Ta, thanks, mate.'

The bloke, he was called Russell, nodded at Bess. 'He house trained?'

'She. Yeah.'

'And you?'

Zak ignored that.

'You can't smoke in here.' Russell nodded to the tins. 'Hazardous chemicals, fire risk.'

'Fair enough,' said Zak.

'Most of 'em are gone by nine in the morning.' Russell indicated at the cars. 'Stay in here till then, then I'll let you out.'

Zak's heart skipped a beat. 'You're not locking us in! No way.' If that was part of the deal, then Zak was walking. He'd go mental. He couldn't be locked up. Never again.

Russell stared at him. He twitched his moustache. 'If anyone sees you—'

'I'll stay in here, I promise.'

He gave a grunt. 'Make yourself scarce after that. Just press the green button for the gates.'

'Right. How'll I get back in?'

'Be here before six, I'll let you through.'

After a couple of weeks Russell gave Zak the code of the gates so he could get in himself. Zak's 'rent' was a nice little earner for him. Zak was a model tenant. When he did smoke he nipped out of the store and did it in the garage, kept his dimps to chuck away somewhere else so Russell wouldn't find out.

It was the worst time of year to be on the streets: the cold and the way it got dark so early. People were tight an' all, the times after Christmas. Often as he could Zak went round to Midge's, a chance to get warm, have a brew and a spliff. Stacey was still there and still had it in for him so he had to be careful, not overstay his welcome. He tried to smooth the way by running errands for Midge: a delivery here, picking a package up there.

Today when he and Bess turned up there was a big gang of lads already at the house. Bikes were piled up in the front garden like a scrap merchant's. Nowhere left to sit in the front room.

Conversation died when Zak walked in. Everyone looked at him and he felt his face burn. He rose on the balls of his feet, nodded to Midge. 'I can come back.'

Midge shrugged. 'S'all right, you can go for some Rizlas, king-size.' He tossed Zak a coin.

Zak went to the shop and when he came back the lads were gone.

'What's going on?' He handed Midge the papers and change.

'Carlton and Sam Millins, they're being done for murder. Danny Macateer.'

Zak stared at Midge. 'You're shittin' me!'

'It's true. Picked 'em up the day before yesterday, charged 'em last night, in court this morning. Denied bail.' Midge ruffled Bess, and Zak blew a long breath out wondering what to say.

'The rest of 'em, they're all freakin' case they get done too, conspiracy and that,' Midge said.

Zak counted on his fingers. 'Eight months it must be. Everyone thought they'd got away with it.' He shook his head.

Midge made a brew and skinned up. When they'd smoked it, he said, 'Wait there,' and went upstairs.

He came down with a shoebox, sat on the sofa next to Zak and opened it. Inside, chamois leather. Zak had been expecting trainers, knock-offs or counterfeits. Midge lifted the yellow cloth out, unwrapped it.

There was a gun.

'Whoah!' Zak said. A handgun, dull, grey steel, a squat shape.

'Feel the weight of it.'

Midge handed him the gun. It was heavy, dense, like a stone in his fist. Zak levelled it at the telly, squinted. 'Is it loaded?'

'Nah. Look.' Midge took it from him, moved something and ejected the clip. 'See.'

'You selling it?' Zak asked. Thinking of the next time someone had a go at him. Watching their faces change as he drew the gun. Watching them back down, back away.

'Nah, just looking after it. Why? Might be able to hire it out, you interested?'

'You expanding the business?' Zak joked.

'Only way to go, see an opportunity, fill it.' Midge sounded like someone off *Dragons' Den*.

'Might do sometime,' Zak said, 'not now though.' He'd have to save up.

After he left Midge's, he walked a different way back into town. Came across a carpet warehouse that had reopened as a food and household shop: Value-Mart. He tied Bess up at the door and went in. It was a bit like a cash and carry, brands no one had heard of, plenty of bulk buys. They had everything from shower gel and biscuits to whisky, even a pile of rugs in the central aisle that they'd probably bought as a job lot off the carpet firm. It was a big barn of a place, breeze block walls, metal roof, the back section where the stock was kept separated by strips of plastic sheeting. A guy was pushing a set of ladders along, the sort you could wheel around to get to high shelves. They almost reached the top of the wall, where it met the pitched roof. A row of skylights ran along one side of the roof.

That's when Zak had the idea. He bought some rissoles, the ones you could eat hot or cold, and asked the woman on the till when they closed. She pointed to a big black and white notice on the wall behind her. 'Eight till eight,' she said. 'Eleven till four on Sunday.'

Outside he sat on a low wall and shared the food with Bess.

The warehouse stood on a plot of its own, an old chain-link fence, broken here and there, surrounding it. There was a drainpipe at the back corner of the building, the corner nearest to him. Across the way was a block of flats and at the other side some other small industrial units. Nothing too close. It wouldn't be easy – but man, it'd be worth it!

Zak and Bess got in through one of the gaps in the fence. Zak had been begging on Deansgate and raised enough money to buy a little headlamp, like a miner's light but LED, and a lump hammer from the discount hardware shop in the precinct. Then they'd waited: half an hour in the café, another in the park. Now Value-Mart was deserted, all locked up.

Zak told Bess to lie down by the loading bay. She was out of sight of anyone driving past and it gave her a bit of shelter. 'Won't be long,' he told her, patted her back, 'good girl.' She licked his face.

The windows on the block of flats were lit up looking like an advent calendar. Curtains and blinds closed against the night. The industrial estate slumbered in the shadows between street lights, their blue-white glow like the colour from a telly. The drainpipe was a doddle but the climb up the roof from there was treacherous. The galvanized metal was slick with condensation, hard to get a grab on, the undulations on the surface not deep enough for purchase and his bad wrist throbbed with the strain. Zak slipped, slid back, his guts churning. He rammed his feet into the guttering to brake, praying it would hold. Sweat broke out all over his body, chilling quickly.

He decided it would be easier to try going up the very edge of the roof to the apex of the gable, then along the top. He shredded his fingers getting up there but he didn't fall, then he sat astride the roof and shuffled along until he reached the skylights. He'd counted when he was in the store, reckoned the third one would be best. He positioned himself close to it and looked down. The light of his lamp shone back at him, blinding stars in the glass.

One thing he didn't know was how the alarm was rigged. Breaking the glass might set it off, some places had sensors for vibration, others only alarmed the entry points, the doors. But even if he was unlucky, Zak reckoned he'd have maybe fifteen minutes before the police showed. Time to fill his bags and get away.

Zak pulled the lump hammer from his pocket and settled its weight in his hand. He gripped the shaft and swung the head down hard on the centre of the pane. There was a ringing noise and the glass crazed a little. No alarm sounded. He hit again, the same spot, and the glass fractured more, lines running here and there, the surface turning white. Three more strikes and the glass had buckled and split, one end peeling down into the maw of the building. Zak used his right heel to hit at the lower end of the frame and the rest of the glass came loose and fell. It made less noise than he'd expected.

Zak peered into the hole. The beams of his headlamp picked up the pile of rugs directly below and the glint of glass on the floor at the side. Zak smiled. He leaned in and flung the lump hammer out to the left, heard it clang against the shelving. He swung his legs round until they were dangling in space. He leaned to his left and bent over to grip the top edge of the broken frame. Then he shifted forward, let go with his hands and dropped, felt the plunge of falling and landed with a whoomp on the dusty rugs. Winded but satisfied he lay looking up, seeing little, only what the thin beams of his lamp picked out. He coughed a bit then clambered down off the pile of rugs.

Waggling his head about to scan as much as he could, he made his way along the central aisle to the front of the store where the public entrance was. There were light switches in the corner there and Zak tried one, then the rest, and filled the place with the blaze of fluorescents.

He had a big laundry bag folded in each pocket. He got them out and set about filling them. Whisky in those cardboard tubes, vodka too. Fruitcakes, some frozen lamb that Midge might like, batteries, a socket set, an electric drill, DVD players and a couple of digital cameras. Dried food for Bess. They didn't sell fags which was a pity.

He picked up a set of earrings and a matching locket for his mam. Put that in. And a trench coat and a fleece for himself.

When the bags were full he went to get the big ladders.

They were padlocked to a ring in the wall, in the storage area.

He couldn't believe it! He went to find the lump hammer and came back. He smashed at the padlock again and again and the hammer just bounced off. Then he went for the ring in the wall, battering the brickwork around it, cursing and nearly bawling with frustration. Then the shaft of the hammer split and the head flew off. Useless.

Zak's head was going to blow up so he sat down on the steps of the ladder and had a smoke. There was no way he could get back up to the skylights, no way. So, he'd have to find another way out. He was worried about Bess, she'd be getting hungry.

There was only one option, he'd have to get out through the roller shutters. Zak ate some fruitcake and drank some whisky while he strung together enough extension cables to reach the shutters that led to the loading bay. He plugged in the drill. His fingers were slippery with blood by now so he fixed up the cuts with plasters from a car first aid kit then turned on the drill. The drill snarled and sparked, dancing off the metal and sheering away, making a shrieking noise swiftly accompanied by the bowel-emptying scream of the alarm system. He kept going, the pain in his wrist gnawing like a cold burn, but the only impact he could make was a series of little scratches and pockmarks on the rippling shutters.

When he stopped he could hear the sound of an engine and Bess barking. He watched the shutters crank open and saw first the legs then the rest of an Asian guy, and two police officers, and Bess wagging her tail.

'I can pay for the damage,' Zak told the Asian guy. 'Or work it off?' The man swore at Zak in English and some other language and motioned for the police to take him. They arrested him and Zak kicked off, refusing to go anywhere without Bess, swearing that there was no one who could look after her. 'You make me leave her and I'll get the RSPCA on yer.'

'She'll go in the pound,' one of the coppers said.

'Fine, I can't leave her here, can't abandon her.'

They walked him round to fetch her and let her into the car with him. Zak told her she was a good girl and she licked his face. 'It'll be right,' he told her. But he knew he was fucked.

They booked him in and put him in a cell and then took him to an interview room. He started trying to tell them that it was a prank gone wrong, that he just wanted a bed for the night, wasn't after robbing 'owt.

'The store has internal CCTV,' one of the coppers said. 'Light activated.'

The other one winked. 'You've been framed.'

Zak imagined it: his plundering the shelves, the action with the lump hammer on the padlock.

He laid his head on his arms.

'Sit up, son,' the copper said. 'I am charging you with breaking and entering, going with intent to burgle, attempted theft and criminal damage.' Then he read the caution. He asked Zak if he had anything to say.

'Will they put us inside?' His throat was aching and his knee jigging all on its own.

'Oh yes. You'll not walk away from this one.'

He'd lose Bess. They'd put him in prison with all the nutters and the hard men. Lock him in. Zak couldn't stop shaking.

'Is there anything else?' the copper said.

'Yeah.' Zak wiped at his nose, pressed his hands between his knees, rocking forward. 'I want witness protection. I seen who shot Danny Macateer.'

CHAPTER TWENTY-FOUR

Mike

Vicky didn't see the letter; Mike watched out for it after Joe Kitson's call. The post didn't come till lunchtime most days and by then Vicky was usually out doing The Perms. He'd been able to hide it and didn't let on when she got in from work.

He needn't have bothered. *Granada Reports* had it as the top story. *Police have charged two men on suspicion of the murder of Danny Macateer in June last year.* Vicky turned to him. 'Did you know about this?'

Mike shook his head slowly.

'You'll have to tell them now, Mike, that you're stepping down, you won't give evidence.'

Stepping down, Mike thought, sounded weird, like he had some smart executive position that he was giving up to 'spend more time with his family'. What she should have said was running away. 'I will,' he said.

'You'd better. Now it's definitely on, we're sitting ducks.' She was paranoid again, her eyes like marbles, her face tight. 'Ring them.'

'They won't be there, now,' Mike told her, 'I'll go in the morning.'

'Promise?'

'I promise.'

She was still looking at him sideways, her antennae on full alert.

'I promise,' he repeated, louder than he meant to.

'No need to yell at me,' she told him.

Joe Kitson kept him waiting fifteen minutes which Mike reckoned was fair enough given he'd turned up on spec and the man must be busy.

Joe came out and shook his hand then took him through and along a corridor past various offices and up a flight of stairs. A different place from last time. There were posters and noticeboards along the way: everything from car crime and property marking to first aid training and Drink Aware.

Joe led Mike into a small room. 'Tea? Coffee?'

'I'm fine,' Mike told him.

'Wise choice,' Joe smiled. 'How can I help?'

Mike had practised what he'd say, tried it out in his mind this way and that but not found any way to make it sound right.

'I can't be a witness,' he said bluntly. 'I can't do it.'

Joe Kitson just gave a half-nod. 'What's the problem?'

'It's the wife,' Mike explained. 'First off, someone broke in, nicked the telly. Then she had this car crash, she reckons they were trying to run her off the road.'

Joe's face sharpened. 'When was this?'

Mike told him.

'You didn't report it?'

'She wouldn't, and she wouldn't let me. She thought we were being warned off. I told her she was crazy. That until someone was actually charged there was no risk.'

'And now someone has been charged . . .' Joe supplied.

'She's freaking out.'

167

Joe Kitson gave a soft breath out, looked down at the table between them.

Mike felt crappy. A henpecked husband with no guts. 'I promised her,' he added. 'If it was down to me—' Mike broke off.

'These incidents – the burglary, the crash – I'd like you to give me all the details.'

Mike waited for him to explain.

'I'm ninety-nine per cent certain there's no link between this case and those incidents but I'd like to nail it one hundred per cent.'

Mike felt a bubble of hope. 'You could do that?'

'Building evidence, particularly in a murder inquiry, means looking at people's actions *after* the actual crime is committed as well as investigating the crime itself. Keeping tabs on potential suspects if you like.'

'You've been watching them.' Mike wanted to be sure he understood properly.

Joe nodded. 'So, take the car crash: with the place and time, your wife's registration, it may be possible to identify the registration of the other vehicle. Trace the owner. Set your minds at rest.'

Mike felt relieved, until he imagined trying to get Vicky on board. 'She won't listen to reason.'

'But if she had proof? Knew for certain there was no connection?'

Mike allowed maybe she'd rethink. 'I can tell you where and when and that.'

Joe nodded. 'Good. Now as for the future – the trial. Like I said on the phone, there'll be special measures in place to ensure you can't be intimidated while giving your evidence.'

'And before the trial?'

Joe held up his thumb, counted it off. 'You're not known to the defendants, correct?'

Mike nodded.

Joe stretched out his first finger, tapped it. 'You work in the area where the crime was carried out?'

Mike shook his head. He didn't work anywhere, any more.

Joe added a second finger to his tally of advantages. 'You live in the area?'

'No,' Mike said.

Joe lowered his hand. 'The defendants will not be given your name or any details that could help them identify you.'

'What about their lawyers? They'll see my statement and that?'

'Yes, but they won't be passing it on to their clients. And remember these guys have entered not guilty pleas. Interfering with independent witnesses would sabotage their position.'

Mike still wasn't sure, and if he wasn't, Vicky wouldn't be. 'What d'you mean, independent?'

'You don't know any of the people involved, you have no possible axe to grind, no ulterior motive, nothing to gain. It's the strongest form of testimony we can get. Other witnesses with a prior relationship could have all sorts of dubious reasons for pointing the finger and the defence will milk that for all it is worth. Rip 'em apart. Have to, that's the way it works. But you, you're the bedrock.' Joe sat back, studied Mike. 'Money's always an issue but if your wife needs further reassurance we are sometimes able to relocate people in temporary accommodation for the duration.'

Mike thought of Kieran, the nightmare that would be. 'We couldn't,' he said. 'My lad, he relies on things staying exactly the same.'

'Perhaps other measures? Panic alarms? Talk to your wife about it. We can always get one of our security guys round to beef things up at the house. Meanwhile I'll get those details from you and set to work eliminating those previous upsets from the picture. How's that sound?'

Mike felt a flare of optimism. Joe agreed with him, they were not being targeted, and with hard proof Vicky would have to see sense. 'Thanks, yeah, do that.'

Vicky grilled him when he got home. Mike bluffed his way through it. Yes, he'd asked to withdraw, retract they called it, and he had to give reasons and then they had to look into it. Lots of paperwork and stuff like that, same as everything else these days. He had decided he would wait to hear from Joe about the crash before he tackled her head on.

A week later Joe phoned him. They had traced the vehicle that hit Vicky even though the crash itself hadn't been caught on camera. The silver Mercedes (not BMW) belonged to a twenty-year-old from Alderley Edge whose parents had more money than sense. Undercover police observation of the major suspects in the murder inquiry had confirmed that all had been elsewhere at the time that Mike's place was burgled.

Armed with the solid facts, Mike suggested a night out to Vicky; they asked her mum round to babysit. They couldn't afford to eat out but went to the flicks instead. Watched the latest action blockbuster and had a drink in the bar after. They talked about the kids for a bit, they always talked about the kids. And Vicky made him laugh telling him about some of the daft things her clients had said. He got another round in and some dry-roasted nuts.

'I heard from the police,' he told her. 'It's good news.'

'Go on,' she said, still pretty easy-going.

'The car crash, they've traced the other car. Nothing to do with the court case at all. Total coincidence. Same with the break-in.'

Her face changed, the colour fading from her cheeks, the sparkle in her eyes dimming. Disappointment, then temper, in the set of her mouth.

'And they'll give us protection,' he said, his voice too eager, too brittle. 'Better locks, panic alarms if we want it, not that there's any risk, just if we want it. And my name, it'll be kept out, I'll be anonymous.'

'I don't believe this,' she cut in. 'Is this what tonight's about? You promised me—'

'Vicky, just listen.'

'No!'

Mike was aware of the hostility between them and how people around were picking up on it: glancing their way, shifting position. The threat of a domestic in the air. 'He explained it all to me,' Mike raced on, a loud whisper, not wanting to shout his business for the entertainment of the bar. 'We are not at risk, we are not a target. We never were.'

'Of course he'd say that,' she countered. 'He wants you up there. People know it's not safe to talk, that's why it's taken so long, why they had to offer a reward. It's not safe. Not when it's a gang thing. And those two are gang leaders!'

Mike groaned, rubbed at his face. Why was she so bloody set on this? 'I think the police know more about it than you do.'

'You are so gullible.' She stood up. 'Well, I'm not going to watch you risk everything. I've already told you – you want to do this, Mike, you do it on your own.' She walked away, pulling her coat on. The people around watched Mike, pretending not to, to see if he would follow.

He rounded on the nearest table, shouting. 'Seen enough? Why don't you buy a bloody ticket?' He saw the bartender look across, ready for trouble.

There was only one thing left for him to do. Tell her why it mattered to him. Why in this he might have to be as stubborn as she was.

He caught up with her outside. The trees were tangled with blue and white lights, the parade of leisure facilities bristled with neon. The night was cold and clear but he could see only one star.

'Vicky, stop, wait. I got summat to tell you.'

She looked at him, sighed. Her face washed out by the neon, miserable. She folded her arms across her front. 'What?'

He shuffled from one foot to the other. The words in his chest like stones, hard to drag up. He blew out. 'It's hard,' he said.

'What? You having an affair?' Her face was pinched, wary.

'No!' He wheeled away, eyes pinned on the sole star. 'I want to do the right thing,' he tried again.

'The right thing is protecting your family,' she shot back.

'Wait,' he said sharply. 'Just listen for once, just bloody listen!'

She narrowed her lips, her eyes mean.

He found he couldn't look at her when he spoke. Anywhere but. 'I've never told you, never told anyone.' He shivered. 'When I was at school, there was this lad, Stuart. He was a bit slow, he was—' Something caught in his throat. 'He was just a kid. He wasn't fat or crippled or mucky, he didn't even wear specs, but there was something about him and he got picked on. Every day.'

She was still. Mike watched a bus pull out, a couple snogging on the top deck. 'They'd wait for him after school, or at dinnertime. He'd never go to the toilets at school or anywhere quiet, sometimes he'd trail around after the dinner ladies. He got quieter, like he was shrinking, but it just made it worse. *Stuart Little*.' Mike named the film. 'Remember that?' Mike glanced at her, she nodded.

'That were his nickname – one of them. A couple of times the teachers found out and people got detention. Or the whole form did. Stuart never told. He knew it'd make it worse. This one day—' Mike stopped. He didn't want to say it. He didn't want to tell her. His fingers were cold, he tucked them under his armpits. Shivered again. 'It was after school. I saw them dragging him into the changing room. He was crying.' Mike swallowed. 'I went home. I didn't go and tell anyone, I just went home. Had my tea, watched the box.' Mike's heart hurt. He tightened his jaw, tried to stop his voice quavering. 'Stuart wasn't in school the next day.' He looked across at the traffic lights, saw them turn to green and the traffic move. He heard a girl's laugh cutting through the other noise, high-pitched, squealing. 'He'd gone home and changed out of his uniform and hanged himself from his bedroom door.' Mike's voice cracked. 'And I still never said anything.' Stuart's father had found the boy, carried him in his arms out into the street, weeping.

'Oh, Mike.' Her voice was full of concern. 'You were just a kid, too.'

'I knew right from wrong. I didn't bully him but I did nothing to stop them. I didn't get help. And even when they'd driven him to do that, I said nothing. That was wrong. This – the court case, it's a chance to do the right thing.'

'It doesn't work like that,' she said sadly. 'You can't change the past. What happened, that's awful, it's really sad, but your responsibility now – it's not to the lad that got shot, it's to Kieran and Megan.'

'The police can protect us.' It was almost a howl.

She shook her head, her lip curling. 'You'd take that chance.' Like he was dirt. Like he'd failed.

They walked home in silence. Not touching. Mike felt soiled, ashamed. All the old feelings. He wanted to weep but he didn't know how.

He looked in on Kieran, peacefully asleep, and thought of Stuart's parents, the horror they would carry with them forever. Of Danny Macateer's parents.

Vicky came in. 'I meant it, Mike.' Her voice was fixed, flat. 'It's your choice.'

He had no answer.

PART THREE

Stand By Me

CHAPTER TWENTY-FIVE

Zak

Soon as he asked for witness protection the atmosphere shifted. They put him back in the cells for an hour or so and then he was shown into a room with a couple of new faces. Plainclothes cops. Little and Large, Zak thought. Little smiled a lot but it was the sort of grin a wolf might have before it attacks. Large never smiled, he looked dead depressed, his mouth turned down, shoulders curled over. He had braces on his teeth. Zak thought he was a bit old for that; most people had 'em done when they were teenagers. But maybe the guy had been in a car crash or a fight or something and the braces were to help repair the damage.

Little and Large went at it for hours: going over what Zak had seen again and again, butting in and trying to trip him up. Almost like they didn't believe him, thought he was making it up to get off the burglary charge.

They videoed him the whole time. Whenever he asked anything, about Bess, or if they were going to give him protection, they ignored him. Said they needed a full and complete statement first.

'I'm not going to court without,' Zak told them. 'They'll kill me, they know me. You got to sort me out, new identity, the lot, me and Bess and me mam.'

'We do this first.' Little showed his teeth.

Finally they let him have a break and he got given

a chicken tikka sandwich and a bag of crisps and a Sprite. Even let him out for a smoke. He wished he had something stronger to take the edge off. He hated being in the cell, locked in. Brought back those sick feelings. Glimpses of memories he didn't want at the side of his head like glitches on a screen.

He remembered the fly on his face, buzzing by his nose. Buzzing in his head too so he couldn't think. Everything fuzzy and fizzy. But he wasn't cold any more. Hot then, lovely and hot. Even with his eyes shut he could feel the line of sunlight, feel the weight of heat pressing him down, heavy as sand. Then the commotion, voices, banging.

Little and Large talked to him again and then they were writing it all out. They wanted him to read it, sign it. 'It'll be okay,' he shrugged.

'You can't read,' Large said like he'd known it all along. 'I'll read it, then you sign.'

It sounded dead weird; nothing that wasn't true but not put the way Zak would put it. He wrote his name on the bottom. He was left-handed and he couldn't help but smudge the letters.

Large looked at Little. 'Could do a video statement?'

Zak groaned. 'Not more.'

'We edit what we've already got, play that in court instead of the prosecution taking you through this.' He put his hand on the paper statement.

'Haven't said I'll testify yet,' Zak said. 'Need some guarantees I'll be safe.'

'We're looking into it,' Large told him. 'It's not a soft option. If we go ahead, accept you on the programme, you'll be relocated, you'll lose everyone: friends, family—'

'I'm not going on my own,' Zak argued. 'My mam?'

'It's possible. Even so, big strain for both of you. And if you break your cover, make a call, let something slip, do something stupid, then we can't protect you. All bets are off.'

Little took over. 'Also, we'd need you to be rock solid for the trial, stand by your evidence.'

'I will, course I will,' Zak promised.

He wondered where they'd send them. If it'd be abroad. Spain maybe. He could work in a bar and it'd be warm all the time and his mam'd maybe work there too, or at a restaurant and Bess'd get the leftovers. People'd be on holiday and give good tips 'cos they were having a good time and soon they'd have their own restaurant and pay other people to work and that. But maybe Bess wouldn't be allowed in Spain 'cos of rabies. So somewhere else. Cornwall? Midge had been down there, he said it was like another country, well chilled and full of surfers and old hippies and that.

It was really, really late when Little and Large came back the next time. They didn't have him brought up to an interview room but talked in his cell. Zak was climbing the walls by now, his skin all twitchy like insects were crawling over him and the room shrinking in on him.

'You've not been completely straight with us,' Little said, sitting next to him on the bench. Large leant against the door.

'I have,' Zak retorted. 'It's all true, all happened like I said.'

'Your mother, you claim to have lost touch?'

Zak's belly ached. 'We did.'

'When was that?' Little asked him.

Zak shrugged. 'Dunno.' He just wanted to see her.

'Fifteen years,' Large said, 'you were seven years old. You were taken into care. Remember that?'

179

Zak began to shake, jittery inside.

'We've seen the files,' Large said. 'Your mother went down for child cruelty and neglect. She got a five-year sentence.'

A flash: his skin hot and dry, quivering, the volley of blows. Flayed until he could barely crawl. 'It's not true,' Zak shouted. He'd been bad, that was all. He'd be good now, she'd see.

'Eleven different fractures, ruptured spleen, malnourished, dehydrated. She kept you chained in a shed.'

Scattered sensations, the bite of metal cold on his ankle, the taste of iron in his mouth, licking his palms for the salt, the crumbs of rubber on his tongue, trying to grind them smaller. 'It was a car crash,' he shouted.

'A car crash that lasted seven years? That what she told you to say?' Large asked him. 'You were starving; you'd chewed up the lino. You were covered in your own filth. You looked like a famine victim. The social workers recommended that there be no further contact. She showed no sign of remorse.'

Zak had his hands over his ears, he wouldn't listen to them.

'She nearly killed you,' Little said. 'Why on earth – this, running off into the sunset, it ain't going to happen, Zak. Even if we could trace her, why the hell would you want to?'

Zak started crying, he couldn't help it. Little shuffled about a bit then got up and said they'd be back in a while.

He must have nodded off because next thing someone was shaking his shoulder and it was Large saying, 'Come on, lad, we're shipping you out.'

'Where to?'

'Hull.'

'Hull? Where's Hull?' Zak knew nothing about the place but the name. He'd a feeling it wasn't Cornwall.

'North-east.' Little flashed his teeth.

'Newcastle?' Zak sat up, swung his legs off the bench, in a daze.

'Down a bit. It's going to be home from now on,' Little said.

'Can I get my stuff?' Zak asked; his sleeping bag was in the underground car park, his other bits.

Large shook his head, looked glum. 'No souvenirs, no goodbyes, no forwarding address. Clean slate. Welcome to witness protection.'

'What about Bess?' Zak began to panic, shaking. 'I'm not going without her.'

Large nodded. 'She's coming.'

That was cool then. He got to his feet. 'Will I have to change my name?'

'Oh, yes.' Large nodded. 'New name, new history, flat, job, whole kit and caboodle.'

'And Bess?'

'I said she's coming,' Large said.

'No,' said Zak, 'will she have to change her name an' all?'

CHAPTER TWENTY-SIX

Mike

'She won't wear it,' Mike had told Joe. Mike had been to sign on and Joe was out of the office, as he put it, so they'd met up at a cafe near the Jobcentre. 'I told her everything like you said, about the crash and the panic alarm, but she won't budge. She hasn't just put her foot down,' he said bitterly, 'she's nailed it to the floor.'

'And if you go ahead?' Joe asked.

'I lose them, she kicks me out.' Mike couldn't imagine it: going home to some bedsit, no Vicky beside him, no kids making a racket. Just himself, the ultimate loser, no job, no family. 'You've got other witnesses?' He couldn't look at Joe, the shame heavy in him, a plea in his voice.

'We need you, Mike.' Joe had spoken simply: no theatrics, just facts.

'How can I?' Mike swung his head to look out of the window: a gang of kids had chalks, were scribbling on the flagstones. There was a CD on in the cafe, Coldplay, the third album *X&Y*, not their best, Mike reckoned, but this particular track a masterpiece, though not the soundtrack Mike wanted to his craven betrayal. Chris Martin's voice, pure as water, intimate as they come, singing 'Fix You'. Not this, mate, Mike thought, no fixing this.

'I'm not sure we could take you on but would you reconsider the witness protection programme? If we go that route,' Joe added, 'someone else takes the reins. I'd have nothing more to do with you. Minimum number of people involved, all very secretive – understandably.'

Mike shook his head. 'My boy . . .' Let alone Vicky. No way would she give up hearth and home and family to be shunted off somewhere like criminals.

Joe sighed, turned his coffee cup round, lining up the handle. 'Retraction isn't an option.'

'Say again?'

'When you signed your statement, you were giving your consent to give evidence if required. You were told that at the time.'

'And if I won't?' Mike demanded.

'You'd get a witness summons, if you failed to attend you could be held in contempt of court, arrested, fined, even imprisoned.'

'What! You wouldn't do that!'

'It wouldn't be up to me,' Joe said. 'I wouldn't have any say. Be down to the judge.'

'And they'd really do that?' The guy was telling him that if he didn't sacrifice his family, he'd end up in prison.

'Oh, yes. This is a very serious matter. Prosecution is in the public interest, a hostile witness would not be tolerated.'

'I couldn't pay a fine, I'm signing on. Get banged up—' Mike pushed his plate away, the pastry untouched, he couldn't eat.

'If you told your wife—'

'You don't know Vicky.' Mike pressed the heel of his hand against his forehead, squeezed his eyes shut tight. This was a total disaster. He sat up, looked across at Joe. 'If it was down to me, if it only affected me, I'd not think twice. That's why I came forward in the first place.'

'I could talk to her.' Joe took a drink.

'No,' said Mike quickly, 'it wouldn't help.' Vicky had him by the balls and now the criminal justice system did too. Pulling in different directions.

'There is another way.' Joe folded his hands on the table, leaned in, his voice a shade quieter but still unruffled, like this was a chat about the weather not Mike's future going in the shredder. Mike looked at him.

'You could testify and not tell your wife.'

'But the papers, the news,' he objected. The murder had been front page stuff all along, it would be again once the trial started.

'You'll be an anonymous witness. Your name won't be used. Mr B or whatever.'

For some mad reason Mike thought of *Reservoir Dogs*, the scene where they got their names, Mr Pink complaining.

'She won't know,' Joe said. 'And you won't be the first person to do it.'

'Straight up?' Mike smelt hope, he felt the prospect of a solution dawning before him. Maybe this could be fixed. He would be able to do what he'd wanted to do all along and still have Megan and Kieran and Vicky.

'I'd say it's your only option.' Joe took another sip of his drink.

He'd have to lie to her, something he didn't like, but then he didn't like the ultimatum she'd given him. The lie would be there between them. Things would never be the way they had been. But that was true already. Vicky's selfishness, as he saw it, her refusal to let him take a stand and the way she'd twisted things when he'd told her about Stuart, had changed things. A side to her he didn't like, a hardness. Not willing to put herself in his shoes for five minutes, or even think about the Macateers, what that mother must be going through. I'm all right Jack, that was Vicky's take on it, looking out for her own and sod the rest. So, Mike's way of thinking, a lie here and there wasn't the be all and end all any more.

'I'll do it,' Mike told Joe, 'but she mustn't know.'

Joe dipped his head, drained his coffee.

'Don't ring the house, and no letters,' Mike warned him.

'I can text you,' Joe suggested, 'will that be all right?'

'Yeah, text's fine.' Mike pulled his plate back, bit into the pastry, famished now, the sweet raisins and currants just the job.

'Good.' Joe took his number and got to his feet, said he'd be in touch.

Mike felt better. So much better that he whistled all the way home: 'Here Comes The Sun'.

He told Vicky that he'd retracted his statement and that the police were not happy with him. She studied his face and he half thought she'd spotted the lie but then she just said, 'It's for the best, Mike.'

A couple of weeks before the trial, Joe texted him to arrange something called a pre-trial visit. It just so happened that Vicky was there when the text came through, doing her books at the kitchen table. Mike was filling in his notes for Jobseeker's Allowance. He had written: *Visited library and searched online for vacancies; filled in an application form for a packer at a fulfilment centre*, and was considering what to put next when his phone went. He picked it up and saw it was a text from Joe. He wanted to kill it but he felt her eyes on him, so he opened the message and skimmed it, his mind scrabbling, like a rat in a tin, for a cover story.

'Who's that?' Vicky's eyes pinned him to his chair.

'Our kid,' Mike's voice was creaky, 'wants to know if I'm up for a pint tonight.' Martin never asked Mike for a drink, they only met up at family dos these days, but it was the best Mike could come up with.

'Thought he did five-a-side on Tuesdays,' she said, one eyebrow raised, her pen tapping the table.

'Not all night.' Mike stood up. 'Anyway, I can't be arsed.' He went up to the toilet, read the text again, then deleted it. And prayed that they'd not have reason to see Martin any time soon.

So many lies, just to tell the truth.

CHAPTER TWENTY-SEVEN

Cheryl

Joe, and this volunteer Benny, showed Cheryl where she'd give her evidence. It was a little room down in the basement, empty apart from a table and two chairs. There was a monitor on the table and a camera fixed on top of that. That was where Cheryl would sit. Benny would sit in the other chair.

Milo was at the crèche at the Town Hall. 'Think of it as a rehearsal for you both,' Joe had said. 'On the day you'll know what's what.'

Cheryl looked round the little room. There were no windows or anything so it felt like you were underground. Everything looked new and clean, like it was for show. With the three of them standing there it felt crowded.

'What will they ask me?' Cheryl said. A sickly, cold feeling creeping through her – not long and it would be the real thing.

'The prosecution barrister will take you through your statement, first,' Joe said.

'I'll see them on the screen?' Cheryl pointed to the monitor.

'Yes. And you'll have a microphone attached to your clothes but your voice will be distorted. The big screens in the courtroom will be switched off and only the judge and jury and the barristers will see you on their screens. Then the defence barristers will question you. You're likely to get two sorts of questions: those that cast doubt on your evidence – did you really see such and such, can you be certain, can you remember clearly – and other questions which will examine your motives, try and cast doubt on your credibility as a witness.'

Cheryl didn't like the sound of that. 'They gonna say I'm a liar?'

'They will imply you might have other reasons for coming forward because of an existing relationship with the defendants,' Joe said. 'A grudge, or an attempt to get the reward money. Don't let them get to you, stay calm. If you do start getting upset count to five before you answer. There's only one thing that matters and that is giving your evidence: what you saw, what you heard, telling the court what happened.'

She had butterflies in her belly already.

'If you get distressed,' Benny said, 'I can hold this up.' He picked up a piece of red card, the size of a cigarette packet. 'It's a signal to the judge.' He was being kind but it made her feel even worse. 'We'll have tissues here, water. Before you start you will swear on a holy book, or affirm.'

Cheryl nodded like she was following but her head was buzzing, her mind cloudy.

Up in the offices where all the witnesses came, Joe went over the arrangements with her again. A week on Monday he would collect her and Milo from outside the supermarket at nine. They would take Milo to the crèche and let Cheryl settle him in then Joe would bring her here. When Cheryl had finished giving her evidence, they'd fetch Milo and he'd drop them both back at the supermarket. She would tell friends and family that she was going into town shopping. Any problems, she had his number.

* * *

It didn't take long for problems to pitch up. Starting with Vinia. She came round at teatime. Nana had made chicken and rice and insisted Vinia fetch a plate and eat some. Milo had eaten most of his and was messing now, dribbling juice into his bowl and making the grains of rice float around. Cheryl took the bowl from him, gave him a biscuit and fussed about clearing up, feeling edgy with Vinia being about.

Nana wiped her mouth, set her cutlery side by side. Cheryl saw she had only picked at her food. 'Rose tells me the trial for Danny will be starting Monday week. All the family will be going.'

Cheryl struggled for something to say, felt the vibes in the room, strung tight like piano wire. Nana had been triumphant when Carlton and Sam Millins were charged. 'At last,' she'd crowed to Cheryl, 'how the mighty are fallen.' But she was fair too, and had continued to welcome Vinia into her house unlike some who cut Vinia dead because she was Carlton's stepsister.

'Will you go, too, Nana T?' Vinia asked.

Nana nodded. 'I think so. Rose would like me there. And the satisfaction of seeing justice done. I know Carlton is family, Vinia, but he took a life and he must pay.'

'If he's guilty,' Vinia said. 'He says he didn't do it.'

Nana didn't reply to that, just sucked her teeth and put the telly on. Nana didn't know Vinia was visiting Sam Millins. Cheryl hadn't dared tell her. Vinia couldn't help having Carlton as her stepbrother but being Sam's girlfriend – that was different. That was a choice and one that Cheryl herself couldn't get her head round. Cheryl had tried to talk to Vinia about it.

'No one would blame you if you walked away. It's not fair for him to expect any more after a couple of dates. He could be in jail for years, Vinia.'

'You just don't like him,' Vinia complained.

'No, I don't. And neither did you, till now.'

'He's different on his own, he's real gentle.'

Cheryl threw her hands up, shook her head. 'You know what he's done! You should get out now.' How could she let him touch her? How could she bear his company?

'I promised him – that I'd stay true.'

Cheryl stared at her friend. Vinia was supposed to be the wild one, never let a man hold her back, reckless and devil-may-care, and here she was like some wet airhead. 'It's your life, Vinia!' How could she make her see sense? 'You stick with him, it's not going to go well.'

'Least I'll have a decent life.'

'With him in prison?'

'He's gonna make sure I'm looked after. Cars and clothes, a nice place to live.'

He could do it, Cheryl knew that, the gangs made money, lots of it. Made it hard for the younger kids to say no when they saw the likes of Sam Millins dripping gold and driving top of the range. 'He's buying you,' Cheryl said.

Vinia's face hardened. 'You got Milo,' she said, 'you got Jeri. You so pretty you can have anyone catches your eye. You don't know what it's like.'

'Back up!' Cheryl protested. 'I ain't had no boyfriend since I got caught with Milo till now, not like I'm married an' all. Jeri – anything could happen, or not. You're saying you will stand by Sam because he's loaded and you're lonely?'

'You don't get it.'

Cheryl lost her temper. 'You bet I don't! He killed Danny!'

There was a silence. Vinia's eyes glittered. 'You don't know that.'

'Everyone knows.'

'He drove the car, is all.'

Cheryl felt sad then, that Vinia was fooling herself, twisting it all to make Sam seem less guilty. They both knew you didn't have to fire the gun to face the charge.

After that day Cheryl didn't expect Vinia to call round any more, thought the friendship was broken, but she kept coming and Cheryl didn't know why or how to stop her.

Now Cheryl cleared the plates and scraped the chicken bones into the kitchen bin. She washed up and put the kettle on for coffee. She stepped outside for a cigarette and leaned against the wall, blowing the smoke up into the air, making smoke rings one time.

Vinia came out and sat on Milo's rocker, her knees tucked up to her chin. 'You want to try these.' Vinia held up a packet of cigarettes. 'I can get you some really cheap, two hundred for twenty quid.'

Smuggled they must be, or stolen, thought Cheryl. 'Ta, can you split them?'

'Yeah, just a packet if you want. They herbs?' Vinia nodded at the troughs along the side wall, full of thyme and chives and oregano.

'Yeah.' Cheryl waited. No way was Vinia interested in Nana's garden. So what did she really want to say? Cheryl blew another smoke ring.

'The trial,' Vinia said, 'will you come with me?'

Cheryl's heart skipped a beat. She couldn't believe she was hearing this. Vinia, Miss Self-Sufficient, asking Cheryl for help. And doing it knowing how badly Cheryl felt about Danny's death, how she despised Carlton and Sam, how she thought Vinia was messing up getting involved with Sam. Cheryl couldn't say yes: she'd be down in that little

191

basement room giving evidence, her voice all gruff, sneaking out afterwards. Was this a trap? A test? Was there some way they'd found out that Cheryl had betrayed them? The possibility made her mouth go dry, sweat prickled under her arms.

Cheryl flicked the ash from her cigarette, tried to ignore her heart bumping in her chest. Suddenly she had the answer. 'I can't,' she said. 'If Nana's going, I won't have anyone to look after Milo. Sorry.'

Vinia shrugged and lit her cigarette. Cheryl took another drag and hoped Vinia wouldn't notice how badly her hand was shaking.

Cheryl got up with Milo at half past three. His nappy was dirty but once she'd changed him, he settled back okay. She sat by his cot a moment, watching the way his eyelids fluttered and the perfect curve of his cheek in the glow from the nightlight.

She had not been down to Bristol yet. She'd put Jeri off, explaining that Nana wasn't great, the doctors had mentioned anaemia and her blood pressure was too high so she tired more quickly; two nights would be too much.

Jeri was disappointed but brightened up and promised he'd get up to see her in Manchester soon, could well be last minute as he was doing a lot of travelling: summer festivals and parties. She should come! He could put her on the guest list for the Spanish one, the last weekend in September. 'Bring the baby. It's lovely,' he told her, 'really chilled. Dancing on the beach till dawn. You'd love it.' He talked about introducing her to people – they were always looking for new talent for the music videos. With looks like hers she'd walk it. She'd be brilliant.

Cheryl didn't have a passport. Milo neither. She had never been abroad and passports cost money they didn't have. She smoothed it over saying she'd have to apply for them, it would be nice to see more of the world.

Cheryl stood up to get back to bed and heard a noise from downstairs. Her belly flipped. She opened her bedroom door and saw, with a rush of relief, that Nana's door was open, her light on. Nana wasn't sleeping too good. 'It comes with age,' she told Cheryl, 'I sleep like a baby again.'

'You're not that old, Nana,' Cheryl had said, 'going on like you ninety or something.'

Cheryl went down to check. Nana was in her chair, eyes closed, a rug over her knees. 'You okay, Nana?'

She opened her eyes. 'Queasy, is all.'

'The chicken?'

'The chicken was fine, fresh and cook through,' Nana objected. Then suspicious, 'Why, you feel sickly yourself?'

'A bit,' Cheryl admitted. But she knew most of it was nerves, the whole business with Vinia and the trial, her insides all knotted up with it. Sometimes it felt like she was the one going to be in the dock. 'Maybe a bug,' she said.

'Dry toast and water.' Nana's remedy for any bellyache.

'G'night.'

'God bless, sweet pea.'

Cheryl dreamt she was at the beach with Jeri. It was warm and the sea was still and aquamarine. She was dancing with him, Jeri's hands on her hips, his face close to hers. Then she was looking for Milo, she had

193

lost Milo, she was begging people to help her find him but they were just laughing at her like she made no sense. Cheryl was running to find him but the sand was dragging her down, her ankles, her muscles burning with the strain, only able to move in slow motion. Sam Millins had Milo! Sam and Carlton had him! In the distance they were walking away. Milo was bigger, almost grown, and he was in the middle, Carlton on one side doing his rolling walk, Sam with a gun in his hand. Cheryl called for Milo again and again but he never looked back.

Cheryl started awake, still wrapped in the dream. The sheets were damp with sweat and she felt greasy, shivery. She still felt sick. She threw up in the bathroom and had dry toast for breakfast. She just hoped Milo didn't catch it too.

CHAPTER TWENTY-EIGHT

Fiona

J oe Kitson came with her to visit the court, at the
beginning of September, a couple of weeks before
the trial. He met her in Albert Square, near the Town
Hall, and they set off to walk down to the Crown
Court. She was grateful for his company. She trusted
him, she realized. And his calm manner, his steadi-
ness, allayed her own anxieties. Good midwives,
good doctors had something of the same quality. She
herself had it at work but in this alien context it
deserted her.

'Do you do this for all your witnesses?'

'Not all,' he said. There was a warmth in his eyes.
Fiona checked: he didn't wear a ring. With a jolt she
understood that she really was attracted to the man.
She felt a flush spread across her neck and cheeks.
It was years. There had been a few relationships
since Jeff but it was awkward with having Owen and
though she liked the men she'd never fallen in love
with any of them. And so she'd never gone all out
to make something long-lasting develop. Shelley
reckoned it was a deliberate tactic. Once bitten twice
shy. Fiona just argued that she hadn't met the right
person yet.

'But a case like this,' he was saying, 'it's very hard
to get people to testify. I'll do all I can to get them
on board, and keep them there.'

'There are other witnesses?'

'There are. But I'm afraid I can't tell you more than that.'

Fiona thought back to the day: she'd been so focused on Danny that she recalled little else. She remembered the churchgoers streaming across the grass, Danny's mum and sister among them. But before that? Kids on bikes. A man on his mobile. She couldn't even remember what he looked like.

They reached the side street and Joe showed her to the entrance which was specially for witnesses; he rang the intercom and a guard opened the door. They had to walk through a metal detector, and the guard searched Fiona's bag.

Upstairs, they reached a suite of rooms. Joe took her in and they were met by Francine, a volunteer with the witness service, who would explain all the procedures and look after Fiona during the trial.

'Come through,' Francine said. 'It's a bit of a warren.'

They went along a narrow corridor with rooms off to the sides. Fiona glimpsed people waiting in chairs, some in the corridor itself. Waiting to give evidence. It would be her turn in a couple of weeks.

Francine took them into the kitchen and made tea for them. There was a whiteboard on the wall, columns with names and abbreviations. Francine noticed her reading it and explained: the case, defendants and witnesses, which volunteers were assigned to who, which court it was in.

The place reminded Fiona of a local clinic: the interface of public and professional, the whiteboard, the waiting area with toys and magazines.

'You can't discuss your evidence with me,' Francine explained, 'but any questions you have about the process I'm here to answer. And if I can't, I'll find someone who can.'

'Are any of the courts free?' Joe asked.

'I'll check,' Francine said. She turned to Fiona. 'It helps to see where you'll be. Sometimes we just use photographs to explain the layout, but I'll find out if we can go in.'

Fiona sipped her tea. People – volunteers, she assumed – were coming and going, chatting to each other. Occasionally someone altered an entry on the whiteboard.

Francine came back. 'Yes, we can get a look now,' she said.

'Are you all right if I leave you with Francine?' Joe asked Fiona. 'I need a word with them in the office.'

'Fine.'

'I'll see you back here.'

The courtroom was more or less as she imagined except for the frosted glass box that surrounded the dock. She remarked on it.

'That's to prevent the defendant from communicating with their supporters. They'll be behind them in the public gallery.' Francine gestured to the bank of seats at the back of the court. 'This is the witness stand. You can go in if you like.'

Fiona did. Opposite her was the jury box and to her right the raised dais where the judge would sit. In the well of the court were the lawyers' benches and then above those to Fiona's left rose the dock and public gallery.

She felt exposed. 'They said there'd be screens?'

'That's those.' Francine pointed to maroon curtains bunched at the back of the witness stand. 'Don't know why they call them screens – sounds better, I suppose. They pull those round before you come in and just leave them open so the judge and jury and the barristers can see you. You'll come in from the stairs there.' Francine showed her a flight

197

of steps that led up to the witness stand from below the court. 'It means you won't need to walk through open court otherwise there'd be no point in the screens.'

The air in the room was dead, sound muffled. Fiona felt a chill along her arms as she imagined it full of people. She wondered what other murder trials had unfolded here, what horrors had been spoken about by people standing on this spot.

'It can be a bit daunting,' Francine said. 'Some people get nervous, then often it's not as bad as they thought. And I'll be with you all the time. You'll be given a copy of your statement to read through when you arrive and then when you get called I'll accompany you. The prosecution barrister will talk you through your evidence then each of the defence barristers will have an opportunity to question you.'

'Each?' It hadn't occurred to her that there'd be more than one, but of course there would.

'Two defendants – they'll be running separate defences.'

Fiona came down the steps from the witness stand. 'How long will it take?'

Francine smiled. 'Hard to say. You're here on Tuesday but they might not call you till after lunch.'

'And the whole trial?'

'A couple of weeks for a murder.' It sounded so mundane, so everyday, the way she said it, though Fiona was sure she would not intend it to sound like that. And this was everyday for the court, she supposed.

'Is there anything else you want to ask?' Francine led the way to the exit.

Fiona decided to tell her, her throat tightening as she spoke. 'After it happened, I had a series of panic attacks. I was off work. I haven't had one in the last few weeks but if it did happen . . .'

Francine took it in her stride. 'We can always stop, ask the judge for a break. It's not unusual for people to get distressed while they're giving evidence. Any problem, you let me know and I'll alert the court.'

'Thank you.'

Joe offered her a lift home. She accepted. It was a high summer's day, the sky a perfect blue, the city traffic impatient, everyone hot and sticky. Joe's car smelt of hot plastic. He wound the windows down. Fiona rested her elbow on the window edge.

'So, you're back at work,' he said. 'How's that?'

'Frantic. We're really short-staffed. They are re-cruiting more people but the birth rate's still rising so we can't meet the demand. It's a constant frustra-tion, not being able to do the job as well as you can because you're spread so thinly.'

'I know the feeling.'

'I thought the police service had lots of money thrown at it.' They passed a pavement café, people seated, the aluminium furniture glaring in the sun.

'Doesn't always land in the right hands.'

She looked at him, shocked. 'Corruption?'

He glanced her way, laughed, a rich infectious sound. 'No, no. Thank God. Just the powers that be deciding on priorities. Terrorism,' he explained.

'Ah.'

'And there's a lot swallowed up with special events: football matches, party conferences, demon-strations.'

'How long have you been in the police?'

'Twenty-four years, near enough. Another six and I can retire on full pension.'

'Pretty cushy.'

He laughed again. 'Maybe. I'm on the old scheme. It doesn't work like that any more.'

'So, what will you do then?'

He didn't reply at first, concentrating on crossing the roundabout, finding a gap in among the lorries and vans. 'I'm not sure,' he said. 'I've a place in France – I've been doing it up. Be nice to spend more time there.'

'Whereabouts?'

'The Pyrenees, the east, not far from Narbonne.'

'Lovely, I was in Provence in July.' The question of what to do with Owen had dissolved when he accepted an invitation to go with a friend and his family to Cyprus. Fiona and Shelley booked rooms in a small hotel next to a spa. They'd taken trains all the way to Avignon and hired bicycles to get about once they were there. Shelley and she had got on famously, accommodating each other's different interests by spending a couple of days apart and enjoying some notably giddy evenings drinking the local wine and setting the world to rights. Back home it rained every day but in France the sun shone and Fiona grew tanned and fit. She slept well but whenever her thoughts turned to the trial she felt herself tense, her sense of well-being drain away. It was a lowering obstacle on the horizon growing ever closer.

'I can't go out there yet, anyway,' Joe said as he pulled up outside Fiona's house. 'My kids live with me and there's no way on God's earth they want to move to France.'

He had kids! 'How old?'

'Seventeen and fourteen, girl and a boy. Never a dull moment.'

'Tell me about it. Owen's sixteen and I keep

wishing we could flash forward a couple of years, people say they improve again.'

'Hah!' He laughed. 'I'm still waiting.' The sage green eyes shining, lines crinkled at the corners.

She didn't want to get out of the car, she wanted to keep talking. 'I guess Manchester has a lot going for it: clubs, bands, uni. Why would they want to give up all that for a backwater in rural France?'

'Exactly. Tuesday, you'll be all right if I meet you there – now you know the way?'

'Yes.'

'Are you bringing anyone with you?'

She was surprised, it had never occurred to her.

'You're allowed: a friend, a supporter, someone to hold your hand.'

'I want you to do that,' she said softly.

His face stilled, he blinked, dropped his eyes.

She'd misjudged it. Oh, God. She felt awful, riddled with hot shame and embarrassment. 'Sorry, that was—' she stumbled over her words – 'I shouldn't, please—'

'It's all right,' he said, looking at her.

'Unprofessional and—'

'Fiona, it's all right.' He caught her gaze, warmth in his again. 'I'd love to hold your hand. But that will have to wait till this is all over.'

She felt like squeaking, running. There was a trace of a smile around his mouth. She was giddy and guilty, blood singing in her veins.

'Thank you,' was all she said.

She'd actually taken the whole day off and it was only lunchtime. She was restless, itching to do something, work off some of the febrile energy fizzing inside her. A day like this, bold with sunshine, was so rare she wanted to make something of it. Even if September yielded an Indian summer, the sun would be lower in the sky, the air softer, the sting of heat gentler.

She made a sandwich and ate it on the move, gathering things together. She called Ziggy and put him in the back seat. Left a note and sent a text to Owen: there was pizza in the freezer.

She no longer used the car to go to work but was comfortable driving again; she'd done some supermarket trips and driven across town to a training seminar but not any further yet. Now she refused to start worrying about whether she'd cope with a longer journey. She was still taking the pills, she reminded herself, and it was nearly three months since her last attack.

The road out of the city to the south-east was always busy; the traffic sped up along the intermittent stretches of dual carriageway then slowed to a crawl as they were funnelled through the narrower parts. She took the turning for the High Peak, climbing out of the valley and up past the big houses close to Lyme Park, the country estate. Out along the road which zigzagged the side of the hills, she admired the tubs and baskets of flowers that spilt bright colour in front of houses and shops. She had all the windows down and Ziggy stood with his nose out, his eyes closed against the rush of air. Why did dogs do that, Fiona wondered, they all seemed to like it. Was it some race memory of life on windswept plains, did it mimic the thrill of running?

It took her almost an hour to reach the parking spot, in the fold of hills. She changed into her walking boots and rubbed sunscreen on her face and arms. She kept Ziggy on the lead for the first part of the walk. The track led up across farmland and there were sheep in the fields: given half a chance he'd have bounded after them, a game to him but a recipe for heart failure for many a sheep.

Fiona's calves, the backs of her thighs, ached as the incline grew steeper, the path now climbing between two old dry-stone walls, the slabs of rock encrusted with lichen and here and there tiny violets and thyme growing in the crevices.

She stopped to get her breath, looking back the way she had come. The hillsides were vivid green, the grass as smooth as suede. The few trees that were above the valley stood sentinel, heavy with foliage, alongside the field walls. In one field she could see a tractor at work and the round bales of hay, small as wooden toys. There was a little mere too, the sun glinting on the water in silver stripes.

When they had climbed over the stile into open country, she let Ziggy off the lead. He meandered ahead of her, head down, in an ecstasy of scent trails. Here purple heather and close-cropped turf quilted the peaty soil and cotton grass danced, white feather-heads shivering even though Fiona could feel no wind. Rushes and reeds marked the boggy parts of the moor. A ridge ran from this point for a couple of miles due south. Huge limestone boulders lay tumbled along it, riddled with fissures and holes, the legacy of centuries of wind and water. Fiona heard the spiralling song of skylarks and spotted a pair high above.

She walked along the ridge, following the path as it snaked between the stones and through small streams where hart's tongue fern lapped at the water's edge. She let her thoughts roam as free as she was. Ruminating upon Joe. Was he interested in her? In a relationship? He said his children lived with him, was it a permanent set-up? It sounded like it. What had happened to their mother? Had she left? Divorced him, died?

Jeff had left her for another woman. The hurt of that had never really gone away. Shelley was right, it had shadowed the relationships she'd had since and made her cling to her independence. If she didn't give them much then little could be taken away. But it was a half-life however much she tried to make of it. In time, and not so long from now, Owen would go out into the world. She would be alone. Walking the dog, delivering babies, climbing hills. It wasn't enough. She wanted more, she wanted love and intimacy.

Joe seemed interested. *I'd love to hold your hand. But that will have to wait till this is all over.* He might be stringing her along, happy to let her believe there might be more to come so she would do her best as a witness. That possibility and the suspicion behind it rankled with her and she scolded herself. When her thoughts lit on the trial, the pleasure she felt at seeing Joe again was dampened by a wave of anxiety. She felt the squirt of panic in her stomach, the clamouring of her mind. She was dreading it. She quickly drew on the CBT techniques that she'd learnt. Stood still and focused on her physiology, her breathing, the set of her muscles, and derailed those responses. It worked; she stopped the panic from growing, from devouring her.

She walked on another mile and found a natural picnic area, a bowl surrounded by a horseshoe of rocks. She took her rucksack off and lay down, stretched out on the grass, wriggling until she found the most comfortable position. Ziggy ran to her and sniffed at her face which tickled and made her laugh. She pushed him away.

The sun was warm on her skin and even with her eyes closed the world was full of light. She could still hear the fluting cadence of the larks and fainter, further away, the piercing, eerie cry of a hawk. She rubbed the palms of her hands over the springy tufts of grass and smelt the sweet, peaty aroma of the earth. She was drifting, lulled into a doze with the warmth and peace of the place.

An aeroplane woke her; she blinked and scanned its jet trail chalked through the blue above. Ziggy was lying a little way away, head on his paws. Fiona sat up and got the water bottle from her rucksack, drank deep. She threw Ziggy a dog biscuit, then ate the apple she'd packed.

The rest of the route took her to the end of the ridge and down through a forested valley, sown with conifers and oak, rowan, silver birch and beech trees, the ground underfoot crunchy with beech mast and pine cones. They passed a waterfall which roared over a cliff and thundered its way on to a plateau of large stones below. Twisted trees and huge ferns at either side of the force were slick with green slime. Fiona sat and watched the sheets of water for a while, the mizzle of spray settling on her hair and clothes. Ziggy drank from a pool near the bottom. They tracked the stream back to the road, the way dappled with shadows from the trees and the golden sunlight.

By the time she reached the car, the blister on her heel had popped, a bite with each step, reminding her how long it had been since she'd given the boots a good outing.

She was honest with herself: those moments with Joe had been a glimpse of the life she hungered for. She might – she hoped she would – live another forty years, that was almost a lifetime for generations who had come before. She would not waste it. It's all there is, she thought, and then we die. She would not let fear or false humility or convenience trap her into a lonely existence. She wanted to share it with somebody. If not Joe, then she would find someone else, actively look for love. Other people did it, dating sites and the like; she would too, a promise to herself. She finished her water and put Ziggy in the car. The dog was shattered, he fell asleep immediately. Then she drove home, the sun, a glorious blood-red blaze, setting in her rear-view mirror.

CHAPTER TWENTY-NINE

Cheryl

Cheryl waited until Nana had been in bed for an hour then she went into the bathroom with the kit. She'd taken forever to buy it, hanging round the pharmacy until the girl behind the counter was giving her funny looks, like she was going to nick something.

After a week of being sick she finally clocked this was not a bug. And it wasn't down to nerves about the trial. The smell of food, meat particularly, brought water to her mouth and convulsions to her stomach. She had to hold her breath when she changed Milo's nappies too, turning her head away to gasp lungfuls of air. And her boobs hurt, tight and tender.

Cheryl unwrapped the stick and peed on it. She closed her eyes and waited. Counted to ten. She was numb and tired, her feet were cold. If the result was negative, what then? Relief. Life would go on in the same old way. She'd get past going to court on Monday then be back to normal. Milo would start nursery school part-time in the New Year. Cheryl would check out the model agency, get a fresh portfolio together. Have a bit more money and not be fretting so much. She'd stopped the nails since the thing with the benefit fraud people. Cancelled those she'd already booked in. Maybe she'd take up Jeri's offer of putting her in touch with some of those video makers.

She'd had to wait for her benefit to go in until she could afford to buy the testing kit. Eight quid a pop. If the test was negative she'd have more freedom, more choices, stuff she could do. Get to know Jeri better, work out if they were heading for something serious, or if they were just having fun for a while.

He'd sent her some music, a compilation from the festivals he'd guested at. Awesome stuff. He texted her most days now, called too. Touching base, he said. Never the other way – she had to watch her credit.

Last night he'd called: how did she fancy a night out on Sunday. He could get a flight late afternoon, be in Manchester for six, fly back Monday night. He was eager, giddy like.

Monday was the trial.

'Oh, Jeri, I'm sorry, I can't. Monday I'm busy.'

'How come?' His voice had gone flat.

She wanted to tell him, imagined the way the weight would lift if she could share this with him. 'I've got an interview at the Jobcentre first thing. If I don't go they cut me off.' She hoped he wouldn't realize that she didn't have regular visits to the Jobcentre.

'That's cool,' he said, sounding more relaxed, 'I can keep the bed warm.'

'But Nana's out Sunday too, so I'll have Milo.' The lies were sour in her mouth.

'Man! Don't they have babysitters up there?' He sounded mean now, the first time he'd ever expressed a cross word to her.

'We'll do it another time, Milo's not used to other people, I wouldn't feel right. It's been so long but I really can't make this weekend, babe. Hey, maybe we'll come to you when you get home, a few days like you said, but I'll have to bring Milo.'

'Deal. And my niece is a highly accomplished babyminder, so once he's settled we can do our own thing.'

He had chatted on and Cheryl squashed any thought of a possible pregnancy into a tight corner at the back of her head. He told her about the advertising company who wanted one of his tunes for an online campaign and the possibility of a Jamaican gig in the summer. 'You could come, catch up with your roots.'

'Oh, man, I'd love that,' she said. She could take pictures for Nana; see all the old home places Nana talked about.

'Good luck, Monday,' Jeri said as they finished up.

Cheryl froze then recalled her story. 'Ta. It'll be cool.'

'Night, babe.'

'Night.'

Cheryl opened her eyes and peered at the plus sign and the bold capitals PREGNANT. Tears stung her eyes. There was always an abortion but she couldn't imagine that, not for her. She thought of growing big again, and the labour. Telling Nana. Telling Jeri. Something like this wasn't part of his dreams. Babyfather when they'd barely spent a month together in real time. She had managed fine without Milo's dad. A boastful boy who had several other kids dotted round the area and who Nana had chased off when he called round feigning an interest in Milo – then three months old. He was in the army now; Cheryl hadn't seen him for over a year. So maybe she would have to do the same again. No exciting new modelling assignments, no man, no trip to the West Indies. Future postponed.

Cheryl worked out her dates. Only one time had she and Jeri taken a risk. The baby would come in April. A girl perhaps. Dark like her or more light-skinned with Jeri's fine almond eyes. Alongside the worry and the sadness, Cheryl felt a tickle of joy. A sister for Milo. She put her hand on her belly, imagined it there, small as a jelly bean.

Sunday night, close to dawn, something woke Cheryl. She groaned and rolled on to her back, waiting for Milo to cry out again, but he was quiet. Maybe it was something outside? There were foxes sometimes that screamed and cats that howled like babies.

Cheryl was turning over again when she heard a thump, felt it shudder through the bed, through her. Not the door, but what? Someone in the house, someone breaking in?

She got out of bed and put her bathrobe on. Her heart going wild. They'd found out she was going to be a witness. They were coming for her! Fear scouring through her veins. She stopped at the bedroom door, uncertain whether to wait where she was. She couldn't just stay here, do nothing. Quietly as she could she opened the door. The landing was dark, the doors shut. She listened, closed her eyes to hear better. Couldn't make out any sounds that didn't fit, couldn't sense any presence. She snapped the landing light on.

She stood, her legs itching from being still, eyes gritty and full of sleep. Still nothing. She looked across to Nana's door, she didn't want to disturb her, she had such trouble sleeping now, but what if someone had broken in and was hiding in there?

Torn, Cheryl tiptoed across the landing and listened, her ear to the door. Nothing. Then she knocked gently. 'Nana?' Turned the handle and went in, looked across to the bed but the covers were thrown back. Cheryl put on Nana's light and saw her, on the floor, at the far side of the bed, on her side. Her eyes were fluttering, her skin a horrible yellow shade to it.

'Nana?' Cheryl felt her own skin crackle like lightning. She knelt beside her; put her arm on Nana's shoulder. 'Are you all right? Nana?'

Nana gave a little whimper, her eyes blinking away, and a bit of drool leaked from the corner of her mouth. Her hands were trembling.

'Oh, Nana. Wait there!' Like she could go anywhere else. Dumb.

Cheryl ran to her room and rang 999, asked for an ambulance, her voice all shaky as she gave her name and address. She went back to Nana, knelt beside her, held her hand, and tried to answer all the questions: *can you confirm the number you are calling from; what's the address of the emergency; can you tell me what happened; are you with the patient now; can you tell me how old the patient is; do you know their date of birth; is she conscious; is she alert and responsive; is she breathing?*

The operator said an ambulance was on its way. Could she make sure the door was open so they could get in?

Cheryl ran downstairs; she unlocked the front door and left the latch off. Ran back, still on the phone, still answering questions, following instructions: *has there been any change; could you please gather together any medication the person uses, the paramedics will bring that with them.*

Cheryl collected the tablets from Nana's bedside table and the ones she had downstairs in the top cupboard in the kitchen.

When she got back upstairs Nana's eyes were closed, and still. Cheryl's guts turned to ice. 'Nana?' She squeezed Nana's knuckles and stroked her head, the hair soft with the oil that Nana rubbed on it.

'She's asleep,' Cheryl told the operator, hearing the terror in her own voice.

'Is she still breathing? Listen and put your hand by her mouth.'

Cheryl put her hand close to Nana's lips; felt a slight, damp stream of air. 'Yes, I think so.'

'That's good; the ambulance will be with you any time now.'

'Tell them to come upstairs,' Cheryl said, she couldn't remember if she'd already said that earlier. Nana was quiet. Cheryl wondered what was wrong. Then there were voices and she felt the temperature fall as the paramedics came in and up the stairs.

One of them got down by Nana and began to examine her, the other talked to Cheryl, lots of the same questions as the operator had asked. Cheryl was still on the phone. 'You can hang up,' the paramedic told her. Cheryl noticed he'd had his teeth done, veneers, a bit too big, too long, like horse's teeth.

The one on the floor said they needed the stretcher.

Nana's eyes stayed closed, she didn't even open them when they moved her. They put all the tablets in a bag and wrote her name on it.

'What's wrong with her?' Cheryl asked.

'Hard to say. Best we get her in and let the doctors see. She allergic to anything?'

Cheryl shook her head.

They took the stretcher down and out into the ambulance. It was growing light, the sun a soft orange ball to the east, the sky a pale baby blue.

'Ask at A&E,' the man said.

It was going to be a nice day. The thought made her want to cry. She rubbed at her face. They closed the ambulance doors and drove away.

Cheryl went inside, the pulse hammering in her throat. Milo was awake, she heard him cry out. A sudden cramp seized her, a rush of saliva in her mouth. She reached the kitchen sink in time. Retched until she was empty. She cleared up then went to get Milo. She changed him and sat him in his high chair with a banana while she got herself changed. She half-filled a bottle with apple juice and diluted it, grabbed a packet of raisins and made a little sandwich with honey in for him to have later. Added extra nappies to his bag, and a change of clothes.

She drank a glass of milk and rang a taxi. There was a tenner in Nana's ginger jar. Rainy day money. If anything counted as a rainy day, today did.

The taxi came straight away, sounded its horn. Cheryl carried Milo out in one arm, his bag and buggy in the other. They settled in the cab.

'Where to?'

'Manchester Royal, A&E.'

The cab pulled out. Milo sat beside her, eyes bright, pointing at the advert on the fold-down seats opposite. 'Woof!' he said and kicked his legs.

'Yeah,' Cheryl managed, trying not to weep, 'woof.'

There was a dull calm in A&E. None of the rushing about or panic Cheryl imagined.

Cheryl gave Nana's name at the window and was told to wait. Someone would call her. They'd no idea how long but it was fairly quiet still. It was eight o'clock and Cheryl was supposed to be meeting Joe Kitson at nine, due at the court for ten. She couldn't think about that now. She just couldn't.

She let Milo toddle about for a bit, watching to make sure he didn't trouble anyone. One woman with grey hair and age spots splashed over her face played peek-a-boo and made Milo laugh. 'Peepo,' he echoed. Then the woman was called through and Milo hauled himself up and sat on her empty chair for a while.

Cheryl kept checking the time, her nerves about to snap. Had they forgotten her? She couldn't stay still any longer; she fetched Milo and went outside to the smoking shelter. She lit a cigarette, the first drag making her dizzy, the second a buzz of relief. The rest tasted foul, her mouth was dry and chalky. She had some of Milo's juice. Milo walked along the yellow lines of the ambulance bay, humming to himself.

'You a car, Milo?'

'Car,' he agreed, then 'Tacta.'

'Tractor.'

She'd have to stop smoking. But not yet. Not today. Not with everything going on. She heard a siren woo-wooing and called Milo closer. Finished her cigarette and took him in as the ambulance pulled up. She didn't want him to see anything scary. Didn't want to see it herself.

Another half-hour. Milo was getting bored and Cheryl was about to ring Joe, and tell him she was stuck at the hospital, when they called her name. The doctor checked out who she was and asked her a few questions about Nana and how she had been over the last couple of weeks.

'Not sleeping well, tired, she thought it was the anaemia,' Cheryl said. 'And feeling a bit sick.'

'And her appetite?'

'She isn't eating much. What's wrong with her?' Cheryl should have seen it, got help. Nana was sick and Cheryl had just let her carry on instead of asking her to go back to the doctor.

'Those symptoms may have been side effects.'

'Side effects?' Cheryl couldn't keep up. Milo wriggled off her lap and climbed into his buggy. She should've brought some toys for him, some books.

'She was on new medication.' Cheryl didn't even know that, Nana never talked much about these things.

'We've admitted your grandmother for assessment; we think this episode may have been a cerebral haemorrhage, a bleed in the brain. There are a number of tests we're doing now to best assess her treatment, starting with a scan.' Cheryl nodded, *bleed, brain* echoing in her head. She felt panic beating against her ribs.

'Can I see her?'

'I'll check for you. I'm not sure whether she's on the ward yet.'

Cheryl waited while the doctor rang someone up. Milo had taken his shoes and socks off. Cheryl put them in his change bag – she couldn't face wrestling with him now.

'They'll ring back down,' the doctor said. 'Shouldn't be long.'

Cheryl sat, the minutes scraping by. She gave Milo his raisins. Then, 'You can go up now,' the doctor said. 'Medical Assessment Unit in the orange zone. Head left out of here and follow the signs.' He made it sound easy but Cheryl took a wrong turn somewhere and had to retrace her steps. She thought of the lie she'd told Vinia – saying she was here when she'd been to the police station. Was this punishment for that lie? Nana sick, blood in her brain. But people got better, didn't they? It was like a stroke: they did rehab and had to learn how to walk and talk again.

She had to use a buzzer to get on the ward. There were signs everywhere about germs and gel dispensers every few feet. Cheryl did her hands but Milo refused. At the desk Cheryl waited for the nurse, who was typing away. When she was done she stared at Cheryl, no smile. 'Yes?'

'Theodora Williamson,' said Cheryl. She could see Nana's name up on the whiteboard behind the desk.

'Are you a relation?'

'Yes, her granddaughter.'

The nurse nodded. 'Room C, just there,' she said. 'And if you can keep the little boy quiet.' Milo was singing softly to himself. Cheryl turned away, a flame of anger in her throat, her hands shaking.

There were four beds, curtains drawn round two, one empty and Nana by the window. She looked the same, eyes closed, but there was a mask over her nose, a tube leading from it to behind the bed. Cheryl guessed it was oxygen. She wheeled the buggy to the foot of the bed. Left Milo there and edged round to the chair at the bedside.

'Night night,' said Milo.

Cheryl took Nana's hand. It was cool and light, the bones frail as a bird's. Did you talk to people who'd had a brain haemorrhage? Was it like a coma where they could still hear you? Cheryl wanted Nana to wake up and smile. Or to snap at her, 'I ain't need no audience, child.' And sort out getting herself home.

'Nana?' said Cheryl.

Milo giggled.

Cheryl's phone rang, the ring tone – a sample from one of Jeri's remixes – startlingly loud and punchy in the room. Cheryl jumped and pressed the screen. It was Joe Kitson.

'Cheryl, where are you?' The signal was poor, his voice breaking up.

'I'm sorry,' she said.

The nurse appeared in the doorway. 'No mobiles,' she snapped.

'It's just—' Cheryl began.

'They interfere with the equipment. You need to switch it off now.'

'Well, where?'

'You'll have to take it outside.'

She'd lost the connection anyway. It was quarter past nine. She should be on her way to the crèche. Tears pressed at the back of her eyes.

'Nana, I have to go now. I'll be back later.' It wasn't enough. 'I'll pray for you, Nana, shall we pray?' Cheryl closed her eyes, bent closer. 'Our Father who art in heaven, hallowed be thy name . . .'

When she had finished the prayer she kissed Nana on the forehead, smelt a trace of bay and rosemary from her hair oil. Nana mixed it up every few weeks, had her own recipe. Cheryl preferred hers over the counter.

'Cheryl, where are you?' Joe sounded worried.

'At the hospital. My nana – she collapsed. Could be her brain.'

'God, I'm so sorry,' he said. 'How is she?'

'She's unconscious. They have to do a scan.' She didn't know what else to say. She watched three lads leave the building. One had a fresh white plaster cast on his leg; another had his arm strapped up. She wondered what had happened, a car crash? A fight? 'I should be here,' she said.

217

'When's the scan?'

'I don't know.'

'Cheryl, I'm sorry but I have to ask you to do this. We only get one chance.'

'But how long—' Her chest felt crushed, her breath thick.

'I don't know. It won't be all day, I'm pretty sure of that.'

'When she wakes up—'

'Please. I can come and get you now.'

A pigeon landed close by and pecked at the floor. Milo clapped at it and yelled with delight when it flew off.

Nana in the bed, still and small and her face all wrinkled. *Every line a story.* That's what she used to say when Cheryl tried to tempt her with anti-age creams and that. Nana in the bed. And Danny laughing with Cheryl about church, flushing at her interest when he talked about the gig at Night and Day. Danny on the screen, singing like a dream, trying to moonwalk, laughing. The life in him!

'Cheryl, are you there?'

Nana furious at people for not speaking out: *like a new set of chains, slaves to fear.* 'Yes,' said Cheryl, 'I'm here.'

Unlike the first time that she'd left him at the crèche, Milo was clingy, wailing when she tried to put him down then grabbing her leg and burying his face in it and sobbing.

'You go,' the crèche worker said, smiling: she must have seen it all before.

Cheryl stalled.

'He'll be fine,' the woman said. Cheryl nodded, biting her lip, her nose tingling. The worker picked

Milo up and turned away with him, ignoring his outstretched arms. 'Mummy's coming back soon; we'll have a look at the toys over here.'

'He loves dogs,' Cheryl called after her, sniffing.

Joe smiled and thanked her again as she got back into the car. But the way his fingers tapped at the wheel as they waited for the lights to change showed he was stressed too. It was almost quarter past ten.

'That's more like it,' he said as the road opened up ahead. He picked up speed.

Cheryl felt the back of her neck burn and her mouth water, then the spasm bucking in her stomach. 'Stop! Please. I'm gonna be sick.' Oh, God.

He didn't need telling twice but pulled up on to the pavement. Cheryl flung the door open and bent over. She retched again and again, thin yellow stuff, until there was nothing left, just a taste like sour cherries in her mouth, her throat raw, eyes watering.

She had a tissue somewhere in her bag. She wiped her mouth and got back in. 'Sorry.'

'It'll be okay, you know,' Joe said.

Cheryl began to laugh, tears in it too.

'What?' He indicated, pulled out.

'It's not nerves – well, I am scared, but I'm pregnant too.'

'Ah, morning sickness.'

Oh, God. It was all too much: the baby, Nana, the room she was heading towards. She was tired and shivery. She didn't want to cry, she wouldn't cry. Not now. She covered her eyes with her hand.

Joe said okay and left it. She was glad he didn't keep talking, didn't ask questions or try and cheer her up.

He parked up and she lit a cigarette as they walked around to the witness entrance. Her eyes flicking here and there, watching for familiar faces, ready to

219

duck or run. 'Can I finish this?' she asked him as they reached the door. He nodded.

'Ta.' She smoked it quickly like it was oxygen and she needed it to breathe. There was no ashtray so she had to chuck it down, grind it underfoot. The pavement was littered with tab ends. Some had lipstick on. Cheryl had no make-up on, hadn't even combed her hair. She wondered if the jury would trust her more looking plain and washed out.

'Ready?'

Her stomach clenched. She nodded once. In through security and up to the office, not the waiting area she'd seen last time.

Benny, the volunteer, explained why. 'The family are here, we don't want them to see you.'

They were here! Danny's twin Nadine, his parents, Nana Rose. Nana Rose didn't know about Nana. Cheryl hadn't had a chance to ring anyone. Nana Rose had a mobile, Cheryl knew that much, Nana had given Cheryl the number; she should ring and tell her. It would look weird if she hadn't. She explained to Joe, who agreed. Did she want tea, coffee?

She didn't know if she dare. She shook her head. 'Just some water, ta.'

Cheryl rang Nana Rose. It went to voicemail. 'It's Cheryl, Nana's not well. They've taken her into MRI. She fell this morning. They think it's a brain haemorrhage. She needs a scan, that's the next thing. I'll let you know. Bye. Bye.'

It struck Cheryl that if Nana had been well, she'd be here somewhere too. Going into the court and hearing Cheryl's voice all disguised and not knowing it was Cheryl.

Benny brought her the witness statement to read. All the stuff she'd said that Joe had typed up and she'd signed. 'Take your time,' Benny said, 'read it through and let me know if there's any mistakes. This is the statement the defence have a copy of; this is what they'll ask you about.'

Cheryl tried to read it but it was hard, her mind kept dancing away, floating off to brood on Nana.

Joe returned with her glass of water. 'How's it going?'

'My mind's in bits,' she sighed.

'Read it out.'

'What?'

'Read it to me, out loud.'

Her cheeks grew hot, was he teasing her?

'It helps to say it out loud, to practise. After all, you've never spoken about this to anyone but me.'

'But I won't have to read this when I go in there?'

'No, you just use your own words to describe what happened, then answer their questions, maybe elaborate if they ask you to.'

She drank some water then did as he said, her voice husky from being sick, tripping over some words and finding others that made her voice tremble and her heart ache. But she got through it.

'How about a biscuit?' Joe offered.

'Or toast?' suggested Benny. 'We have a toaster.'

Cheryl covered her mouth, blinked and nodded. 'Dry,' she managed as Benny reached the door. 'Dry toast.'

Before she could finish the toast Benny came to tell her, 'It's about ten minutes now, we should go down.'

Cheryl couldn't swallow. The food lodged in her mouth. She felt embarrassed, face burning as she had to spit out the wad of toast on to the plate.

'Good luck,' Joe told her. 'Soon be over. You need to leave your phone.'

'Oh, yeah.'

Then they were going downstairs, this way and that. Into the box. The cell. That's what it felt like to Cheryl: underground, warm and lit and carpeted but still like somewhere you were locked up. Cheryl was trembling, she kept thinking of Carlton now, her guts iced-water at the thought he might find out she was here. Benny reminded her about the red card in case she got upset. He asked her if she would make the oath on the Bible and she said yes.

Cheryl sat on the chair.

'A bit closer,' Benny said. 'Good, and when you talk just look at the screen, don't worry too much about the camera – if you're looking at the screen then they will see you. Can you clip this on?' Benny passed her the little microphone and Cheryl stuck it to her top. Then Benny handed her a plastic cup of water.

There was a feeling running through Cheryl and she tried to place it: like the moments before the dentist, or waiting for a test at school, or the week before Milo was born. The sensation of something looming, no escape, no way back. A steamroller rumbling towards her, the ground shuddering.

When she was having Milo, when the pains got really bad, she was crying and saying to Nana, 'I can't do this, Nana, I just can't.'

'No goin' back,' Nana had said. 'Baby's coming and no one can stop it. You nearly there.' Nana had rubbed Cheryl's back, really hard, and that had helped a bit then she felt the pain rolling inside a different way and they told her to push.

Afterwards Nana was always coming up with home remedies for Cheryl and the baby. Old wives' tales from back home. When her breasts got sore and swollen, Nana told her to comb them with her Afro comb and stick plantain leaves in her bra. Cheryl was scandalized. 'I ain't combing 'em! Nana, that is so gross.'

'Is sense, you'll see.'

The midwife said that massage did help, Cheryl could do it in a warm bath, apply steady pressure towards the nipple where the lumpiness was worst, express a little of the milk. She tried that and it got better. But she drew the line at stuffing vegetables in her bra. And now, what would Nana think of a second child? Would it be too much for her now she was sick?

'Okay,' Benny said. 'They're putting the cameras on now.' Cheryl shuffled in her seat. Rubbed her palms on her jeans. The screen went from black to colour. She could see the courtroom, the judge. Somewhere there, out of sight, were Carlton and Sam Millins. Vinia. And the Macateers. Cheryl took a sip of the water, it was lukewarm, the plastic cup felt oily in her fingers. She rubbed her hand on her jeans again.

Then the sound came on, she could hear the rustle as people moved, the hum of chatter. Then the judge spoke.

'Ladies and gentlemen of the jury, the prosecution's first witness will be giving evidence from a video link and their voice will be distorted. In certain cases these special measures are adopted but it is of the utmost importance that you do not assume from this any prejudice against the defendants nor attach any greater weight to the prosecution evidence. Your judgment will rest solely on the strength of the evidence you hear, not on the manner in which it is presented.'

The usher in the court stood up. 'Witness A will now swear the oath.'

Benny nodded and held out the Bible to Cheryl. Cheryl placed her hand on the book and read the card. 'I swear by Almighty God that the evidence I shall give shall be the truth, the whole truth and nothing but the truth.'

One of the men in wigs, a tall, skinny man, stood up and spoke to Cheryl: 'Please tell the court in your own words what you saw on the twentieth of June last year.'

'I saw Danny Macateer.' Cheryl's tongue felt too big for her mouth, her lips were dry. The room was cool and she felt goose pimples flare on her arms. 'I was on Abbey Street, near the shop, on the corner with Faraday Street. We said hello and that and he went on.'

'Which way did he go?'

'Along Abbey Street towards the main road.'

'And what did you do?'

'I set off home, down Faraday Street.'

'You knew Danny?'

'Yes.'

'How?'

'From around, from church and that.' Cheryl couldn't tell them that their nanas were best friends, nothing had been kept in her evidence that might give a clue to who she was.

'How did he seem?'

The question floored her. His smile, the way he laughed when she mimicked Nana Rose. His quiet pride in his music. She swallowed. 'Good. Happy, he was going to a rehearsal.'

'Tell us what happened then.'

'I was walking down Faraday Street, a car came past the other way; it was Carlton and Sam Millins.'

Cheryl could hear voices in the court, reactions to what she had said.

'Derek Carlton?'

'Yes.' No one calls him Derek, she thought. She wanted to laugh. 'They went the same way as Danny, turned into Abbey Street.'

'How did you know it was Derek Carlton and Sam Millins?'

'I saw them. And it was Sam's car – the BMW.'

'How do you know both these men?'

'They live in the area. Everyone knows them, their gang runs the place, they cause a lot of trouble.'

One of the other lawyers got to her feet. She had a round, pale face and round glasses. 'Hearsay and prejudicial,' the woman said to the judge.

The judge told the jury to disregard the last statement. Cheryl felt her skin tighten. This was stupid; she couldn't tell them what mattered. The whole gang stuff had killed Danny. It didn't just hurt the people running round with drugs and guns, it made things bad for everyone.

'Are you sure that the men you saw that day were Derek Carlton and Sam Millins?'

She spoke as firmly as she could: 'Yes.'

'And you were able to pick them out of video IDs when you were first interviewed by the police?'

'Yes.'

'Who was driving the car?'

'Sam Millins.' She looked straight at the screen, unblinking.

'Please tell us what happened after that.'

'I heard a shot.'

'Where were you then?'

'Further down Faraday Street.' She imagined Vinia listening, knowing that she and Cheryl had been there that day, trying to remember who else had been about, who might have turned grass. There'd been plenty of people out and about and Faraday Street ran for several blocks, Cheryl hoped that Vinia would imagine this witness had reached a different stretch of the road. Would not put together what she was hearing with her best mate Cheryl.

'You recognized it as a gunshot?'

'I guessed it was. I've heard them before.' Welcome to my world, Cheryl thought. 'And then the car came across Faraday Street really fast, along Marsh Street. They'd been round the block.'

'Did you go to see what had happened?' the man asked.

'Yes. I saw it was Danny, he was on the ground.' A lump filled Cheryl's throat. He should have been getting on the bus, going off to his rehearsal, playing his music, growing up, falling in love.

'Were you shocked?'

'Yes. He was a good kid; he wasn't mixed up in any bad stuff. They should've left him alone.' Her voice broke.

The lawyer thanked her and sat down.

Cheryl felt wiped out, tense, her back ached and she'd a metallic taste in her mouth.

After a moment the woman lawyer stood up, the round-faced one: she was defending Carlton. Cheryl almost blurted out a laugh when she introduced herself as Miss Mooney. 'You say you knew Danny Macateer?'

'Yes.'

'You liked him?'

'Yes.'

'You knew Derek Carlton and you believed him to be involved in criminal activities in your neighbourhood?' Miss Mooney spoke quickly, like she was spitting out facts, knew where she was headed. Cheryl sensed a trick, felt her belly twist.

'So perhaps you thought blaming Derek Carlton for Danny Macateer's death would be a convenient way to get rid of Derek Carlton?'

'No!' Cheryl said. 'I only blamed him 'cos of what I saw.'

'Really?' Miss Mooney making her out to be a liar.

'Yes,' she snapped back.

'Let's take a look at what you saw, shall we? You claim you were on Faraday Street that day. What was the weather like?'

'The weather?'

'You don't recall?'

'Hot, really hot and sunny.' Cheryl remembered the shimmer above the tarmac as they set out, how high the sky seemed, the big bowl of it and Nana's roses full of perfume. Oh, Nana.

'Which side of the road were you on?'

'The other side from the shop.' Vinia had come out of the shop, they'd crossed over. Milo was in his buggy. She'd turned the buggy away but that was after she saw the car.

'And exactly where on the street were you?'

'I don't know.' She had to be careful, Vinia was listening, Vinia who was now Sam's woman.

'You don't know,' Miss Mooney drawled as though this was exactly what she expected. Like one of the teachers at school, all sarky and disappointed in people. 'What made you notice the car?'

Again she wasn't sure what the right answer was. She hesitated. The goosebumps still prickled her arms but she was sweating too. 'The noise, I think. It was going fast.'

'How fast?'

'Maybe forty?'

'Forty miles an hour and the sun was high overhead, am I right?'

227

'Yes.'

'How far away was the car when you first noticed it?'

'Not far.'

'You say you don't know whereabouts on Faraday Street you were – had you passed the hairdresser's, were you closer to Abbey Street at the top or Marsh Street?'

Cheryl felt trapped. She had to say something. 'Marsh Street, past the salon, I think.' Being as vague as she dare.

'Barely yards. I refer the jury to the map of the area.' There was another screen in the court, a map drawn on it, streets marked. The woman moved a computer pointer to indicate Faraday Street. 'This is reproduced in the papers you have,' the woman told the jury. 'A hot summer's day, the car came out of the side road, Marsh Street, only yards away and was travelling at speed past you, the sun glaring off the windscreen, how could you possibly identify who was inside?'

'Because I saw them! I saw Carlton. On my life!'

'Was he wearing sunglasses?' she asked crisply.

Cheryl's mind scrabbled for the picture in her head. She'd been looking away most of the time, shielding Milo, eager to make herself invisible, not wanting any contact with Carlton and his mates.

'I don't know,' Cheryl admitted.

'You don't know,' Miss Mooney smiled. 'And I put it to you that you don't know because you didn't actually see who was in that car.'

'I did!'

'What about when the car drove past a second time. Could you see the occupants then?'

'There were two people still in it.'

'Could you see them?'

Cheryl paused. She bit her tongue, reluctant to answer. She'd sworn to tell the truth. 'Not really.'

'Did you get the registration of the car on either occasion?'

'No.'

'You told the court you heard a shot, you then saw a car travelling at speed away from the direction of the gunshot and you didn't think to get the registration number?'

'No, I didn't,' Cheryl said defensively.

'You didn't go to the police, that day, did you? You went home?'

Cheryl cleared her throat. 'Yes.' Like everyone else, she'd scurried away to hide.

'You didn't go to the police for eight months, in fact. Were you waiting to see if the police caught the culprits before you falsely accused Derek Carlton?'

'No!'

'The reward then. You were waiting for that – and you saw your chance to make money by coming here and telling us a pack of lies. Maybe settling an old score.'

'That's not true,' Cheryl shouted. 'That's lies.'

'I submit that you are misleading this court. You can't remember where you were when you heard the car, it drove past you at such speed it would be nigh on impossible to see who was in the car, even without the likely glare of the sun on the windows. You claim Derek Carlton was the passenger in the car yet you are unable to tell the court whether that person was even wearing sunglasses or not. You see Danny Macateer lying dead after hearing gunshots yet you wander off home without any thought for reporting this supposed sighting—'

'I was scared,' Cheryl interrupted. 'I thought they'd kill me!'

There was a commotion in the court with lots of people shouting at once. The judge told the jury this was inadmissible as evidence. His voice was sharp as he instructed Cheryl not to speak except to answer a question put to her.

What could she tell them? That the bang of a firework had finally shown her how scared she was, would always be as long as the gangs held sway. That she didn't want her son growing up only to see him sucked in or mown down. That somehow she had found enough courage to pick up the phone.

Miss Mooney came after her again. 'Some months later, only after a substantial reward had been offered, you finally approached the police. And for some malicious design of your own making you dreamt up these claims which bear little scrutiny.'

'They did it,' Cheryl said, 'everyone knows—'

The judge stopped her again. 'We are only interested in your eyewitness testimony. Rumour and gossip have no place in this courtroom.'

'What did you really see that afternoon?' asked Miss Mooney.

'What I told you—'

She cut Cheryl off. 'Were you even on that street?'

'I swear. I saw them,' she said fiercely.

'If Derek Carlton had been wearing sunglasses would you still have been able to identify him?'

'Yes.'

'How?'

'Because I know him, I know his hair and how he walks, everything.' She felt hemmed in by the questions.

'Are you close?'

'What? No!'

'You have never been in a close relationship to him?' she asked waspishly.

'No.' Like Cheryl was some jilted girlfriend.

'You don't like him?'

'I hate him,' Cheryl said. 'He's a gangster.'

There were shouts and objections in court.

'And you'd go to any ends to see him convicted of a crime he didn't commit. Because this is a vendetta, isn't it?' Her tone was harsh.

'No!'

'No further questions.'

Cheryl felt like someone had knocked her about, shaky again and sick. Her stomach growling with hunger, her breasts sore. She wanted to go, get back to Nana, fetch Milo. She felt dirty.

But the other defence lawyer was on his feet. Mr Merchant. Young but big with double chins and a small brown beard, too small to hide the chins. A posh voice.

'When the car first drove past you, you were at the passenger side, am I right?'

'Yes.' Cheryl's nerves were thrumming, her pulse stuttering.

'And you have told the court that the car was travelling at speeds of forty miles an hour or more, is that correct?'

'Yes.'

'The road is narrow, would you agree?' he asked briskly.

'I suppose.'

'It's a residential street, small terraced properties, just room for two cars to pass on either side?'

'Yes.' What did it matter? Cheryl wondered.

'Then you would have been close to the car?'

'Yes.'

'So close that any passenger and the bodywork of the car itself would have obscured your view of the driver, isn't that the case?'

'No, I saw him.' It was like everything she told them was crumbling, dissolving.

'With your Honour's Permission?'

The judge nodded and then Mr Merchant explained he was now showing a reconstruction filmed on the same street using a similar model of car with volunteers taking the roles of driver and passenger and a camera filming the witness's point of view.

Cheryl watched as the film played out. It was stagy and cheap, like one of those health and safety films they'd watched in technology. Someone in court laughed aloud. The film showed just what the witness could see: the car drove by and there was the blur of the passenger but nothing of the driver.

'You would have to bend down to peer in and see the driver,' announced Mr Merchant.

'I must have seen him before they got to me, then,' Cheryl said crossly.

'But not five minutes ago you told this court that only the noise alerted you, and given the short distance and the speed the car was travelling at you would scarcely have had a chance to see anything, isn't that really the truth?'

'No.' He doesn't believe me, she realized, he thinks I'm a liar. The risk she was taking, the fear she carried, leaving Nana on her own in the hospital – all that and he made her out to be some scheming bitch.

'Remember you are on oath.'

'I saw them,' Cheryl repeated, her jaw stiff, her mouth gluey.

'What was my client, Mr Millins, wearing?'

'I don't know,' admitted Cheryl.

'Nothing? Not one item?'

'He was sitting down, driving.'

'Presumably he was dressed?'

232

People laughed and Cheryl wanted to spit at the man making her feel stupid. 'I can't remember his clothes.'

'Was he wearing a hat?'

Sam Millins often did, a little pork-pie type, but it would be dangerous to guess. 'I don't know.'

'You don't know a considerable amount, it seems to me. I put it to you that the reason you don't know so much is that this is all an invention, a web of lies concocted for your own ends.'

'No!' What could she say to make them believe her?

'Because you bear this defendant some sort of grudge, you'd like to see him punished and you'd like to get your hands on the reward money.'

'That's not true.' Cheryl was close to tears, her fists were clenched, her shoulders rigid.

'My client stands to lose his liberty and his reputation. The charge of murder is the most serious of all. You place him close to a murder but your account is full of holes. Beyond alleging that you saw him there, that you saw his car, you have not been able to give one shred of supporting evidence to back up that assertion. You don't know, you can't remember: that's all we are hearing. No further questions.'

He turned away and Cheryl was left shivering, tears burning the back of her eyes. They were done with her.

'Let's get you a cup of tea,' Benny said. 'You deserve it.'

Cheryl cleared her throat, took off the microphone.

Upstairs Joe was waiting. 'How'd it go?'

'They didn't believe me.' A nugget of rage boiled inside her.

He smiled. 'You can't know that, the jury will make their own minds up.'

'They made out like I was in it for the money, that I had some issue with Carlton and Sam Millins, and all these stupid questions—'

'It's their job, it's not personal.'

'It felt personal!' Cheryl shook her head, disgusted with it all. Weary. 'I've got to get to the hospital.'

'Tea's here.' Joe nodded as Benny came in with tea and a plate of toast. 'Only take a minute.' All fatherly.

Cheryl tried to smile but her face was all wonky. She sipped the tea and ate the toast. She turned her phone on but there were no messages. Then Joe drove her to the crèche. This time Milo kicked off because he wanted to stay, he'd found a play set with Dalmatian puppies and a kennel and was in woof heaven.

'Go see Nana,' Cheryl told him. She put him under one arm and he kicked his legs and yelled. She struggled outside and he calmed down when they got to the car.

'Whatever happens with the verdict,' Joe said as he drove towards the hospital, 'what you did today will make a real difference. The more people speak out, the more people will in future. Like a snowball. The community protect the gangs out of fear – what you did today helped change that. They'll see it is possible to be a witness and be safe. You should be proud of yourself, you really should.'

Cheryl blinked. 'I'm glad it's over. They were so mean, really tight.' She felt drained, hollow.

'That's what they do, they have to try and discredit the witnesses to save their clients. But you did good. Think what it means to the Macateers.'

He was right, that was something, that was important. Despite her exhaustion she felt a surge of pride. A lift in her mood. She'd done it! Been bold. Stood up to Carlton, borne witness for Danny. Oh, if only Nana knew – though she could never tell her – how proud that would make her.

'I'm sure you'll be fine,' Joe said, 'but you know how to reach me if you need anything.'

'Like getting rid of benefit investigators?'

Joe laughed. He pulled up outside the main entrance. 'I hope your grandma's better soon. And good luck with the baby,' he said.

Cheryl nodded. He was the only person who knew. She'd tell Nana as soon as she could. It'd be something to look forward to. When Cheryl had found out she was carrying Milo she had been so anxious about Nana's reaction, even wondered about an abortion. But when Cheryl, in tears, told her, Nana just said to dry her eyes. 'A child is a blessing—' she'd touched Cheryl's cheek – 'a gift.'

Milo was drowsy but not asleep; she put him in his buggy and waved as Joe drove off. She felt a sweep of fatigue. The day had gone on forever. If Nana was okay maybe she'd take Milo home, they could both have a nap then come back to visit after tea.

When she reached the ward, the nurse she'd seen before was at the desk. 'Miss Williamson,' she said, 'we were about to ring you. Doctor would like a word.' She pointed the way.

Cheryl wheeled Milo into the small room and parked him beside her. There was a woman there in a white coat.

'I'm afraid I have some very bad news,' the doctor said. 'Your grandmother suffered a second cranial bleed just over an hour ago. We did all we could but attempts to revive her failed and she died.'

Cheryl's heart tore, the pain ripping through her like an electric shock, taking her breath. No! Her eyes swam. Nana died without her, she should have been here, and she should never have left her. Now she was dead. No! Please God, no! Nana was dead. Cheryl placed her hands over her eyes, leaned her elbows on her knees.

'Peepo!' Milo said.

Cheryl burst into tears.

CHAPTER THIRTY

Mike

*D*ANNY MACATEER TRIAL OPENS. It was on the front page of the *Manchester Evening News*, with pictures of the boy's family arriving at court. Decked out smart but sober. Mike bought a copy on his way to the tram after he'd finished work.

The story carried over on page two with more background to the case and the pictures of the lad they'd used before. On the tram Mike counted maybe a third of the people reading the paper, and this time tomorrow it'd be in again and it'd be Mike they were reading about; Witness B. It made him feel good, a glow inside.

The new place he was working was a temporary contract – three months, minimum wage, £5.80 an hour. A fulfilment centre for a batch of online shopping outfits. The work itself wasn't exactly fulfilling: matching orders from the stacks in the warehouses, wheeling them through to Despatch. Seven hours a day. But the other staff were okay, a right mix: Polish, Latvian, African, couple of Somalis and a lad from Congo, a Scouser, the rest Mancunians of all creeds and colours. Mike liked Jan, the Polish lad. He was into chess and soon had most of them playing to pass the lunch break. Mike hadn't won a game yet but he was getting better at it. Mike had met up with Jan a couple of times after work for a pint. Jan was thinking about going back home now the bottom had dropped out of the employment market in the UK. They were all on temporary contracts, made it easier for the company to respond to fluctuations in demand – they just let them go when orders dropped off.

Mike had got a text from Joe confirming that he would still be needed Tuesday. Mike had replied and then deleted it. He had booked a day's leave and told work it was a family wedding. He hadn't told Vicky anything and that's the way it would stay.

Tuesday he left the house as usual at seven fifteen. Then he had to hang about in town until ten when he could get into court, the back way like before. This volunteer Benny showed him into the waiting room. There were a group of lads there already and pretty soon the place filled up. Seven trials on, Benny told him, a couple due to finish today.

Mike read his witness statement through. There were bits he'd forgotten, like the dog barking at the house at the edge of the rec, and there were other bits that were bigger in his head than they were just written down. Like the shooting – in Mike's head it was almost slow motion, the man stepping out of the car, raising his arm, Mike seeing the lad walking over the grass, his back to the shooter, the way the lad jerked and spun round before falling. It must have been quick but in Mike's head it took forever.

After he'd got to the end, he read a magazine for a bit, aware of the tension in the place. Each time one of the volunteers came in to call someone, everyone was on pins, swapping glances, on the verge of wishing each other good luck though they were all strangers. Mike wondered if he should feel more sense of worry or dread about it. He didn't share Vicky's paranoia and believed Joe when he said there was no link between the bother they'd had and the

238

gang. But should he be more wary about being in court?

Joe arrived and asked him how he was, if everything was okay, and Mike said fine. Then Benny said it was his turn and Mike's nerves kicked in, but nothing too heavy.

They went down through the building. Mike reckoned he'd a good sense of direction but he'd lost his bearings by the time they got to court. It all speeded up then, he went into the witness box and Benny sat behind him. There were curtains round the box, just the front open, and he felt like a horse with blinkers on. He'd a daft urge to whip 'em back and eyeball the guys in the dock. He swore the oath then the prosecution barrister asked him to tell the jury what he'd seen.

He laid it out, driving up Princess Road, seeing the man step out of the car, the shot, Mike slamming on his brakes and pulling over. He remembered The Clash was playing but he left that out. Then running to help, the nurse already with the boy, Mike calling the ambulance. Mike felt his heart pick up pace as he talked but he thought he sounded calm enough.

The barrister asked what else he could remember and he mentioned the dog because that was in his statement, and the ambulance coming, then the churchgoers, the boy's family, arriving. Mike's chest was tight then, remembering the woman crying over her son, and the older one, the grandma, on her knees on the grass. Mike was thinking what it would be like if they lost Kieran or Megan. Massive.

Next, the woman who was defending Derek Carlton questioned him. Had he been able to identify the man who'd fired the gun?

'No,' Mike replied. 'He was a black guy but I couldn't make his face out.'

'You were some distance away. How far do you think?'

'Thirty yards?'

'More like fifty,' she corrected him, a glint in her eye like she'd scored a point. 'So, it could have been anyone firing that gun.'

'I suppose,' said Mike. 'He was a big bloke though and I remember his clothes. A yellow top, and dark shorts.'

'Are you sure about that?'

'Yes.' Was she messing with him?

'Not a red top?'

Mike was sure. Was he sure? 'Yellow,' he said.

'But you couldn't see his face?'

'I could see it, just not very well. Not enough to describe him.'

'Do you recall his hair?'

'No.'

'You were driving at the time, yes?'

'That's right.' He'd probably still be doing it, if it hadn't been for the murder.

'So any sighting of this man would have been fleeting, a second, perhaps less?'

Mike hesitated. 'I'm not sure.'

'Presumably you were also watching the road, negotiating traffic and so on?'

'Well, yeah.'

'Your attention was divided?'

Mike felt like his story was slipping away from him. 'Yeah, but I saw him shoot the gun.'

'Which hand did he have the gun in?' the woman asked.

'You what?'

'Don't you understand the question?' Patronizing.

'The right hand,' Mike said tightly.

'Are you sure?'

'Yes.' He saw what she was doing; trying to trip him up, make him muddled. Best not to think too much about the answers. But had he blown it? What if the guy was left-handed and Mike had just delivered him a get-out-of-jail-free card? Shit.

'And the car – can you describe that?'

'Silver BMW, X5. I couldn't see the plates though, it was side on.'

The woman looked a bit unsure of herself at that and Mike loosened his fists.

'You know your cars!' she said drily. Some of the jurors smiled at that. Mike thought back to the other Beemer he'd seen, the one that distracted him and led to the bump and him losing the driving job. Had that been the same car? The police had never said anything about finding the car. The wise move would have been to get rid of it straight after the murder. Ship it abroad or break it up for parts. Or maybe it had been a stolen car, though the witness in the paper yesterday had identified it as belonging to one of the defendants – but she hadn't seen the reg plate either.

'What about the gun, what sort was that?'

'No idea.'

'Any detail at all, colour, size?'

'I couldn't see, really, not at that distance.'

'So it might not have been a gun?'

Was she serious? 'He shot it, he shot the lad.'

'You assumed that from what you saw—'

'More than an assumption,' Mike argued. 'He had his arm up like this and then the lad was hit, fell down, that's common sense, that's not an assumption.'

'I beg to differ,' she said stiffly. 'Did you make other assumptions too?'

'Like what?' Mike was getting ratty, all this nit-picking.

'You couldn't see the man's face but you assumed he was black.'

Mike bridled. 'No way. I could see his face – just not clearly. And he was black. I could see his arms too, and his legs. They were black an' all, they matched.' Someone began to giggle and the judge raised his head and looked daggers. 'I didn't need to assume anything,' Mike went on. 'I'm sorry I couldn't make out his face, I wish I had but that's how it is.' He didn't think she liked his answer, she went all pinched mouth then handed him over to the other defence bloke.

He had only one question for Mike. 'Did you see the driver of the car?'

'No,' said Mike.

And that was it.

Mike had the rest of the day to kill. Vicky would be suspicious if he got in early. He was ravenous and found a little cafe off Deansgate that served all day breakfast for £3.99. He got that – no mushrooms – and a cup of tea to wash it down. As he ate he considered the morning. In one way it had been an anticlimax, like Mike was just one in a long line of people saying their ten penn'orth and the exciting bit would be at the end when the verdict came in. And Mike's contribution hadn't amounted to much. He hoped to God they had someone who was there and could describe the men, both of them, someone more reliable than yesterday's witness who sounded like she was in it for a fast buck. It wouldn't have gone to trial if they hadn't got enough evidence, surely?

It was hard to know what the jury had thought but he hoped they'd be able to tell that Mike was being straight in spite of the way the defence woman had rubbished what he'd said.

It was nearly one o'clock. Three hours till he could get the tram. He'd do a bit of window shopping. He was thinking of getting a bike for work, cost a bit upfront but he'd save on the fares and cycling an hour a day would keep him in shape. Day like today, fair and bright, nothing better. Different story on a dark winter's morning in the pissing rain. Still, others managed: waterproof clothes and the lot. Mike was disheartened when he saw the cost of bikes. He could go for something bottom of the range but would it take the welly?

Wandering round the Arndale Mike realized that the reason it felt like a let-down was that he'd no one to share it with. No one waiting for him after it was done to pat him on the back. Couldn't sit with someone and pick it over, brag about the bits when he'd got the upper hand, complain about the things the woman said. Then he felt guilty for thinking like that – it wasn't about him, was it? It was about a lad being murdered and trying to get justice. Mike'd go through the rest of his life carrying this secret. Just like the other one. One at each side, like scales. Or maybe not. It didn't work like that; the good didn't balance the bad. What he'd done today made no odds to Stuart's family, couldn't change what had happened back then: the child coming home from school, humiliated again, going to his room, changing his clothes, not able to face another day, another hour. Tying the knot and slipping the home-made noose round his neck. Mike groaned. There was no penance would right that wrong, remove his guilt. *You were a child*, Vicky had said. But that wasn't enough of an excuse. All he could do was be a better man, a good man.

Mike browsed the music shops up on Oldham Street. Drew up lists in his head of what he'd get when he could afford it. Jan downloaded stuff and had an MP3 player on his phone. Mike told him all about the Manchester Greats: bands he had to listen to, Joy Division, The Smiths and Happy Mondays. The music still as powerful as it had been all those years ago.

Finally it was home time.

Vicky was waiting for him, face like frost, when he got in. 'Where've you been?'

Mike's pulse went stratospheric. How the hell did she know?

'Work,' he managed.

Vicky shook her head, a sneer twisting her lip. 'Good wedding, was it? Anyone I know?'

What the fuck?

Vicky pressed the answer machine. An accented voice, male: *Mike, it's Jan. Your phone's off. They offer overtime tomorrow, extra four hours, thought you like to stay on. Hope wedding was good. Bye.*

Mike's brain was scrambled; he studied the carpet, helpless.

'Well?'

Hole in the ground. And he was in it, right down the bottom. There was a noise from the kitchen, Megan ran in, grabbed her doll's pram and dragged it after her back outside.

'You're seeing someone, aren't you?'

'What!' She was off her head. He felt a laugh blistering inside him but knew he had to be very careful. 'You know I'm not, I'd never.'

'So what else is it? You've blobbed work, lied to them, lied to me. You're always sliding off with your phone.'

244

Twice! He'd done it twice, maybe three times tops. When Joe got in touch and Vicky was there, she had a knack of always being there, spooky bad timing. And she was nosy, always had to know who was texting him. Mike had to sneak off for some privacy and to come up with an alias for who sent the text. 'I'm not sleeping with anyone, I swear.'

'Where were you?'

'An interview.' Mike coughed. 'A new job. I couldn't let work know – they'd be brassed off, so I fed them the line about a family wedding.'

'What job?' She wasn't buying it but it was all he had to sell. 'Why didn't you tell me?'

'Didn't know if I'd get it, didn't know if you'd like the idea.'

'Why?'

Mike's brain was doing a Basil Fawlty, John Cleese lurching around in blind panic. He tried to find something suitably disgusting. Gross. 'Abattoir.'

'Is this bullshit, Mike?'

How could she tell? 'No!'

'You can't stand blood and guts.'

'I know. More money though. Didn't get it,' he added. 'It was horrible, nearly chucked up.'

She stared at him. 'Is this the truth?'

He tried not to blink. 'Yeah, honest.'

'Give me your phone.'

'What?' He wondered if he could pretend it was missing, that Kieran had squirrelled it away some-where.

'Something to hide?' Her lip curled.

'No, just be nice to be trusted, seeing as I haven't done owt wrong.' He was sinking.

'We'll see, shall we?'

'Vicky—'

'Give it here.' She'd got her face on, hard as stone, eyes all glittering.

He handed it over. He'd deleted all his messages, made a habit of it, and his call register. She was going through his contacts.

'Who's JK?'

Joe Kitson. 'What?' Mike's skin fizzed, his bowels loosened.

'You heard.'

'Oh, bloke at work, John King. I'll prove it, shall I?' He put his hand out. 'Like a word with him, would you?' Irate himself now.

'Yeah, I would.'

Mike felt sick. He called Joe Kitson, praying the man would be quick on the uptake. Mike spoke quickly, a laugh in his voice. 'John mate, Mike here, from work. Do us a favour, say hello to the missus, will yer? Settle a bet. I'll tell you the rest at work tomorrow. I'll put her on. Cheers, John.'

Vicky's turn to look a bit sick. Mike passed her the handset.

'Hello?' Vicky said.

'What's this bet then?' Mike could hear Joe ask.

'Nothing really,' she said awkwardly. 'See you.' Her face flared crimson as she handed Mike his phone. 'I don't remember you mentioning a John,' she said, still not admitting defeat.

'Course you do.' Mike's knees were weak and his heart was going like a pump hammer. 'Worse at chess than I am. Quiet bloke.' He grinned. 'You daft cow.'

'I'm sorry,' she said quickly.

'I should think so an' all.'

She snatched the paper up from where he'd left it and started walking towards the kitchen. 'Next time just bloody tell us, then.'

'What? That I've got a bit on the side?'

Vicky turned and hurled the paper at him and then began to laugh. He loved her laugh, rich and dirty. He loved her. And he'd got away with it. 'Get us a beer,' he said.

'Get it yourself,' she told him. But she went to the fridge, anyway.

Oh, God. It was all going to be okay.

CHAPTER THIRTY-ONE

Zak

Zak gave his evidence via video link from Hull County Court. Hull was a dump. Freezing cold and nothing going on. It was by the sea and the wind blew from the east. Little said it came all the way from Siberia. With knives in it. Even the rain fell sideways. Zak's bones hurt deep inside.

Little also told Zak it had been an important port for hundreds of years, a big trading post and a fishing port until the Cod Wars, but there were still working docks. Zak wasn't impressed. Okay there was a marina and arcades and stuff in the town but the rest of it, the places Zak lived and worked, were minging.

Zak had been in one place for a couple of weeks, straight after they arrived from Manchester. Like a safe house with no personal stuff anywhere and alert alarms in all the rooms. From outside it just looked like all the other houses in the row. Little and Large took turns with him in the days, talking him through his new identity and what he was to tell people. At night another guy came, a minder. He stayed up all night watching the nature channel on satellite TV. He only spoke when Zak spoke to him and then never gave anything away. Like words were money and he was skint. The worst thing was no drugs, not being able to have a puff or a snort and chill out. He even had to have his cigs out in the back yard.

They let him walk Bess, always one of them following him. At first he had felt safe, a bit like the hospital but the food not so good, then he got bored and by the end of those two weeks he was close to exploding just for summat to do. Then they got him the flat, and the job. The flat was in a three-storey block. Nine flats each floor, beside a dual carriageway. Zak's was at the back so he could hear the traffic but his view was just rooftops, rows of them. He'd a bedroom, kitchen, living room and bathroom. Low ceilings, dark carpet. He got excited thinking about decorating it, making it comfy. Never had a place of his own for more than a few weeks, and most of those just a room in a squat or a place that only the desperate would pay good money for. Then something would happen, like gatecrashers turning the place into a war zone, or kids stealing the lead piping so there was no water any more, or a shortfall in the rent and he'd be off.

Little and Large made it clear that wasn't an option. Banged on and on about it being his responsibility, his side of the deal. Large kept saying it was his big chance, turn his life around, settle down. But it was Hull, he didn't know anyone, he didn't belong. He missed Manchester.

Zak asked them about other destinations but Little snapped it was witness protection not a sodding travel agency. Same with his new name. Ryan Wilson. Ryan! He hated the name. There'd been a Ryan in one of the homes, a psycho bully who robbed everyone's stuff and had pointy, baby teeth and asthma.

But they forced him to have the name and he had to practise writing it. He told them he didn't go in for much reading and writing but they insisted he'd need a new signature. Not being good with reading limited the jobs they could find him. In the end he started at a recycling centre: sorting glass and metal. The rubbish came in on a wide belt and the 'operatives' as they were called stood either side picking off items for the different crates. You had to wear full protective clothing: overalls and gloves and boots. The place was cold and the work made a right racket, the crashing of glass and the metal clanging. It stank too from the bits of old booze and food and that. You got all sorts coming on the belt. A dead dog one time, just a pup. That cut Zak up to see it.

Zak's new life story was that he'd grown up with his mam in Wigan. 'I don't talk like I come from Wigan,' he'd told Large.

'No one over this side'll know the difference,' Large said, fiddling with the braces on his teeth.

Then they'd moved to Hull.

'Why? Why would anyone come here?'

'For work.'

'There isn't any.'

'She worked for Woolies before they went bust, transferred here. Died of cancer three years ago.' Large looked at him carefully. Zak didn't like him peering like that. Knew he was thinking about Zak's real mam and all that bother. What did they know? She was all he had, her and Bess. He'd been really naughty, must have, and she had to punish him. Went a bit too far, that's all. Zak shuddered, got up and stretched.

'Her name was Julie Wilson. You never knew your dad.'

'You got that right.'

They began to call him Ryan and he hated it. 'Can't I have a nickname?'

'Like what?' Little laughed. 'Fingers?'

'Behave!' Zak said.

'Willie – short for Wilson.' Little kept laughing.

Zak went outside for a fag.

'A middle name, then?' he asked when he got back in.

Little shook his head.

'Why not? Does it cost more or summat?' Zak felt like crying. He did not want to be Ryan.

They wouldn't budge. 'It's all sorted now, birth certificate and all. No can do.'

Ryan Wilson had no other family and had dropped out of school, drifted about for a bit. They kept it simple.

Once Zak got settled at work, he told the rest to call him Matt, said it was his middle name. He carried on like that. Only used Ryan for the official stuff. Handy in a way: if someone called asking for Ryan he knew it wasn't a mate. Not that he'd much to do with the others outside work, the odd kickabout with the younger ones but mostly he'd go home, take Bess out then have some scran and watch telly. Little and Large had warned him not to get too pally too soon. Keep his distance. They'd be checking up on him. So once or twice a week he'd get a call from them, or one of them would pitch up at the flat unannounced.

A couple of months after he'd started the job, he heard one of the lads bragging about some weed. Zak asked if he could get him some. It arrived the next day. Zak got home, saw to Bess, had a pot noodle then fired one up. He was catatonic by 9 p.m. Next thing, Large is on the phone, on his case. Why wasn't he at work?

'Migraine,' he told him. 'Happens now and again.'

Zak should have been happy: he had Bess, he had a warm flat, a place of his own, didn't have to look for

251

somewhere to crash every night. He could lock the door and keep the world out, get up when he liked at weekends, watch telly all night long if he liked. He could afford to eat three times a day. But he felt lost and lonely. Zak accepted he'd have to stay in Hull till the trial.

'What about after?' he asked Large.

'It's not that bad,' Large told him.

'Compared to what? When can I move?'

'We'll talk after the trial. Look, we've sorted you out: nice flat, regular work. Not easy.'

Then it was the trial. He had to be kept close, they said. It was like going back to those first two weeks with Little and Large babysitting him. They took him to a motel outside town. Bess had to go into kennels.

'No way,' Zak said. 'She's never been in kennels, she'll hate it.' Why couldn't they stay at the safe house again? Why couldn't Bess stay at the flat and them take him back there after the trial? He tried facing them down, saying he wouldn't go ahead if they sent Bess to kennels. Little went ballistic and Large sent him out to cool down and told Zak he was on very thin ice and that protection could be withdrawn if he wasn't fully cooperative. So they were at the Travelodge for two nights and the day in between. Adjoining rooms. There was nothing to do but drink and watch telly. Then the second night Large told him they'd an early start in the morning. His time had come.

Zak didn't sleep much. It was hard without Bess around. When he did nod off he had dreams that woke him up again, shadows coming after him, blows landing on his back, on his arms and his belly, words raining down like stones. Chained and he couldn't get away. Bits in his mouth and flies on his face. The dark swallowing him.

* * *

At Hull County Court he had to sit in this room with
a man and talk into a monitor. They showed him the
room was bare, no picture on the wall, no notices,
nothing that could give anyone in the court in
Manchester a clue as to where Zak was. It hit him
like a thump in the guts: Carlton's crew would be
doing all they could to shut people up and what Zak
was doing today was painting a massive target on his
chest. That's why he had to be poxy Ryan Wilson
once he walked out again. Ryan Wilson who didn't
know Manchester much and had led a blameless if
aimless life.

The usher read out the oath and Zak copied him
then they played Zak's video statement that Little
and Large had cobbled together from their early
interviews with Zak. It meant Zak wouldn't have to
go through it all for the prosecution. Man, it was
embarrassing: he looked a mess and he kept stum-
bling over his words and that. It covered the basics:
that he'd been in the middle of a house burglary
when he'd seen Derek Carlton shoot the boy crossing the rec. That Zak knew Carlton by sight, by
reputation, and had scarpered, taking his dog and
the proceeds of the robbery with him.

One of the lawyers told the court that Zak had
been arrested in the process of committing another
burglary and had volunteered information about the
murder in return for immunity from prosecution and
witness protection.

Then they played more of the video, the bit where
he was saying how everyone knew it was Carlton and
Millins who did it and how when they were picked
up someone brought the gun to Midge for safe
keeping. Zak hadn't wanted to say that but they kept

253

on at him; that it was all or nothing and the gun was vital evidence.

He'd seen it in his head, what must have happened next: the SWAT team raiding Midge's. Midge and Stacey pulled out of bed and cuffed. The police finding the gun. Midge getting charged then realizing he'd not seen Zak for a while and putting two and two together and coming up with Judas. Midge, who'd always given him a brew or shared a spliff, who'd fenced his stuff. Midge, who'd taken Bess to the PDSA when Zak had the pneumonia. And he had to dob him in. That was the worst of it.

The woman asked him where he'd been living last June.

'No fixed abode,' he said. That's what they called it.

'Were you employed?'

'No.'

'In receipt of benefits?'

'No.'

'You were surviving on the proceeds from your criminal activity?'

'And begging,' Zak agreed.

'Were you having regular eye examinations?'

She was cracked. 'No!'

'So you don't know whether your vision is impaired?'

'I can see fine,' Zak said, catching up. Her making out he was short-sighted: shabby.

'Can you read the sign above the exit?' She pointed.

Zak stalled; he could see it fine on the monitor but reading was another matter. Then the other lawyer, the prosecution guy, was up complaining as Zak said, 'I can't read all that good.' And the judge called the lawyers up and they had a bit of a barney then the woman carried on. 'We don't know how well you see but the house was about thirty yards away. Even with good vision it may have been difficult to identify who you saw.'

'It were easy,' Zak said, 'I'd know him anywhere. He wears those baggy shorts and he had a yellow wife-beater on.'

'What?' demanded the judge.

'It's a sort of vest,' Zak said, miming the shape on himself, sketching the armholes. 'Big pits. And it was Sam Millins' car, an' all.'

'Please confine yourself to only answering those questions put to you,' the judge said.

'Had you consumed any drugs that day?'

Took Zak a moment to remember. 'No.' He'd scored later at Midge's.

'What about alcohol?'

'Just some cider. White Lightning.'

'How much?'

'Half a bottle?'

'What size bottle?'

Zak sighed. 'Three litres.'

'How strong is that?'

'Pretty strong.'

'Seven and a half per cent proof, to be exact. And you drank a litre and a half. You would have been drunk.' Her nose turned up, a flicker of disgust in her eyes.

'No! I'm used to it,' Zak said.

'What about the previous night, did you take any drugs then?'

Zak shrugged. 'I don't remember.'

'Try.' Her mouth set tight.

He came clean. 'Maybe a bit of weed.'

'Skunk?'

'Yeah.' He could do with some now.

'For the benefit of the jury, skunk is the strongest strain of cannabis known and it remains in the system for up to ten days in regular users. Would you say you were a regular user?' she asked Zak.

'Yeah.' He didn't like the way she was painting him, a druggie, an alkie.

'So when you broke into the property on Booth Street, when you saw events on the recreation ground, you were under the influence of drink and drugs. Surely these would affect your ability to see and remember what you saw?'

'No,' Zak contradicted her.

'Did you work with Derek Carlton?'

'No.'

'But you were involved in stealing goods and the handling of stolen goods?'

'Sometimes,' he conceded.

'And the supply of drugs?'

'Not the drugs, well, not much. Personal use only.' Zak grinned. No one else did.

'Do you find today's proceedings amusing?' she asked him, her face all sour.

'No.'

'Then please refrain from making jokes. You are aware this is a murder trial?'

'Course.'

'And that we are here to get to the truth of the matter. You deny being involved with Derek Carlton but is it not the case that on more than one occasion you ferried packages between suppliers and dealers?'

Zak had done Midge the odd favour. Small scale. 'Maybe a couple of times.'

'I beg to differ. I suggest you were up to your neck in illicit drug dealing and associated violence and it would be very convenient for you to blame Derek Carlton for this murder thereby getting rid of the competition.'

'No way! That's mental!' Zak said.

'Is it true you said nothing until you were arrested in the course of breaking into a supermarket and attempting to steal goods?'

'Yeah, but—'

'Blaming Derek Carlton would be a way of evading justice.'

'No, it's not—'

'I think it is. Two birds with one stone. You save your own neck and you see off a rival at the same time. You are a known criminal with a history of drug abuse, why should anyone here believe a word you say?' Her words lashed at him.

'You calling me a liar?' Zak could feel the hot rush of rage in his guts.

'Aren't you a liar?'

'Piss off!'

There was a flurry of reactions in the court and the judge told Zak he would be held in contempt if he was abusive.

'I'm not lying,' he shouted, his skin crawling, roaring in his ears.

The judge said they would take a brief break to enable the witness to compose himself and then resume.

The usher tried to calm Zak down – offered him a drink. Zak felt boxed in. He asked if he could take a leak – just needed to move, get up and out – but the guy said it'd be better to wait. They'd start again soon, he said, just answer the questions, don't let it get to you.

Zak shuffled in the seat, muttered a bit, then the woman, skanky bitch, was back in his face again. 'You knew Derek Carlton's accomplices?'

'Like who?'

'Michael Revington? The man you called Midge?'

Zak didn't want to talk about Midge, he felt bad. 'Yeah.'

'You stayed at his house, spent time with him?'

'Yeah.'

'You claim in your statement that Michael Revington took possession of the handgun used to shoot Danny Macateer?'

'I think it was, no one said that—' Zak couldn't finish, she talked over him.

'I suggest another version of events: I suggest you played a far greater role in things than you are admitting. I put it to you . . .'

Her voice banging on and on, Zak could feel his nerves jangling, sparking.

'. . . that it was you who delivered that gun for safekeeping to Michael Revington and—'

'No way! That's slander that is, you can't say that!'

'And that you know a lot more about the murder of Danny Macateer than you have told the court and you have twisted everything round to suit your own ends,' she said vehemently.

Zak's head was bursting. She was saying he'd been in on the shooting, that he'd do something like that. 'I'm not havin' this—'

'You didn't actually see who fired that gun but that doesn't matter, does it, the truth doesn't matter, only saving your own skin – even if you send two innocent men to prison. This is a tissue of lies, why don't you admit it?'

'I'm not doin' this. You can go fuck yourself.' Zak got to his feet, ripped off the microphone. The usher stood up, trying to calm him.

'Sit down!' thundered the judge. Then everyone was yelling. Zak reached the door of the room and wrenched at it. It was locked. He kicked it hard, bastard pain in his foot. Slammed his hands against it. Smacked his head into it, hard, harder, blotting out all the thoughts, the avalanche of feelings, the thumps and slaps and curses.

Then the door was unlocked and Little was yanking him out and spitting words at him. His wolf's grin looking like he was ready to rip Zak's throat out. In the end Zak had to go and sit back down. It was that or be arrested then and there and banged up for contempt. He was tempted but he had Bess to think of.

There was another ten minutes of slagging off from the woman and then the other brief, the one looking after Sam Millins, started in on him. More of the same: trashing Zak's reputation, liar, con-artist, beggar man, thief. He'd invented a pack of lies to escape the law, he was a completely unreliable witness and his account could not be trusted. The fact that his evidence was even being admitted today indicated how weak the prosecution case actually was. Whoever killed Danny Macateer that day it was not his client and the garbled rag-bag account they had just heard was simply the desperate imaginings of someone who told the police what he thought they wanted to hear to escape jail himself.

'Crap!' Zak said.

'Precisely,' replied the brief. People sniggered and then he was done.

Little and Large were not pleased. He'd come within a hair's breadth of being done for contempt and if that had happened he'd have been off the programme, beyond their protection. Plus his antics on the stand (as they called it) had been bloody atro-cious. Zak couldn't be bothered to defend himself any more.

'You've done it now, your name's out there,' Large said, 'in lights, Blackpool illuminations. Keep your head down and your nose clean, Ryan. There's a lot of people would like to take you apart for what you've done. They'll be looking for you.'

'What about the reward?' Zak asked them. 'I kept my end of the bargain.'

Little went red, like he'd burst, and Large laughed. 'What planet are you on, lad? *Evidence leading to a conviction* – could go either way thanks to your performance. There might not be any conviction. If these guys get sent down, it'll be in spite of you not because of you.'

Zak shook his head, a bitter taste in his mouth. Shafted.

They dropped him at his flat and went to bring Bess. She danced around him like a mad thing.

'What about a move?' Zak asked Large. 'You said maybe after the trial?'

'No chance.'

'Well, a better job then,' he wheedled.

'Doing what, exactly? No skills, no qualifications.'

'I like animals.'

'Try the Jobcentre, keep an eye out. It's time to stand on your own two feet, Ryan.'

Stop calling me that, Zak thought.

'Any problems, any bother, call the number,' Large said. 'We can get you to safety.'

'So you'd move me if there was bother,' Zak asked, wondering if that was a plan.

Large sighed. 'Genuine bother, and a move could be worse than here.'

How? thought Zak.

Large got up to go and Zak said, 'Can you give us summat to get some grub in? No money till tomorrow.' He'd get something to take the chill away, something to make him relax.

Large shook his head but came up with a fiver anyway.

'I need dog food an' all,' Zak complained. Even though he had plenty in the cupboard.

Large signalled for him to give the fiver back and gave him a ten. 'That's your lot,' he said, 'you have to make your own way now. Don't mess up, lad.'

Zak took Bess up to the park but he couldn't shake off the feeling he had. A dirty shame at the way they'd talked about him in court, how they'd treated him. Like he was rubbish, no respect, nothing. Like he wasn't even a human being with feelings. He needed something to help him forget, to rub out the feeling.

He settled Bess and headed out once it got dark. There was a pub on the far side of the dual carriageway on the estate. Bit of a dive but exactly the sort of place where he could score. A bit of weed or some coke. Something to take the edge off. No – more than that. Something to help him get completely off his face. That's what he needed now. And a tenner should cover it.

CHAPTER THIRTY-TWO

Fiona

F iona had been following the trial in the newspapers and on television. First there had been
two anonymous witnesses, one a passer-by like she
was and the other a local woman who knew both
Danny and the men accused of killing him. She had
given her evidence by video and with her voice
distorted so she wouldn't be recognized. That took
real guts, Fiona thought.

Then yesterday had been a shambles by all
accounts. The man who was on the witness protection programme appeared on remote video link
losing his temper and swearing and trying to walk
out of wherever he was and almost getting arrested.
His behaviour was a gift to the defence. He'd come
over as chaotic and unreliable and much had been
made of his criminal background.

Joe had rung her last night. He didn't go into any
details, said nothing that she couldn't have got from
the media, but he told her the guy hadn't done them
any favours and it was a godsend she'd be on the
stand the next day, redressing the balance.

He sounded weary, she thought.

'It must be a strain for you,' she said, 'not knowing
how it will go.'

'Yeah, but it's worse if you don't even get to court.
Some cases, they eat away at you.'

She thought he might say more, the wistful note in

his voice, but he changed topic, picked up the pace. 'Still, everything all right for tomorrow?'

'Yes. I will get the tram but the early one.'

She'd been dillying and dallying over whether to get a taxi or the tram, fretting that if there was any disruption to the tram service she'd be late.

'You sure? I can sort out a lift.'

'I'm sure.'

'I'll see you there then. Goodnight.'

Owen had come in then, he'd been walking Molly home. Molly who'd been there after school one day last week coming down from Owen's room with him when Fiona got home. Chatty and giggly with dyed black hair and panda eyes. Owen's girlfriend. Owen blushed as he introduced them. Molly was in his English class, music too. Delicate-featured, half his size, Molly volunteered fulsome replies to Fiona's pleasantries. A dark-haired pixie. Fiona peeped out of the living-room window when they'd left and saw them kissing, Owen stooping over to cuddle her. Fiona was moved to see him so affectionate, delighted.

Fiona presented Owen with a box of condoms the next day. Well, she left them in his room while he was skateboarding and told him as they were finishing dinner, let him eat first. She knew there'd likely be some awkwardness and he'd want to escape.

'I know you might not need them yet but they'll last a while. And it's important you use them when you do have sex.' She'd seen her share of young parents-to-be, still kids themselves, lives knocked sideways with an unexpected pregnancy.

Owen groaned and shook his head. Got to his feet.

'Sex is great—'

'Ugh, Mum!'

She felt her own face warm. 'It's a beautiful thing. It's even better when you stay safe. Now that's all I need to say,' Fiona told him. 'And don't forget the dishwasher,' she called after his retreating back.

This evening she reminded him about her court appearance.

'Right,' he nodded and kept on nodding as though if he did it for long enough he might dredge up something to say.

Fiona laughed and Owen scowled. 'What?'

'Nothing. You make me laugh, that's all.'

'Why?'

'I don't know.' It was something to do with his awkwardness, the gap between the size of him and his childishness, the clumsiness and naivety. She found it funny when it wasn't driving her to distraction.

The day of her court appearance was cool and grey with a fresh wind and she walked Ziggy early. Just a short run about the meadow, down to the bridge and back. There were gulls soaring high and circling over the river, the birds the same colour as the clouds. A cormorant took off from the far bank; its large wings made long slow strokes, powering it up and into the trees.

Fiona could smell the dark, sweet scent of water: earth, a hint of sewage and something flowery, reminiscent of shampoo. She wondered if wastewater ever got into the system, all those chemical fragrances. Ziggy chased a squirrel, then set out after a magpie. She called to him and they went back.

She had dreamt about Joe; a shameless, sexy dream that felt so real that when she woke she could feel the physical effects, the glow of warmth between her legs, the excitement fizzing on her skin, in her veins.

Now, when she met him at the witness suite, she was riddled with embarrassment, her greeting forced and brittle, barely able to take in what he was actually saying. He went to fetch her tea and Francine came into the waiting room. A Chinese couple were sitting in one corner with someone Fiona assumed was another volunteer. The other seats were empty. Francine gave Fiona her statement to read. Fiona's hand shook lightly as she took the papers. A family passed along the corridor and with a start Fiona recognized them: the Macateers, Danny's parents, Nadine, the grandma.

Fiona began to read. Remembered how she had sat with the police at the edge of the recreation ground, telling them what had happened. The sun high above, her palms, her knees, rusty with blood. Her eyes seized on the phrases stark and shorn of detail: *they almost knocked me down, he wasn't breathing, he was losing a lot of blood, I performed CPR.*

The room was warm, airless, no hint of the wind blowing outside. Fiona felt a stir of anxiety, a band of heat across her shoulders. She took a slow breath. Joe appeared with her tea. It was hot and she scalded her lip, the burn bringing tears to her eyes.

'All okay?' He nodded at the statement.

'Yes.'

'And you?' he asked gently.

'Just want to get through it.'

He wore a dark shirt, charcoal grey with a thin lilac stripe in it. No tie. Top button undone. No hair visible there. She was appalled at her own shallowness. A murder trial and she was like some lovesick girl. This was his job, that was why he was here. Nothing more. She wondered about his kids again, was tempted to ask what they were like. Tell him about Owen and Molly.

Joe's phone beeped and he excused himself, went out to take the call. Francine came back and chatted to Fiona – would she want to swear on a holy book or affirm? 'Affirm,' Fiona said. She'd no religious affiliation, didn't believe in a God.

'It shouldn't be much longer,' Francine reassured her. Fiona drank her tea. The Chinese couple said something to the volunteer, who got up to leave with them. 'Just going for a smoke break,' the volunteer said to Francine.

'Maybe I'll join them,' Fiona joked.

'Do you smoke?' Francine asked her.

'No, but I could start.'

Francine smiled. 'I'll go and see where we're up to.'

Fiona stretched her neck, rolled her ankles, then Francine was back. 'Yeah, they're ready. We'll go down.'

Fiona felt dizzy, heard the hum in her ears, took a breath and blew out slowly and followed Francine into the corridor. Joe was there. He nodded at her. His soft green eyes shone. 'Good luck,' he said. 'You'll be fine.'

She couldn't speak. She kept one hand against the wall as they went downstairs, not trusting her balance. It felt as if the building was listing to one side, and that she would make a misstep.

The humming in her ears grew louder, a static that interfered with her sight as well as her hearing. They went along and down some other stairs into a room where Francine asked her to wait a minute. Then she took her up a narrow wooden staircase and into court.

The drone in Fiona's head persisted as she read out the affirmation. She could see the piece of card trembling in her hand and her own words sounded muffled. She took another slow breath, tried to focus on what she could see rather than the turmoil inside.

The jury sat in front of her across the court, two rows of them, a mix of men and women, different ages, most of them white but there were two black women and an Asian man. The judge up on his dais at Fiona's right was looking at papers, and below, slightly to the left between her and the jury, were the benches with lawyers and clerks. Fiona could sense but not see the crowd of people in the public gallery; there were whispers from there and an occasional cough.

The prosecuting barrister, a tall, skinny man, began talking Fiona through the main points of her testimony. The questions were easy, her replies straightforward, and the swarm in her head sub-sided. If she stuck to simple facts, didn't submerge herself in the memory, she could keep it together.

'Yes, I heard this bang, the shot, and looked out of the window.'

'What did you see?'

'I saw him falling,' she answered.

'What did you do?'

'I asked the woman I was with to ring an ambulance then I ran outside. To go and help.'

'If I can refer the jury to the map, Your Honour,' said the barrister. 'The witness was at this point here when she crossed the street.'

Fiona watched him identify the place on a large map that was on the screens.

'Tell us what happened as you crossed the road.'

'A car came along, very quickly. I nearly ran into it. They braked and swerved then drove on.'

'Which direction did they come from?'

'My left, erm, from the north.'

'From here.' He indicated on the map.

'Yes.'

'Can you describe the car?'

'It was a BMW, silver.'

'Did you see the occupants?'

'Yes. There were two people in the front but I only got a good look at the driver.' She had lurched to a halt inches from the vehicle, seen his face, angry and intense.

'You later identified this person as Samuel Millins?'

'Yes.'

'Did Samuel Millins communicate with you in any way?'

'No – he just glared at me.'

'And when the car drove off, what did you do?'

'I went to try and help.'

'What did you find?'

The boy lay on his back, one leg buckled to the side, his arms outflung. 'The boy, Danny, there was a wound in his chest; he was losing a lot of blood.' *Pooled in a slick beneath his shoulders, soaking into the grass, into the hard earth among the daisies and dandelions.*

'What did you do?'

'I took my cardigan off, tried to use it to stop the bleeding.' *His eyes locked on hers.*

'What happened then?'

'He stopped breathing. I couldn't find his pulse. I began CPR, tried to start the heart.' Her voice cracked a little; she cleared her throat. *The smell of soap on his skin, the fine down on his cheek. The sun on her neck, his blood warm on her hands.* The memory clawed at her. She blinked and tried to relax her shoulders.

'And then?'

'The ambulance came and the people from church – his family.' They were here, Fiona thought, listening to her, drowning in their own memories. How could they bear it? To wake every day with that loss in their hearts, the absence, the child missing from their world. At work she had dealt with women who miscarried, whose babies were stillborn limp and blue, or whose babies were sick and couldn't be saved. Fiona had witnessed their grief, offered what comfort she could, but to lose a child after fifteen years – to lose him to violence, the bite of a bullet tearing his future away. She thought of life without Owen, squashed the thought.

The barrister representing Sam Millins was a podgy man with a beard. He thanked her for coming but he was a little concerned with some points of her evidence and he'd like to examine these.

Fiona swallowed and felt her ears pop.

'How would you describe your state of mind when you left the house to attend to the victim that day?'

'Well, I was worried, frightened and shocked, I think.'

'Yes. Thank you. And when the car almost ran you over, is it fair to say that added to your shock?'

'Yes.' She had been shaking, her nerves electric, senses sharp as glass.

'You say the car used its brakes. Did it come to a halt?'

'Not completely, it slowed then went faster again.'

'So you only saw the driver momentarily?' he asked.

'Yes,' she agreed.

'When the victim sadly died you were eager to help the police?'

'Of course,' Fiona said.

'You wanted to do anything you could to bring those responsible to justice?'

'Yes,' she answered.

'And you were asked to see if you could identify the driver of the car from video records held by the police?'

'Yes.' Remembering the smooth way Joe had organized it so she wouldn't get a chance to freak out.

'So you were determined to find the culprit among the records you were shown?'

'No,' Fiona objected with an eddy of dislike at the implication she was on some sort of vendetta, 'only if he was there.'

'You glimpsed the driver for one fraction of a second, in a state of deep shock, yet you expect us to accept that you could identify his face many days later?'

'Yes,' she insisted.

'And you had absolutely no doubt?' He almost sneered, implying her certainty was preposterous.

'No. He was just like I remembered.'

'Witness identification is notoriously unreliable, you could have been mistaken, after all.'

'I don't think so. In my experience shock heightens the senses, it was like seeing a snapshot of him and he was distinctive enough for me to spot him immediately when I saw him on the video.'

'Distinctive?' The man frowned.

'He looks like Johnny Depp,' said Fiona, slightly embarrassed, 'but different hair.'

There was whooping and cheering in the court and the judge got irritated. The clerk called for quiet.

'So your identification was based on the notion that the man driving the car looks like a film actor?'

'One particular film actor.' She would not be made a fool of, she'd not back down. 'That makes him memorable.'

Someone wolf-whistled and the judge put his hand to his head and then said gravely, 'If there are any more interruptions from the public gallery I will clear the court. That is not a threat, that is a promise.'

'You work in the area for the NHS. That is correct?'

'Yes,' she agreed.

'For how long?'

'Twenty-one years.' Where had the time gone?

'You must know the community well.'

'Yes, the families.'

'And we all have families,' he said. 'You would know my client then?'

'I don't think so.'

'You can't be sure?' He seized on any inference he could.

She had to be alert, not lose a jot of concentration. 'I'm sure.'

'You hadn't ever seen him in the neighbourhood before that day in June last year?'

Each question was chipping away at her certainty. 'No, I don't think so.' Had the man proof that she'd met Sam Millins before? Could she have forgotten? Had she visited his mother, his sister, in the course of work? The ringing started in her ears.

'But you can't be one hundred per cent sure of that?'

'I don't recall meeting him, seeing him ever.' Fiona fought to hide her irritation.

'You see, I think you may well have come across Sam Millins. My client is not denying he has a reputation in the neighbourhood and you may well have had him pointed out to you over the last few years and then in the heat and confusion of the tragic and violent incident in June 2009 imagined that he was the man driving the car.'

'I didn't imagine anything,' Fiona said hotly.

'You were aware that there were gangs operating in the area?'

'Yes.'

'But you never heard who was involved?'

'It's not something people talk about.' She remembered the new mother turning her away, the day of her panic attack. *I just don't want any trouble. That's how it is.* Closing the door.

'No?' He acted sceptical. 'So you had no idea that Derek Carlton, a black man, and his friend Sam Millins, a white man, had a reputation as gang leaders in the area?'

'No.'

He gave a little smile and shook his head, implying she was not being honest with her answers. Fiona felt annoyed.

'You didn't see the car until it was almost upon you?'

'That's right.'

'You couldn't see it when you heard gunfire and looked out of the house?'

'No, I don't remember seeing it,' she stuttered, flustered.

'You don't know where it came from? Only the general direction?'

'That's right.'

'You don't know who shot Danny Macateer?'

'No.' She made an effort to calm herself, not show how wound up she really was.

'How did you get here today?'

'On the tram.'

'How long did that journey take?'

'Half an hour.'

'Where did you sit?'

'In the front behind the driver.' She was puzzled by the turn of questions.

'There is a window between the driver's cab and the compartment?'

'Yes.'

'So, the driver would be visible to someone sitting where you were?'

'Yes.' What was he on about?

Mr Merchant nodded his head slowly, solemnly. 'Can you describe the driver of the tram?'

'No.'

'Even though you would have seen him pass you as the tram slowed to stop at the station platform, then had half an hour in close proximity? Considerably longer than the fleeting glimpse of my client.'

'I know what I saw.' Doubt was nibbling at her stomach but she could not buckle now. He was trying to undermine her. She *had* seen Sam Millins. She closed her eyes. She remembered the huge rush of horror as she ran from the house, the sick feeling, the blur of motion and the snarl of brakes. Sam Millins' face. The jaw, the chiselled cheekbones, his eyes flashing with rage. *The wild beating of her heart, the roar of adrenalin.* That man had murdered Danny Macateer, along with his accomplice. He sat just yards away now.

Fiona began to shiver, numbness gripped her mouth, dizziness swirled, clouding her vision. *Blink,* the skitter of fear in his gaze and the bloom of love, *blink,* her shoes full of blood. She gripped the wood that framed the stand, trying to fight the tide of terror rising inside. Sweat broke cold across her back and on her scalp and the pressure built, a fist crushing her heart. Her heart jerking, jolting. There was no air, a vacuum. Fiona gasped, gulped. Sensed movement beside her as Francine leant forward. The judge asked if she would like to stop and have a break. Fiona shook her head. She couldn't be sick, oh, please not here. People were talking, buzzing sounds in her head. *The sky in Danny's eyes, pupils rimmed with gold, copper in her throat, the loss of his breath, the loss of his life.* She struggled to breathe, won a sip, fought her way through the acid panic, through the screaming in her nerves and the white hot fear. When her words came she forced them out, stammering through clenched teeth, stones of truth hard in her mouth. 'I saw Sam Millins in that car. I saw him. I swear. He drove that car.'

She made it downstairs with Francine's help. 'Take your time,' said Francine. 'It's done now.'

Fiona nodded, her teeth chattering, her arms and legs rigid with tension, a din in her head. She didn't feel triumphant or relieved, just angry. Angry at the way he'd tried to trip her up and ridicule her story. Angry that the truth about Danny's death was reduced to jousting and cheap comments about film stars. Angry that she had been overwhelmed again by another attack. She was so angry she wanted to scream or break something.

'I need to go home.'

'Take a minute,' Francine suggested, 'then we'll go and get your bags.'

'How was it?' Joe was waiting for them.

'Bit rough,' she admitted, and allowing to weakness made her eyes fill up. She sniffed and blinked. She would not weep now.

'Well done,' he said. 'And thank you. Really, it is so important, having a witness like you.' He smiled, glanced at his wristwatch. 'Now, I'm sorry, I'm going to have to go.'

Oh yes, she thought, game over. She'd done her bit and he was moving on. Why did she ever imagine there might be anything more than that? 'Okay,' she said.

'I'll be in touch.' He nodded, he didn't even shake her hand, just walked away.

Or not, she thought. And gathered up her belongings.

PART FOUR

I Can See Clearly Now

CHAPTER THIRTY-THREE

The Verdict

There was no quick result: Mike knew that was a bad sign. It was a Tuesday when the lawyers did their summing-up speeches and the judge asked the jury to retire to consider their verdict. They didn't return one by the end of the day and they were sent to a hotel for the night.

Mike could feel it all turning to dust. The thought of the murderers getting away with a not guilty verdict or of the jurors failing to agree was like a fist in his guts. They had to convict, even if some of the witnesses had been a bit ropey, even if the forensic evidence was no great shakes.

Mike wondered if the jury had been got at. That happened. And unlike the witnesses, the jurors were there on display, in full view of the public. The defendants' cronies could eyeball them across the court; follow them home if it came to it. And if you were being intimidated and they knew what you looked like, where you lived, where your family lived, then it would be hard to report it. Risk bringing trouble on yourself, on your family.

All day Wednesday at work Mike waited, listening to the hourly local radio news bulletins, on an old Walkman radio cassette he'd dug out. Jan laughed at the sight of it. Mike pretended he was keeping up with the cricket scores.

Mike didn't know the exact rules about how the

votes had to go for a murder trial but he knew most of them had to agree. The jury were sent to the hotel again for a second night.

Thursday, and in the lunchtime bulletin came news that the jury had failed to agree unanimously and had sought direction from the judge. He had instructed them to see if they could reach a majority verdict, of ten or more in agreement. Mike wondered how big the gap was, how many wanted a not guilty.

When he got home he was wound up. Vicky told him Kieran had hidden the landline again and Mike snapped at him which didn't do any of them any good.

Mike knew what he'd seen. He'd seen the guy shoot and kill the boy, the other independent witness, the nurse who'd done CPR, had seen the man driving the car, picked him out and everything. What more did they need? What was taking so long?

Fiona was coming back from her break when her phone rang. The unit was busy; she'd two first-timers to look after: one a breech presentation and the other an elderly primigravida, a woman in her forties who was pregnant after three rounds of IVF. Fiona was worried about the breech but wanted to give the mother a little longer before raising the issue of a Caesarean. No foetal distress yet and the woman was strong and fit.

Fiona's heart flipped as she read Joe's name on the display. 'Hello?'

'We've got the verdicts,' he said. 'Guilty on all counts.'

'Oh,' she gasped and tears sprang into her eyes. She turned away from the ward, faced the notice-board, the collage of photos and thank-yous. All the babies and their parents.

280

'I thought you'd like to know.'

'Yes.' She blinked. 'Yes, thank you. That's brilliant.' She hadn't expected to feel so emotional about it. Then the student midwife was signalling to her, her face stark with panic. 'I have to go,' Fiona said. 'Thank you, thanks, bye-bye.'

'We've lost the heartbeat,' the student said quickly.

Fiona ran.

'You see.' Vicky nudged Mike, nodded at the telly. 'Guilty.'

Mike watched the film of the Macateer family outside the court; the father was reading a statement. 'And we would like to thank all the witnesses . . .'

'They didn't need you, Mike. They managed fine without you.'

'. . . without them we would never have got justice for our beloved son.'

'I suppose,' Mike said, trying to sound reluctant. He'd already had a text from Joe and had punched the air several times to the astonishment and amusement of other commuters travelling home.

'You made the right choice,' Vicky told him.

'Yep.' Mike sighed and picked up the remote, changed over to the footie. 'Reckon I did.' Drummed his fingers on the edge of the couch, accompanying the fanfare in his head.

Cheryl got in and switched on the telly. She'd been at the funeral home making the arrangements. Nana had a fund with the Co-op that would pay for it, a plot at the cemetery and everything. Cheryl felt lost, like she was walking in someone else's shoes, someone else's world. Her mind scattered and dopey, her reactions unpredictable. Cheryl saw the headline scrolling across the bottom of the picture – *GUILTY – TWO MEN CONVICTED OF KILLING MANCHESTER SCHOOLBOY DANNY MACATEER* – and started to cry. It was all too much. Oh, Nana.

Nana Rose had called the evening of Nana's death, she'd got Cheryl's message. Nana Rose was distraught at the news of her old friend's passing and anxious to know the details. 'You were with her, Cheryl, yes? She was not alone.'

Cheryl couldn't lie. 'Not exactly. I had to leave her for a bit. I was as quick as I could be . . .' Cheryl let the sentence trail, her eyes stinging.

'This is a disappointment,' Nana Rose said. 'I hate to think of her alone.'

Cheryl thought Nana Rose was saying Cheryl was a disappointment and for a moment she almost took it on but she went back to why she'd had to leave and she knew Nana would have been proud of her. So proud of her. And she held on to that. It kept her strong.

Vinia had come round after the trial was over. 'I worked it out,' she said after they'd talked about Nana and everything for a bit. 'The witness, the one I told you knew Sam and Carlton, the one that saw the car and had their voice disguised. I know who it is.'

Cheryl, who had been trying to sort the kitchen out, froze, the rubbish bag heavy in her hand. She swallowed. 'Oh, yeah?'

'Genevieve,' Vinia proclaimed. 'She was there that day, remember?'

Cheryl opened the back door, carried the bag out, her heart pittering in her chest. 'Genevieve went to the States, didn't she?' Cheryl called. 'To those cousins in Atlanta?' Cheryl hoisted the bag into the wheelie bin, slammed the lid shut.

'When did she go?' Vinia was scowling, pulling out her cigarettes, as Cheryl went in.

'Summer. Still there. Can't have been her.'

Vinia sucked her teeth. 'Damn!'

'There were loads of people out that day,' Cheryl told her, 'could have been any one of them.'

Vinia held the packet out to Cheryl. 'Smoke?'

Cheryl hesitated. She was trying to cut down but with Nana gone and all, it was so hard. Vinia screwed her eyes up, craned her neck back examining Cheryl. 'What?'

'I'm pregnant,' Cheryl told her.

'Oh. My. God. Whoa! What you gonna do?'

Cheryl pressed her tongue against the roof of her mouth, shook her head.

'Does he know?'

Cheryl shook her head again.

'Aw, girl. I reckon you need this then.' Vinia handed her a cigarette, pulled out her lighter. 'I sure as hell do.'

Now Vinia was back with news about the sentences. Cheryl was up to her eyes sorting out things for Nana, notifying the post office and utility companies, cancelling some things, transferring others. She'd had a lot of help from people at church: some making meals for her or taking Milo for a couple of hours, others driving her places.

'Life, both of them, and a minimum of twenty years.' Vinia said. 'I'll be thirty-nine when he gets out. I hadn't planned on living that long!'

'They deserve it,' Cheryl said.

'Well, yeah, but—'

'Don't make excuses, Vinia.'

'What's eating you?'

Cheryl felt a glow of rage, a steady burn, something righteous and fierce. 'Apart from my nana gone and a baby on the way and no money, you mean?'

Vinia sighed.

'Carlton and Sam killed Danny, now they get to pay. I'm glad I won't see either of them for the next twenty years. I don't want to know about them or hear about them.'

Vinia's eyes went hard. 'What you saying?'

Cheryl cleared her throat. 'The crew doesn't exist any more, all those other arrests since. No one would care if you walked away now. But if you're going to stick by Sam, don't come round here again.'

Vinia turned away then back, making Cheryl flinch. 'You asking me to choose? Without me you're on your own, Cheryl.'

Cheryl said nothing.

'It's not like you have to go visit anyone, innit?' Vinia pouted.

'I have Milo,' said Cheryl, 'another baby come April. I'm thinking of them. I don't want them growing up mixing with guns and gangs and—'

'You're picky all of a sudden,' Vinia said.

'That's how it is,' Cheryl folded her arms. She felt dizzy.

Vinia didn't speak. She picked up her bag and walked out.

Cheryl let her breath out. She closed her eyes for a moment, then straightened up and went to clean the sink.

EPILOGUE

Zak wondered how people stuck it: going to work in the dark, coming home in the dark. Animals hibernated. People should too. He managed up until Christmas but after that he found it harder to get out of bed in the mornings. Especially if he'd had a few the night before.

He got a warning, then a written warning. Not that he could read it. Then he got the push. The Jobcentre wouldn't let him sign on for Jobseeker's Allowance because he was voluntarily out of work; he would be sanctioned, they said, though he could appeal for hardship payment. He couldn't face it.

He tried some of his old scams but it was tougher up here: either people were tighter with their cash or he was losing his touch. Wouldn't need to bother if they'd given him the reward. Tight gits. Zak still couldn't believe he wouldn't get a penny, all he'd done.

Now he got letters through, some official with red lettering. He knew that wasn't good. Then a bloke came round, a bailiff. Zak had till the end of the week to pay his rent or he'd be evicted. He had the numbers for Little and Large but all they'd do was slap his wrists and stick him in some other poxy job. Maybe not even that. They had warned him over and over like some stuck record, that if he messed up he'd be thrown off the programme. He sold the TV and DVD player to a pawn shop, made enough for the train and a bit left. He had to buy a ticket for Bess as well.

He felt better as soon as they got off the train and were walking down Piccadilly ramp into town. The place hadn't changed. Like he'd never been away. It was raining, a fine drizzle. A tram hooted. He'd have to steer clear of Midge, if Midge wasn't locked up, avoid Hulme way but there were other places he could try. He wondered if Russell was still caretaking at the flats.

Once he got himself sorted out he could maybe try and find his mam, see how she was doing. She might have somewhere he could stay. A nice house with a conservatory and fish in a pond and big leather sofas.

First things first and that meant something to help him sleep and then somewhere to kip. He bought a bottle of White Lightning at the mini-market and some rolling tobacco. There used to be a place down the other side of Victoria Station, under the bridge, that he'd used a couple of times, in between a dumpster and the wall. Arranged right you could open the lid of the dumpster and prop it against the wall, make a roof to keep the rain off. Yeah, he'd try there – he'd a good feeling about it.

He walked down Market Street, Bess at his side. The African guys were still selling umbrellas and the old guy who did rock 'n' roll under a fishing tent was belting it out. Zak bought a sausage barm from the cart at the bottom of the hill. ''Ere, have one for the dog,' the woman said, 'on the house.'

'Ta,' he said.

'Ey, I'm sick of this bloody rain,' she said, handing him his change. 'Drives you mad.'

Zak checked the sausage wasn't too hot and gave

it to Bess. Then took a bite of his own and set off along Corporation Street where the Ferris wheel was turning. The white framework and the lights blurry in the misty rain.

A woman stopped to make a fuss of Bess and a bit further on Zak could see the emo kids in little groups hanging in the rain outside Urbis. Home, thought Zak, smiling. How could he ever live anywhere else?

Jeri came for Nana's funeral. Cheryl didn't ask him to, he just said when is it and I'll come up. He couldn't come for the whole nine nights but he would come on the eve of the final ceremony and stay a few days.

She hadn't told him about the pregnancy yet but she knew she'd have to. She'd do it after the service, when it was all over. She didn't want it interfering with giving Nana her send-off.

He arrived into chaos: people crammed into the sitting room, others clattering in the kitchen, clearing up and serving food, Milo writhing in her arms, on a crying jag.

Cheryl's heart jumped at the sight of him. He made his way through the crowd and kissed her, touched Milo's cheek. The gesture brought an image of Nana, her palms stroking Milo's face, singing his name as Cheryl swung him. Cheryl had to blink hard and rein in her tears.

They were barely alone that first night. Not until the early hours when the last of the tipsy mourners had left.

'You look tired,' Jeri said when he came in from the shower, a towel round his waist and his chest, his skin a golden caramel colour, dotted with droplets of water.

'Mega.' She kissed him. His lips were soft, tentative. His arms went round her and she closed her eyes, leaned into him, kissed his neck. His skin was smooth and warm and she felt the bump of his pulse through her lips.

'You want to sleep?' he murmured.

'In a little while.' She raised her face and looked at him. The swirl of desire washed through her spine and her limbs and deep inside her. She felt weak.

He nodded and led her to the bed.

Vinia was at the funeral. Cheryl was glad she'd come even though the friendship was in tatters. Nana had been like a grandmother to Vinia, who'd not known her own, both of them dying when she was still small. Nana regularly fed and sheltered Vinia when Cheryl brought her back from school. Times in Vinia's own home were always stormy and Nana's was a refuge of sorts.

Cheryl felt spacey all day, reeling between hot tears and a cold, shattered, numb sensation. Jeri wore a beautiful black suit made of fine, soft wool and a white shirt. He looked wonderful, Cheryl thought, like a model himself in a glossy magazine, advertising a watch or men's fragrance. When they first arrived at the church she could sense the ripple of interest from the congregation. She could imagine the gossip.

At the cemetery, Vinia came up to them. Cheryl's heart sank. Not now, she thought.

'Jeri,' Vinia greeted him. 'Hi, Milo.' Milo grunted. He'd got a cold and he was grumpy with it. Vinia's eyes were red, her nose puffy. She'd been crying. 'Cheryl, I am sorry,' Vinia said.

'Thanks.' Cheryl tried to smile, moved to walk

away but Vinia put her hand out, touched Cheryl's arm. 'You were right.' Vinia lowered her voice, glanced at Jeri.

About what? Had Vinia found out Cheryl had testified? Cheryl's belly churned, her pulse rate rose. Instinctively she drew away from Jeri, turned her back to him, blocking his view of Vinia.

'I've written to him,' Vinia said. 'It's over. You happy now?'

Cheryl shrugged. ''Spose.'

Vinia's bravado faltered. Her eyes grew wet. 'I miss you, girl.' She looked ashamed.

Cheryl swallowed. Gave a nod.

'We good?' For the first time she saw the need in Vinia and the fear too, the apprehension that Cheryl might still rebuff her, and Cheryl understood that this had not been easy for her friend.

'Yeah,' Cheryl nodded.

Vinia gave a little breath, found her cigarettes and held them out to Cheryl, who hesitated then shook her head.

Vinia signalled towards Jeri with her eyes, raised her eyebrows in a silent question: you told him?

Cheryl shook her head and shot Vinia a warning look then turned to go. 'We'll see you at the hall.'

They sat in the living room, Jeri and Cheryl, side by side, drained by the day. Milo was asleep upstairs. Cheryl was on edge, running versions of her announcement in her head while Jeri talked about Jamaica and how they might travel.

'I can't come,' Cheryl said, the words blunt.

'Why?' He frowned. 'We can sort out the passports. I know you don't like taking money but—'

'I'm pregnant.' Her voice shook.

289

Jeri turned to her, his face blank with amazement. Time stretched out. 'Oh, man,' he said eventually.

Cheryl searched his face, looking for clues to revulsion or pleasure or annoyance. Finding nothing.

'I thought you should know,' she said flatly. 'Doesn't mean I expect anything.'

'It's a surprise.' He got to his feet. He had his back to her, still in his white shirt, his suit trousers. His hands in his pockets. 'Oh, man,' he said again softly.

Cheryl had her hand over her mouth. She had no more tears today but her lips were trembling. She didn't want him to know how much this hurt. She'd been such a fool to think she could hold on to a man like him with his glamorous job and his money and his fine looks.

The silence yawned between them. Then, 'Do I get a say?' His voice was tight.

'In what?' Whether she kept the baby? Did he want her to get rid of it?

He turned to look at her; his face was drawn. A line furrowed his brow. 'You don't expect anything from me,' he said steadily. 'Is that because you don't want anything from me? You'd rather be on your own? My part's over?'

He thought she'd used him. She shook her head, she didn't know what to say. 'It was an accident,' she told him.

He pressed his hands to his head, squashing his dreads. Sighed. 'I don't know where I stand with you, Cheryl. We get on real well, it's going fine, then suddenly you're busy, you can't get to Bristol, I can't visit you here. You make stupid excuses about babysitters. You treat me like a yo-yo.'

'No!' She had to put him off because of the trial, that was why. Mostly why.

'You were happy enough for me to come for the funeral but now that's done, I'm not needed. Yeah?'

She couldn't tell him about the trial. She couldn't ever tell anyone. That secrecy was all that kept her safe, her and Milo and the little baby to come. And the rest? Holding him at arm's length? Not getting too close, too eager. How could she explain that?

'Why me?' She found her voice. 'You could be with anyone. All those talented people, musicians and dancers – all those places – your life . . .' She knew she wasn't making sense. She pressed her temples. 'I thought you'd drop me, even before the baby, thought you'd hurt me.'

'Why?' His eyes flashed.

'Because I'm not like you.' Her eyes burned. 'I don't even have a pay cheque. I haven't got a passport. I was trying to be realistic. This . . .' She flung her arm out, taking in the room. 'This is it!'

'You think so little of me? Of yourself? I started out in a place just like this!' He raised his voice. 'There was never enough money. You think I've forgotten all that?'

'But you could have anyone,' Cheryl said.

'Most of them, the hangers-on, the groupies, they're takers, Cheryl. They like the image, the lifestyle. It's all skin deep. You're different. You're real.' When he spoke again his voice was very quiet. 'Least, I thought you were.'

In the pause that followed she heard an ambulance siren. She wondered who was hurt and what had happened to them. If there was more trouble.

'I was scared,' Cheryl said, 'I'm sorry. And I really didn't know you, if I could trust you. I still don't.' She stared across at Nana's chair, empty.

'I could say that too,' he said.

'I'm not ashamed of who I am,' she added, 'I'm not. I'm as good as anyone else. I care about you,' Cheryl cried, 'I really like you but it's all mixed up and I don't know what's going to happen.'

'Hey.' He moved to sit beside her, pulled her into his arms. 'Hey.'

She wept dry tears, for herself, for Nana.

'I'm here,' Jeri said, 'I'm here because I want to be with you. You're beautiful, outside and in. I can't get you out of my head, girl. First time I saw you, blew me away, I knew. That feelin' – man . . . I really like you, Cheryl, and we're having a baby. You and me. We're having a baby, yeah?'

Cheryl nodded, choking on a sob.

'We'll work it out, yeah?'

'Yeah.'

Cheryl pulled away and looked at him. He held her eyes, his own bright and steady.

Joe Kitson rang Cheryl. He was putting her forward for the reward money. If approved, and he'd do his damnedest to make sure it was, she'd be given a code to take into a city centre bank so her anonymity would be preserved.

'You'd have to be careful with the money,' he said. 'Don't want people asking questions.' He sounded flat, tired. 'Say you'd inherited it or something.'

Cheryl's throat ached. 'My nana, she erm . . . she died. I could say she had some savings put away.'

'Oh Cheryl, I am sorry.'

'Yeah.' Cheryl pressed her tongue against the back of her teeth.

'I know it wasn't about the money,' Joe said, 'what you did was amazing. You remember that.'

Cheryl sniffed hard.

She sat for a while after the call. So tired. The house quiet, Milo having his nap. She pulled the throw round her and curled up on the sofa. *God bless, sweet pea.* She slept.

Zak was getting chips. He asked for scraps as well: the little bits of crunchy batter you got for free, and lots of salt and vinegar. He'd found a place to score just before and was looking forward to getting off his face once his belly was full.

He was heading for the corner, opening the chip paper, Bess by his heels when he saw them. Three lads. One held a baseball bat. Didn't recognize them though there was something familiar: maybe he'd run into them before at Midge's or somewhere.

Zak yelled at Bess to stay and ran, dropped the chips and ran, into the alley, his feet beating on the flagstones, the wind in his ears blocking out sound. They were behind him. He didn't need to look. He pelted to the end of the alley, gulping air, and darted across to another one opposite. There were wheelie bins near the end of it, a cluster of them. Zak ran between them, tipping them over as he went, a barricade to try and slow his pursuers. As he gained the end of the alley he turned right and out of the corner of his eye, caught the flurry of motion behind.

Faster. Faster. He ran, feeling the spike of pain in his chest, his breath rasping, a stitch in his side. A junction. He swerved sharply to the right and along the cul-de-sac, into someone's front yard, swung himself up and scrambled over the wooden door which led into the back garden and crouched, waiting, trying to halt his breath, the crackling sound it was making.

He waited. The slick of sweat cooling tight on his skin, the smell of his own fear high in his nostrils. His throat was parched and his guts hot liquid. He listened, straining to hear beyond the pulse throbbing in his skull and the drone of a plane above. He waited until cramp bit at his calves and he'd begun to shiver with cold.

Unsteadily, he got to his feet and put his face to the high, wooden door, an eye to the gap between the edge and the frame. He couldn't see anything except the low wall opposite, some of the house beyond.

He'd have to make himself scarce, fetch Bess and get down to Wilmslow Road, take the first bus that came. Shame about the chips. He wondered if the dealer had recognized him (even though Zak had introduced himself as Matt) and called up the goons. Man, he needed a drink.

Carefully, Zak took hold of the door handle and heard the tiny snick as he raised the latch. Suddenly, the door burst backwards, slamming into him, breaking his nose and knocking him to the ground. There was a blur of blows, one to the back of his head exploded white starbursts in his eyes. Kicks and thumps to his spine and his ribs and his face. He tasted pennies. Felt the dam of pain burst over him, robbing him of speech, emptying his bladder and his bowels. He heard the snap of bones and the snarl of curses. The smack and thud of boots and the thwack of the bat. He heard barking. Something barking. I'm sorry, Mam, he begged, I'll be good. I promise. But the blows came faster. He couldn't remember. His eyes were full of blood and there was no air. Screams of terror died in his throat, shuddered through him. Then there was no pain. Nothing.

*   *   *

DANNY MACATEER WITNESS KILLED. Mike saw the caption on the newspaper sandwich boards outside the cafe. His heart stopped, then racketed on like it had lost the right rhythm. He and Kieran had been at the museum while Vicky took Megan to a birthday party. Mike bought a copy of the paper and took Kieran in, bought drinks and settled at a table. He passed Kieran a straw and once the lad was sipping away, Mike turned to the paper. He skimmed the front page, the newsprint rippling and distorting so he had to keep going back over it:

> Zak Henshaw, who testified at last year's trial into the murder of sixteen-year-old Danny Macateer, has been found beaten to death in the Anson Road area of Longsight. Henshaw (23) had been offered witness protection and a new identity in exchange for his cooperation with the police who charged gang leaders Derek Carlton (25) and Sam Millins (24) with the brutal shooting of the innocent schoolboy. At the trial the judge allowed special measures for several eyewitnesses. All gave evidence anonymously apart from Henshaw who appeared via remote video link from an undisclosed location. For unknown reasons Henshaw had returned to the city, breaching arrangements for his safety. Police are trying to establish if the attack on Henshaw was linked to the successful prosecution which saw Carlton and Millins each sentenced to life for the murder. Henshaw, a petty criminal and drug user, was homeless at the time of the murder in June 2009. A spokesman for housing charity Shelter stated that homeless people were disproportionately likely to be victims of violence.

Mike left the paper in the cafe.

Vicky had bought one. 'You seen this? You thought I was imagining things, didn't you? But one of them's been killed. They're not saying that's definitely why but it doesn't take a genius, does it?'

'They knew him, though, didn't they?' Mike couldn't resist. 'He was involved and then grassed them up to save his neck. That's why he was on witness protection.'

'Yes.' Vicky nodded her head as if he was proving her point. 'Some protection!'

Mike shook his head. Best not to get into it or he might say too much. 'I'll do Megan's bath,' he said. And escaped.

It went round in his head that night. They'd known this witness, his name, his face. He'd not been anonymous like Mike had. He'd been one of the gang, reading between the lines. He'd been in hiding but he'd come back to Manchester for some reason. Maybe he had a death wish. Whereas Mike – completely different situation. And what he'd done – taking the stand and hiding it from Vicky – he wouldn't change it for the world.

Fiona heard the newsreader, heard the words, *a witness in the Danny Macateer murder trial has been found murdered*, and felt a lurch of anxiety. She set the iron down and stared at the television. Joe Kitson was there talking, explaining how they were still conducting an investigation and fending off comments about the competency of the witness protection programme.

Fiona was trembling. It could have been her – or Owen. He was out with Molly. She'd an overwhelming desire to call him, to check he was safe. She knew she mustn't. She couldn't infect him with her own fears. What if she was wrong? What if he was in danger now and she did nothing? He might be lying somewhere bleeding to death.

She carried on ironing but the sense of dread clung to her, a miasma she couldn't shift. She still had Joe Kitson's number. She had come close to deleting it a few times since September, dispirited that he had never got back in touch, but she held on to it. She was perplexed because he had seemed to return her interest – at least that time in the car. Surely she hadn't imagined the spark between them.

Now she debated whether it was reasonable to ring him in the light of the news and got cross with herself for prevaricating. Of course it was reasonable.

His line was busy, his answerphone picked up: *Please leave a message.*

'It's Fiona,' she said, 'I'm er . . . I need to talk to you, please can you ring me?'

The minutes inched by. She finished ironing and put the clothes away. As she returned to clear up she misjudged and kicked the leg of the ironing board. The iron teetered and as she grabbed for it, catching the handle with one hand, the edge of the metal grazed her other arm inside her wrist. The burn was fierce and brought tears to her eyes. She ran it under cold water for a while, watching the shiny skin pucker and redden. She'd some Germolene some-where which would dull the stinging.

She was rifling in the medicine chest when the door bell rang.

'Forgotten your key again,' she muttered. Owen was getting more disorganized as he grew older, not less. She felt a wash of mild relief that he was back.

In the hall she saw the silhouette at the front door. Not Owen. The hairs on her neck stood up and her pulse went wild. She stood for a moment, indecisive, giddy. Then stepped closer. 'Who is it?' She tried to sound strong, calm.

'Joe Kitson.'

She wanted to hit him for frightening her. She opened the door, her greeting flustered and awkward. 'Come in, erm, I thought you were Owen, and then you weren't.' He looked older, thinner.

'You okay?' he asked.

'Yes. No. I don't know.' She went into the kitchen with him. 'Would you like a drink?'

'Tea would be wonderful. Just milk, no sugar.'

'You've come from work?'

'Still at work but the beverages there are undrinkable.' He slid his coat off and draped it over the chair back. Sat down.

'The witness, Zak,' Fiona said.

Joe nodded.

'It's never going to go away, is it?' She tried to keep her voice level. Switched the kettle on.

'They don't know who you are,' he said.

'But it's possible that one day someone could find out.'

'It's extremely unlikely,' Joe said.

She put the tea bags in the mugs, got the milk out.

'Carlton and Millins are behind bars, along with several associates on related charges. What's left of the gang is in disarray, defunct to all intents and purposes.'

'But they killed Zak.'

'They knew him,' Joe said. 'Face, name, the lot. He was connected to the gang, loosely but even so when he appeared for the prosecution he knew he'd have to hide for the rest of his life. He would have been safe if he'd stayed in the programme.' Joe leant forward, his palms on the table. 'They don't know

298

you, not your name, not your face, you are not one of them.'

'But some people do.' She turned to make the tea. 'The woman I was visiting, other mums in the area probably.'

'No one's saying anything,' Joe said. 'We got a result. Imagine the difference it makes to those women's lives, to those families, not having Carlton and Millins terrifying the community. They stand to gain, everyone does. I give you my word, you'll be all right.'

She passed him his drink. 'I still get the panic attacks,' Fiona said. 'I was so hopeful, with the therapy and the drugs. I so wanted it to work. To be better.'

He nodded. 'I'm sorry.' He sipped his tea.

She imagined the talk sliding into pleasantries, chit-chat about jobs and holidays, and then him leaving. Maybe she should just let it be. But she had to know. 'You never got in touch.'

'No.' He coloured and cleared his throat. 'I . . . er . . .' He sighed, placed his mug down, twisted it, lining the handle up just so. 'I've been on leave.'

'Oh?'

He met her gaze. 'Stress,' he said drily but there was a different look in his eyes, a wounded look. 'Just started back.'

She scrabbled for something to say. 'It's very common.'

'The job, it's erm . . .' He faltered, tapping his finger against the handle of the cup. 'It got to me. But,' he brightened his tone, 'according to the occupational shrink I am fit for purpose.'

She was full of questions. Had it been the Danny Macateer case that had got to him or another? Had he been in hospital? Was he taking drugs for his

299

trouble, too? But she sensed that it had cost him to tell her at all and that he was not comfortable talking about it. 'Good,' she managed.

'I didn't feel up to socializing.' He wrinkled his nose.

'Yes, of course.' And now? 'We are a pair,' she joked. 'Stressed and petrified.'

He smiled and the warmth of it turned her stomach. She drank some tea.

Then Owen and Molly were back wanting toasties and hot chocolate and Joe said he had to get back.

Fiona saw him to the door. There was a pressure tight in her chest, fluttering in her stomach. Don't make a fool of yourself, she thought. He's not interested. Can't blame him. 'Perhaps we could go for a drink, sometime,' she said quickly.

'I'd like that,' he said.

Her heart skipped a beat and a glow suffused her cheeks.

'I can't say when,' he apologized.

'No, of course, you'll be busy. But you'll call?' She heard the uncertainty in her tone. So what, she thought, that's how it was, how she was.

'I will.' He put his hand out to reach hers, squeezed her wrist and she screamed in pain. Joe dropped her hand and reared back in alarm. 'Fiona?'

'It's all right,' she gasped, tears springing in her eyes. 'Just my wrist. I burnt it on the iron.'

He blew out a breath. 'Sorry.' Nodded at her. 'I'll ring you. Promise.'

She nodded back, beaming, embarrassed at how touched she felt and how elated. Her nerves alight, dancing on tiptoe and her wrist stinging like hell.

Cheryl felt another contraction start, the dull cramp growing tighter as it built, a band around her belly and her back. She blew out, leaning forward and pressing the hot water bottle close.

Milo, with his Dalmatian doggy hot water bottle, mimicked her, frowning and hissing.

'Look at him!' Vinia laughed. 'Still got belly ache, Milo?' He nodded. Then as Cheryl's contraction ebbed away, he turned back to the TV where Wallace and Gromit were after the Were-Rabbit.

'Forty seconds.' Vinia was timing her.

'How long since the last?'

'Four minutes. Should we call?'

'When I had Milo it was like this for ages. If they get any longer, maybe then.'

Vinia went back to flicking through the free newspaper. Cheryl paced about the living room, her hands at the hollow of her back.

'Hey, we could get a dog,' Vinia said.

'No way! Nutjob! With two kids—'

'This one's good with children. Listen.' Vinia read it out: '*Bess is a reliable and friendly dog with a lovely nature and is ready for rehoming*—'

'Oh!' Cheryl winced and clutched the top of the sofa. 'Another?'

Cheryl nodded; too busy riding the pain to say anything. It lasted longer, she was sure. It hurt more. 'Call now,' she said.

Babies didn't pay attention to shifts, Fiona had learnt that way back when she'd first done her training. And with some labours she would carry on working after her shift had finished because the continuity mattered to her, to the mother, to a successful outcome. She anticipated tonight was shaping up like that. Cheryl Williamson was booked in under the domino scheme: she would spend the first stage of labour at home then transfer to hospital for the delivery and third stage and be discharged within hours if there were no complications. For someone like Cheryl, with another child at home, it meant less disruption and for the hospital it meant a bed freed up for a woman who might need more medical assistance.

The housemate, Vinia, opened the door. Fiona had met her once, wanting to make sure that Cheryl would have some support in the days after the birth. Fiona had been seeing Cheryl for the last two months, ever since she'd returned to her role working in the community. And, boy, was she glad to be back. The first few days had felt like a trial, a test. Was she tempting fate coming back here, was she trying to induce a panic attack? She had to prove to herself that what Joe had said was true: she was not a target and she would not let the fear define her. True, her world was a harsher place since the murder: the experience had left her raw – as if someone had peeled back a protective layer to expose her vulnerability, to expose everybody's vulnerability. The sense of security she'd had before was gone forever. The death and then the trial had changed her, as they had so many others. There was no way back. Only forward.

She always thought of Danny Macateer when she drove past the recreation ground but these days there was no splintering of confidence or shortness of breath, just sadness, an ache that the boy had died. Sorrow soft inside.

'How's she doing?' Fiona asked Vinia.

'Fine but they're speeding up. She's upstairs now, needed the loo.'

They went up to Cheryl's room. Milo was lying on the floor, flying a toy plane around with one hand.

'Okay, mister,' Vinia said. 'Bedtime.'

Milo got to his feet, stared at Fiona.

'Hello,' she said, 'remember me? That's a lovely plane. You flying off to bed now?'

He nodded and Vinia took him out. Fiona put her bag down and Cheryl came in.

'How are you?' Fiona asked.

'Okay.'

'Any show?'

'Yes. And the pains are getting closer.'

'Okay,' said Fiona. 'You pop on the bed and I'll do your temp and BP, then if that's all right with you I'll do an exam, see where you're up to.'

'Thanks. Ooh!' Cheryl's face changed, shutting down as she focused on a fresh contraction.

Fiona placed her hand on the top of Cheryl's bump and timed the contraction. Cheryl grasped her other hand, squeezing it tight. The girl was breathing well, steadily, moaning softly.

'That's it,' said Fiona, 'that's good. Eighty seconds.' Substantial. 'How long since the last one?'

'Not long. Three minutes?' Cheryl said.

Fiona handed her a thermometer and asked her to place it under her arm, then she checked her blood pressure. Both were fine.

'We'll have a listen to the baby.' She got out her sonic aid and placed it low on Cheryl's abdomen. The baby had been fully engaged for the last three weeks so Fiona was pretty sure where she'd find the heartbeat. The whooshing of the womb and the galloping sound of the heartbeat echoed in the room.

Cheryl smiled. 'So fast,' she said.

Fiona nodded. 'Your waters haven't gone?'

'No.'

'Great. Can you lie back for me?' Fiona put on her apron and snapped on the thin gloves. She used

303

some gel to lubricate her fingers then bent to examine Cheryl. With a little spike of surprise she realized that the rim of the cervix was thin, almost fully effaced, and as she gently spread her fingers she estimated it was about nine centimetres dilated. It wouldn't be long till second stage. 'Nine centimetres,' she told Cheryl. 'We should take you in straight away. Is Vinia staying here with Milo?'

'Yes.'

'And Jeri?'

'He should be here any time, he got the train.'

'You might want to tell him to go straight to St Mary's.'

'Ooh!' Cheryl bent over, another contraction sweeping through her, her fist balled on her knees, face contorted.

'Breathe through it, that's good.'

When the pain left Cheryl said she needed to wee again and Fiona gave her a stick to use so she could check her urine. Fiona texted Owen telling him she would be late home and asking him to make sure Ziggy got a walk.

She was about to ring Despatch for the ambulance car when Cheryl called out from the bathroom. Fiona went to her. Cheryl was standing clinging to the wash basin, the spatter of liquid pooling at her feet. 'It's my waters,' she said. 'I think the baby's coming. Aah!' She gasped and her legs trembled.

'Okay, darling,' Fiona said, 'just breathe, that's lovely. You're doing really well. I'm just going to have a look.'

Fiona got to her knees and lifted Cheryl's nightdress: what she saw confirmed every instinct. 'Okay, the baby's in a hurry so we'll stay here. I've some things in the car, I'll bring those. We'll be fine.'

Vinia came out on to the landing. 'Cheryl?'

'Can you find some spare sheets and towels, the older the better,' Fiona asked her.

'She having the baby here?' Vinia looked appalled.

'Yep. Just wait with her while I fetch my things.'

Fiona called one of the other midwives on the rota and asked her to come, then set about preparing for the delivery. Vinia helped her cover the floor and the bed with plastic sheeting then old sheets and covers. She checked the room temperature and Vinia organized the baby things, pulling them out of the bag Cheryl had packed for the hospital.

Cheryl stood swaying, holding on to the footboard of the bed. 'I want to push,' she said. She began to moan: long, deep sounds.

'Just let it come, Cheryl, try and open up, try and relax, good girl.'

Fiona turned to Vinia. 'Rub her back, low down.'

Three more contractions and the head was crowning. Cheryl was crying, tears dripping down her face. 'Good girl,' Fiona reassured her, 'you're doing brilliantly, really good. Won't be long now and the baby'll be here. Have you got any names?'

Cheryl sniffed. 'Dora for a girl, after my nana. I think it's a girl.' Then she wailed again. 'It's coming,' she screamed. 'It hurts!'

Fiona stroked her shoulders; let her settle instinctively on all fours on the floor. It was a great position for delivery but awkward for the midwife who had to hunker down behind and monitor what was going on. The room was cramped with the three of them there but she'd just have to deal with it.

'That's it, push now, Cheryl, long and steady, keep going, keep going, that's great, that's lovely.' Fiona could see the cap of dark hair, the ball of the baby's skull, see it straining to emerge. She asked Cheryl to wait, telling her to pant. This would allow the

305

perineum to stretch and she'd be less likely to tear. When the next contraction came she let her push again, urging her on, and saw, with pleasure and relief, the head crown.

'The head's out, Cheryl. Well done.' Fiona watched the head rotate, the natural preparation for the birth of the shoulders.

The door bell rang, it would be the second midwife, and Vinia went to let her in. It was customary to have two of them at the birth. If there were any problems one could tend to the mother and the other to the child.

Cheryl began to groan again and Fiona instructed her, 'Push nice and steady, that's good. You're doing really well. Keep going.'

Cheryl yelled and bore down. She felt the pressure between her legs, the shocking sensation of the baby, bone and muscle, forcing her way out. The tearing pain that made her scream and then Jeri was there, coming in with Vinia, his face wide with apprehension and fear flashing his eyes.

'Aw, Cheryl baby.' He knelt before her.

'She's coming,' Cheryl panted. 'Oh, Nana, help me.'

'Aw, man,' said Jeri.

Cheryl rocked back slightly, grunting, and put her arms around Jeri's neck. 'It hurts,' she cried.

'Okay, babe,' he whispered to her, 'it's cool, all cool. You're good.'

Cheryl yelped. Another rippling pain.

'Push this time,' Fiona said, 'good and strong, hard as you can.'

Cheryl locked her arms tight round Jeri's neck and burrowed her face into his shoulder, strained and keened, the solid weight of the baby splitting her open. She would tear apart, she would die from this.

'Good girl, keep going, baby's coming, keep pushing, good girl,' Fiona said.

Then with a shocking rush the baby came, slithered out in a stream of fluid and blood and mucus.

'Baby's here, well done, good girl.' Fiona helped Cheryl turn, undid the buttons on her nightdress and placed the baby on her chest. Covered the baby with a thick towel.

Cheryl looked down at the fine sweet face, the damp, black hair, looked into the dark eyes, pools of ink, shining bright. 'Hello, my little one, hiya. Hiya.' She kissed the baby's head and each eye, its nose, breathed in the strange smell: like toast and brine.

Cheryl lifted the towel and looked at the baby, tiny limbs, the knees still bent up, and between them a penis, a little spiralled shell. 'A boy,' she said to Jeri.

Jeri's eyes were soft, tears on his lashes. 'He's perfect,' he said. He grabbed Cheryl's hand and kissed it. 'Oh, baby. Oh, man. Blow me away.'

'Would you like to cut the cord in a minute?' Fiona asked him.

He nodded.

Vinia was sitting in the bed now, shaking her head. 'Man, I am not ever going there. I'm going to tie my knees together. You tell me I so much as look at a man.'

Cheryl laughed.

Jeri used the special scissors to cut through the twisting rope then Fiona attached the clip.

'I brought this.' Jeri held up a silver fifty pence piece. 'My mum said I have to give the baby silver, keep it safe.'

'Go on then,' Cheryl told him. He placed the coin in the little fist and the baby waved its hand.

'He's holding it, look at that,' Jeri crowed.

'There are lots of traditions with silver,' Fiona told them. 'And some of the Jamaican families used to bury the placenta or the cord and plant a tree.'

'Nana told me that when I had Milo,' Cheryl said. 'I didn't fancy nothing like that in the garden but we took some of his hair and put that in one of the tubs.'

Fiona asked Jeri to hold the baby while she helped Cheryl deliver the placenta.

'There's more!' Vinia groaned. 'Lord have mercy.' Then the bell went and she escaped downstairs. This time it was the other midwife.

The contractions for the placenta hurt just as bad as the ones for the baby but Cheryl knew getting it out would be easier. When she was done and cleaned up, no stitches even, Jeri handed the baby back and Cheryl put him to her nipple. The baby latched on and sucked.

'Been here before,' Fiona smiled. 'So, if it's not Dora what will you call him?'

They'd not agreed any boy's names; she'd been so sure she was having a girl. She looked at the baby, its eyes steady on her face as it suckled. 'Daniel,' she said. Jeri looked at her, head tilted, questioning. It was right, she knew. It just felt so right. 'Daniel,' she said again. Then to Jeri, 'You can pick a middle name.'

Jeri nodded, moved closer, stroked the baby's head with his fingers.

'That's a lovely name,' Fiona said.

It was dark when Fiona finally left. She was shattered, her eyes gritty and sore, her back stiff. She'd shared sandwiches and tea with them and they'd christened Daniel with a tot of rum. Now she needed her bed.

There was a full fat moon silvering the roofs and the parked cars and the trees at the end of the street. Fiona put all her bags in the boot and started the car. She drove to the recreation ground and parked there. She got out and stood by the car. There was barely any traffic across on the main road. The night was cool but not cold. It was almost May. She looked across the grass and thought of the boy who had died there, of delivering the twins, Danny and Nadine, so many years ago, and of tonight's birth. The tiny infant who shared his name. She closed her eyes and remembered: *his large boy's hands, the smell of spearmint on his breath, his gaze, the brown eyes, tawny, reflecting her silhouette and the blue sky beyond her. A rim of gold edged each iris. The bloom of love. The sky in his eyes.*

She looked up at the moon, caught the flash of a silhouette. Thought for a moment they were bats. Then saw: the spinning, swooping dives, the scissoring of wings, arcing across the moon. Her heart soared, a pinwheel of joy. The swifts were back.

Discussion Points

(1) There are four different points of view in *Witness*. Were these easy to follow? Were the voices distinct enough from each other?

(2) Which characters did you enjoy reading about most and why?

(3) Witnessing the crime and then testifying affected the characters in a number of ways. Did you find their reactions believable?

(4) Vicky argues that Mike's first and overriding responsibility is to protect his family rather than perform his civic duty. Do you agree?

(5) Fiona fears for her son Owen in the wake of the murder. Is this a realistic fear?

(6) What made Cheryl change her mind and contact the police?

(7) Who had most to lose in coming forward?

(8) Why does Zak lose his temper when he is being cross-examined? Why does Zak imagine a happy future with his mother? Why does he return to Manchester?

(9) There are different family structures in the book. Both Fiona and Cheryl are lone parents. The breakdown of the traditional family is

sometimes cited as a cause of increasing social disorder and crime. What are your views?

(10) Were there any scenes in the book that you found especially moving or effective?

(11) Did anything surprise you about the procedures involved in appearing as a witness?

(12) At Danny's funeral the community leader talks of 'the need for hope and vision, the need to take the guns from the hands of the boys who were lost and brutalized and deadly and give them work, hope, life'. Is this an effective way of tackling gang crime?

(13) *Witness* depicts different communities, cultures and lifestyles in the city of Manchester. Were any of these new or unfamiliar to you? Do you enjoy reading about people with very different lives from yours or do you prefer stories about characters whose lives are similar to yours?